I0612667

THE NIGHT HOUSE

HOUSE OF MOON & STARS

J. C. McKenzie

The sole of a shoe poked out from under the bush. Taya froze.

George's shoe. Attached to George's leg. Attached to his body under a bush.

"He's not dead." A deep voice spoke behind her.

She whirled around.

A Tarka.

The Tarka.

She'd recognize the beautiful beast from the supply cart anywhere. He stood well over six intimidating feet with a powerful build from a lifetime of training. Where the hell had he come from?

"I don't make a habit of killing children." The Tarka held perfectly still, gray gaze flashing, platinum-blond hair shining under the setting sun. He looked like a warrior angel sent to Earth to smite the pest-like humans.

She clutched her staff and brought it up with numb fingers.

He raised a dark eyebrow. "You plan to fight me with a stick?"

"I can hand it over and tell you what to do with it, if you promise to follow directions." She moved the stick slowly. Not fast enough to give away her skill, but enough to warm her wrists and get blood flowing back into her limbs.

"I'll take option number one, thank you," he said.

PRAISE FOR NOVELS BY J. C. MCKENZIE

Conspiracy of Ravens
"Raven is my kind of people. Half hot-mess, half bad-ass, all awesome... the story had plenty of humor, action and mystery rolled up in a nice paced story."
~ Urban Fantasy Investigations

Nevermore
"The dramas, dangers, intrigue, and tension of NEVERMORE will have you glued to the pages, and when it is finished, Ms. McKenzie will have left you satisfied yet wanting more." ~ Fresh Fiction

Queen of Corvids
"It has all the classic comedy, angst, and drama that I have come to expect from J.C. McKenzie, and then it piles on mystery and more interesting characters."
~ Lady with a Quill

The Call of Corvids
"This is a fascinating read that brings together a world that has been marred with fae wars" ~ Fresh Fiction

Cormorant Run
"CORMORANT RUN by J. C. McKenzie is an amazing dystopic science fiction read that will have you mesmerized from the first word to the last."
~ Fresh Fiction

The Night House
"From the very first page till the very end I was hooked on this book and read it in less than one day...it had everything you could want from a story romance, secrets, lies, suspense, surprises and more."
~ Paranormal Romance Guild

Shift Happens
"SHIFT HAPPENS has excitement, intrigue and lots of danger. I love the whole cast of characters and how they played a part in the story" ~ Fresh Fiction

Beast Coast
"I loved this book as much as the first. There are secrets, surprises, and all manner of supernaturals."
~ Paranormal Romance Guild

Carpe Demon
"The story keeps the adrenaline pumping and spine tingling tension building throughout the story with well written scenes full of vivid details that capture the imagination and make it easy for the reader to become engrossed..." ~ Literary Addicts Book Community

Shift Work
"It's a terrific series and if you like supernatural reads, with a side of romance, the sort with solid and intense plots, gripping and very real dangers, hard choices, supernatural people some of whom can be selfish, cruel and bloodthirsty...You'll be hooked."
~ Jeannie Zelos Book Reviews

Beast of All
"This time out, J. C. McKenzie has outdone herself with high-velocity action, soul deep emotions and one of those finishes that you want to replay over and over!"
~ Tome Tender

BOOKS BY J. C. MCKENZIE

Isle and Eyrie

Cormorant Run

Heir of the Eyrie (forthcoming)

House of Moon and Stars

The Night House

House of Chaos (forthcoming)

Crawford Investigations

Conspiracy of Ravens

Nevermore

Queen of Corvids

The Call of Corvids

From the Shadows

Into the Fire

Dark Legacy

Embrace the Flame

The Carus Series

Shift Happens

Beast Coast

Carpe Demon

Shift Work

Beast of All

Obsidian Flame

Dangerous Dreams

Dangerous Liaisons

Dangerous Decisions

That Old Black Magic

The Good Griffin

Standalones

Immortal Throne

Call of the Deep (Shucker's Booktique)

Stormbound (Be My Love)

THE NIGHT HOUSE

HOUSE OF MOON & STARS

J. C. McKenzie

This is a work of fiction. Names, characters, places, and incidents are either the product of the author's imagination or are used fictitiously, and any resemblance to actual persons living or dead, business establishments, events, or locales, is entirely coincidental.

The Night House

COPYRIGHT © 2018 by J. C. McKenzie

All rights reserved. No part of this book may be used or reproduced in any manner whatsoever without written permission of the author except in the case of brief quotations embodied in critical articles or reviews.

Contact Information: jcmckenzie@jcmckenzie.ca

Cover Art by Jacqueline Sweet

Alternate Illustrated Cover Art by JV Arts

Publishing History:

JCM Publications First Edition, 2019

ISBN-13: 978-1-7752251-7-1 (digital)

ISBN-13: 978-1-7752251-6-4 (print)

ISBN-13: 978-1-990143-18-2 (hardcover)

To my daughter, V.

We named you after the last colour in the spectrum of light because you are the bright rainbow after a storm. It's only fitting that I dedicate the first book I ever wrote to my last child. You will always be my rainbow baby and I will always love you.

AUTHOR'S NOTE

As I'm Canadian, and this story is set in Canada, I will subject all my fabulous readers to the wonderful world of Canadian spelling. We use a combination of British and American spelling in the True North. It's "colour" not "color" and "organization" instead of "organisation." We love the letters U and Z and have a fondness for the double L. To add to the confusion, the balance between British and American spellings varies from region to region.

Also of note: Although we are technically a metric nation, our proximity to our American neighbours (see how I spelled that?) means we are well versed in the imperial system. Many of us still use feet and inches to describe our height and pounds for our weight.

Canadians...we're complex and full of layers. Like tasty Nanaimo Bars.

PART ONE
REMAIN

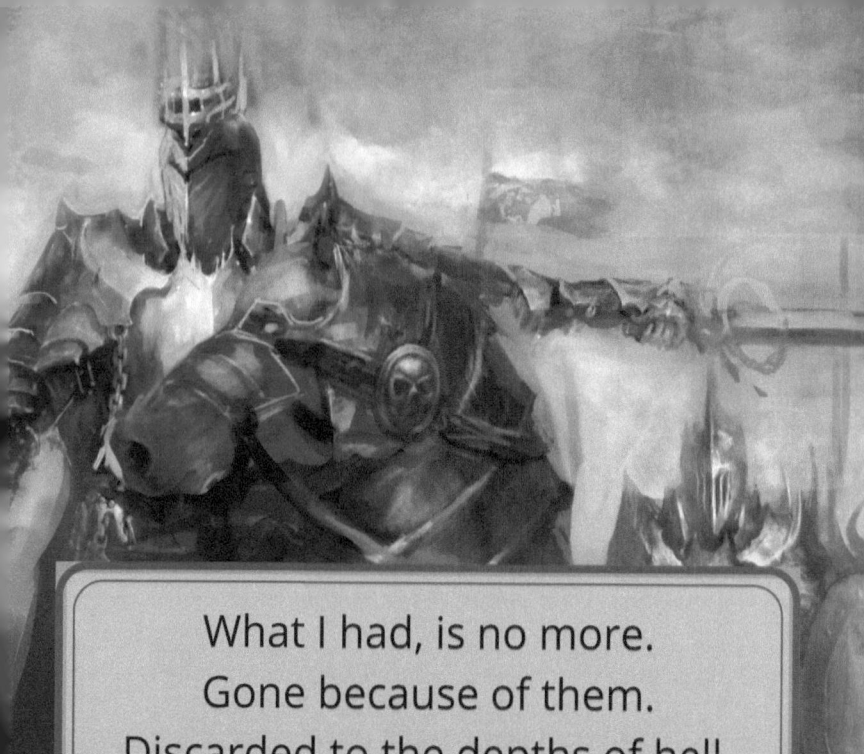

What I had, is no more.
Gone because of them.
Discarded to the depths of hell,
Painting dirt a dusty crimson.

I look back at the past,
As something I should've cherished.
Now, only memories,
Those realities have perished.

~ J. C. McKenzie

CHAPTER 1

THE REAPING

AUGUST, WILDERNESS OF VANCOUVER ISLAND, CANADA, BEFORE ARKAVIA (BA)

Taya stood knee-deep in a glacial-cold river with a beer in one hand and watched the world end. Of course she didn't know at the time the wall of sparkling blue dust moving rapidly through the evergreen forest like some sort of science fiction force field heralded the collapse of society. Instead, she mocked her drunk girlfriends from the river while her feet grew numb.

A sonic boom reverberated through the woods followed by a whoosh of fragrant summer air. Taya's platinum-blonde hair flung back and her eyes watered. She turned to the source.

"What the fuck is that?" Amy dropped an armful of firewood in a heap and brushed dirt from her shirt.

A wall of blue ballooned out and barrelled toward them through the now-still trees.

"Quick, Taya. Use some of that Ninjutsu against it," Michelle yelled out, slurring her words a little.

The women laughed.

"It's not Ninjutsu." Amy threw her hands on her hips in what must be her impersonation of Taya. She flicked her brown curls out of her face.

"It's Kung Fu." All her girlfriends recited in unison before erupting into peals of laughter. Ashley and Monica made terrible karate kicks at one another and shrieked, "Hiyaaaaaaaaah."

Technically, Kung Fu was only one of the styles she trained in, but there was no name for the style her father taught. She gave up trying to explain the finer intricacies of martial arts and fighting styles to her friends long ago.

Taya pointed her beer bottle at them. The bitter smell of booze tickled her nose. "Laugh all you want now, ladies, but when the zombie apocalypse happens, you'll beg to be my best friend."

Ashley snorted. "We're already your best friends, you—"

Her words cut off. The blue wave had reached them.

It hit Amy first. The serene fairy-like mist glittered under the summer sun and travelled through Taya's friend in slow-motion. The last expression on her face was one of horror. She crumbled into a small pile of reddish dust.

No sound. No shrieks of agony or crack of bones. One moment she stood there gaping, and the next, she was ash.

Monica screamed. Then Ashley. Both their cries cut off the moment the wave reached them and turned them to dust. Michelle glanced at Taya.

They smiled at each other, a sad smile that said everything in their hearts. This was it. Taya would die here. In the forest with her best friends. She gulped.

The wave hit.

Taya's skin vibrated. Her gut twisted. Her heart spasmed. The floral pine scented wave passed through.

She still stood in the shallow glacial water. Her heart raced. She patted down her body. Still here. Boobs still there. Her friends? She whipped around to face them and her breathing stopped.

Piles of ash sat around the campsite where her friends stood moments ago.

The blue wave spared Taya, but it took everything from her in one fell swoop. She sank to her knees. The cold water rushed past, just as it had before, as if nothing had changed. The river kept running, the trees swayed and even the birds chirped.

The hoppy taste of beer turned sour in her mouth. She threw the bottle to the side where it smashed against the rocks. With a wail, she scrambled up the river bank. She reached Ashley's crimson-gray remains first. The ash, dry and slightly warm, flittered through her fingers. The soft scent of wild roses slid along her skin. A sob wracked her body.

This couldn't be happening. This wasn't real. How could it be? Had she drank too much on the first night of camping? Was this some sort of sick booze-induced nightmare?

The rocks poking out from the packed dirt dug into her exposed knees. The cold river water still dripped from her skin.

No. This was real.

There was no rewind button for this horror show.

Whatever swept through the forest targeted her friends. Why was she spared when they weren't? Was she some sort of statistical anomaly? A mathematical remainder from someone's deadly calculations?

Taya swiped her hair from her face. Her parents hadn't raised her to be soft. She needed to steel herself from this moment and *survive*.

She pulled her numb body from the ground and brushed off the dirt clinging to her shins and shorts. The death wave was well on its way south from here.

South.

Toward her home. Her parents. Her brother. They weren't close. They had time. Maybe the blue wave wouldn't reach them. Maybe it would fizzle out. Maybe she had time to warn them.

She scrambled to her phone. She fumbled the device in her shaking hands. It slipped through her fingers and smacked the ground. She scooped it up and pressed the screen. Nothing. *Tap. Tap.* Still nothing. She flipped it around in her hands. No damage. No cracked screen. She tried again. Dead.

She found Amy's phone next. Dead. She tried the others. None of the electronics had any battery power. They were all dead. Like her friends.

Foreboding clamped around her body, locking it straight. What the hell was going on?

She raced to Monica's truck and grabbed the keys from under the driver's seat. She slid the key into the ignition and turned. Nothing. Not even a sputtering engine. She tried again. Silence greeted her.

What. The. Fuck.

No engine sounds. None of the lights came on to flash a silent "fuck you" like they normally would when she did something stupid like leave her lights on.

Was the blue death wave some sort of magical electromagnetic pulse? Didn't an EMP only work on technology when it was running? Chills racked her body. Her knowledge of anything techie like that was limited to what she saw in movies and read in books.

The cabin of the truck closed in on her. She needed to get out. Her lungs hurt. She threw open the door and leapt from the vehicle. She stumbled on the dirt and her knee slammed into the gravel.

Breathe.

Focus.

Think.

The empty campsite greeted her. She couldn't stay here. Not with her friends lying in piles of dust and some unknown force sweeping through the trees and obliterating people in a single pass. Staying in the campsite left her vulnerable and exposed.

What if more death waves came? What if something more deadly followed? Icy shivers ran up her spine until it gripped her skull.

Hell if she'd sit around and wait. She pulled her numb body from the ground, brushed her legs off and straightened. Her parents pushed her to excel not just in school, but survival skills and a variety of martial arts. When she was younger, she'd resented them sometimes and didn't understand why she had to work so hard when others flittered through life. She needed to rely on her training now and think smart.

Okay, brain. Think.

The death wave originated somewhere to the north. Whatever caused it lay in that direction. She'd head south.

The glittering clear water of the river flowed past the campsite, mocking her with its carefree frolic along the rocks. Leaf-dappled sunlight cascaded down and danced along the rippling surface.

The only difference between her and her friends was she stood in the flowing water while they were on dry land. Had the river saved her? Were the icy depths of glacier run-off the reason her life was spared?

Taya found her backpack and gathered her

camping gear in record time. Setting up the tent had taken an hour and three beers. Not because Taya couldn't do it, but because she'd chatted with her friends and they'd teased each other mercilessly. This much-needed girls' trip started with laughter and love.

Taya sniffed. *Okay, here are the tears.* She let them roll down her face.

Only the subtle sounds of nature surrounded her as she packed her supplies. Did those birds mock her along with the river? How come they were spared, too, but not her friends? Was it only humans who were affected?

She swung the heavy backpack onto her shoulders and snapped the chest and waist clasps. With her compact tent, food and a change of clothes, the thing weighed at least thirty or forty pounds. She eyed the gravel road they'd come in on. A gentle wind brushed over the ground and stirred up dirt. She turned to the campsite. The same gentle breeze teased the piles of ash that had been her friends. Her best friends.

Should she dig them graves? She hesitated. They were already ash. Let nature free them. Let the Earth embrace them. The dust played in the soft wind, spreading across the campsite and into the bush before whispering across the river.

The road would be an easier path, but more dangerous. She needed to stick by the water in case another blue wave came even though traveling along the riverbank required more energy. She didn't know what to expect when she reached civilization.

If any civilization remained.

More fear. More chills. She rubbed her arms frantically. How far did the death wave go? Was anyone else spared?

The river had saved her life. She was sure of it now. She walked through the campsite toward the river. The last remains of her friends danced in the air and brushed against her legs.

Her tears stopped. She had no more to give. If it was within her power, though, if she ever faced the person responsible for the deaths of her friends, she'd avenge them. She'd gut the blue death wave wielder and make him or her pay.

CHAPTER 2
APOCALYPSE FOR ONE

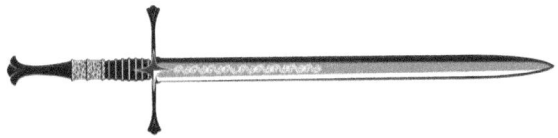

Taya wiped the sweat from her brow and leaned down to refill her water bottle from the icy river. The warm air brought the sweet smells of sun-ripened berries. It had been two days since the death wave, and traveling along the rocky, jagged river bank had been as exhausting and unforgiving as she expected.

Her backpack rested against the rocks nearby, looking significantly lighter than when she started this journey. Forgoing the beer, chips and hotdogs, there hadn't been a lot of nutritious food left to choose from when she'd packed her bag. Her food stores ran low, but she wouldn't panic. Not yet. When she drove into the wilderness with her friends, days ago, they'd passed a small town on their way to the campsite.

If she made it to the town, she'd find a bigger backpack, stock up on supplies and find out what the hell was going on. In the meantime, she rationed and questioned her decision making. The campsite she left had tons of junk food remaining from the ill-fated girls' trip, sitting where she left it, unattended. Should she turn back? Should she have taken the wieners and risked them going bad without a cooler?

She hesitated. No. Knowing her luck, scavengers already raided the supplies and she'd end up worse off than she was now. She had to be close to the town.

She drank some water as the river rushed by her bare legs and the heat from the hot summer sun beat down on her. Dragonflies zoomed over the surface of the water, butterflies fluttered around the fragrant wild flowers lining the banks and cicadas sang from their lofty perches on the neighbouring conifers. So far, people and technology appeared to be the only casualties of the blue wave.

A branch snapped. She froze.

"Lookee what we have here," a scratchy male voice spoke from behind her. "Another survivor."

She whirled around, her bare feet turning on slick river rocks. A man with a shaggy beard and greasy hair glared at her. Baggy clothes decorated with dirt and tears hung from his lean frame. The stench wafting off his skin hit her. Dirt, piss and body funk. He was too straggly for only two days into an apocalypse, or whatever this was. He had to be one of the homeless that lived along the river—the ones the tourist sites warned travellers about. Had the flowing water saved him, too? Another mathematical remainder?

How many people lurked in the woods around her? And why didn't he sound happy to find another survivor? She scanned the bank. He said "we," but no one else appeared to be with him. Figure of speech, then? At least he wasn't a zombie. She couldn't deal if this turned out to be an actual zombie apocalypse.

The man's gaze flicked to her backpack where it rested against a large rock. His stomach growled loud enough for her to hear more than ten feet away.

He planned to steal her food.

He snarled and dove for her pack. Instinct kicked in. She lunged and snatched her stuff from his grasp, and dodged out of his way, but she was too slow. His fist smashed into her face. Pain exploded behind her eyes. She spun with his strike and flung her elbow out. It contacted the back of his skull. The man lurched forward. She completed her turn, grabbed the back of his head, fingers curling around his greasy hair, and slammed his face into her knee. *Crack!* She shoved him into the water and away from her. Her heartbeat pounded in her ears.

The man flailed and staggered to his feet. He pulled a pocket knife from his pants and unfolded the rusty, dirty blade.

"You don't have to do this." She squared off to face him, weaponless. Her head throbbed.

The man held the knife out to the side. His stance desperate, not trained.

"There's a campground two days up the river," she continued. "Less if you take the road. It's full of supplies. Food, tents, clothes, backpacks to carry it all. I only took what I could carry and my friends..." She swallowed. "And my friends no longer need it."

"Are you going to cry?" He tilted his head and sneered. "Give me your stuff and I won't hurt you."

"Why? There's a town nearby."

"Not anymore."

What the hell did he mean by that? Had she travelled all this way for nothing? Dread clawed at her insides. The throbbing behind her eyes eased away and her vision focused. She gnawed on the inside of her cheek. "You can have everything if you keep heading north."

"Toward the source of that blue shit? No thank you." He leaned to the side, coughed and spat bloody mucus into the river. "A pretty thing like you probably lies all the time to get your way."

"I'm not lying."

"I don't care. Throw the bag over. You can try your luck with town or go back to the campsite."

"No."

"I'll kill you."

He'd probably done all sorts of things to survive on the streets and along the river. The detached, hard gaze told her he spoke the truth. He would kill her. He'd shove that old, dirty blade into her for a water bottle and three days' worth of food.

"You can try," she said.

He growled and sprang forward. He slipped on the smooth river rocks. Water sprayed her shorts and T-shirt. Taya took the opening. She stepped and turned into his body, grabbing the knife arm and elbowing him in the head again. He grunted and buckled forward. She ducked under his arm, stepped back and wrenched his arm behind him.

Control the weapon, her dad's instructor voice played in her head.

She twisted his wrist. His hand opened and the knife clattered against the rocks at their feet. She drove her knee up, and kicked the man and his stench away from her.

The man stumbled forward, spun and swore.

"Colourful. But not very original," she said. "Leave now."

The man screamed and dove forward. His body slammed into her midsection and his momentum carried them into the river. Cold water rushed around her. His hands snaked around her neck, thumbs digging in and held her down below the surface.

He was going to kill her.

He was going to kill her.

She thrashed her arms and legs. The ineffective blows glanced off his body. He straddled her and pinned her to the river floor. The sharp edge of a rock dug into the back of her shoulder. Cold water continued to rush over her face. She bucked, but he braced his wiry arms against her throat. Her vision narrowed, blackness closed in. She couldn't breathe.

She needed to breathe.

Groping the riverbed beside her, she gripped a smooth river rock and bashed it against the side of the man's head. He toppled over. She pushed him off and sat up, gasping for air.

The man snarled again and surged forward. Sunlight reflected off metal. The knife. He'd found it. He wouldn't give up until he killed her.

She blocked his downward stroke with her forearm and drove the rock she still clutched into his face. He cried out and fell back. She scrambled over the slippery rocks, splashing ice cold water and pinned him down. Her lungs screamed.

He swung his arm toward her, driving the knife at her neck. She leaned back, grabbed his wrist and redirected his aim. Her heart raced. Time slowed. Her entire focus narrowed in on the weapon as she pushed the blade into his chest and straight into his heart.

His eyes bulged. His head lifted out of the water. Not letting him up, she slammed the rest of the blade in and held it there. The air scraped her lungs as she drew in ragged breaths.

His hands fell away from the hilt and he fell back limp.

The river hadn't saved him this time.

It carried his blood away as if cleaning up this horrific act of violence. She waited for more adversaries to rush from the forest and attack her. No one came.

Taya remained sitting, panting for breath and straddling the dead man as he bled out. She let the river cleanse her, too.

CHAPTER 3
THE PATH LESS TRAVELLED...

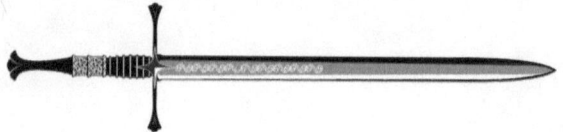

Taya didn't know how long she remained sitting on the dead guy while the world rushed past and her body and mind grew numb. She was raised to fight and trained daily. Competed in tournaments, won championships, and sparred regularly. But she'd never killed before. Only criminals murdered people.

The man wouldn't have let her go, and giving away her supplies meant a slow death instead of a fast one. She had no choice. But still...

Her insides contorted as if trying to wring out the taint of her actions. Her vision swam. When she finally dragged herself from the icy water of the river, shivering and trembling, the sun had slipped over the horizon. No way in hell would she set up camp near the body.

With numb limbs, she pulled her other set of

clothes from her pack, and changed into fresh pants and a long-sleeved shirt. Even after wringing out the water, the river had drenched her shorts and shirt. If only she hadn't fought—

No.

Don't go there. Not yet. Too soon. Focus on the current problem and make a plan.

She strapped the wet clothes to the front of her bag so they'd dry without getting the rest of the supplies soaked. The summer heat would take care of the rest.

She slung the backpack over her shoulders and trudged up the river bank. The last thing she wanted to do was hike through the woods in the dark, but staying with the body wasn't an option and travelling along the river at night wasn't ideal, either.

The body.

Her stomach lurched.

Her memory replayed the man's final moments— the sick sound of the knife stabbing into his flesh, his bulging eyes and the blood.

She squeezed her eyelids closed and counted down from ten. When that didn't work, she focused on the sounds and smell of nature around her. This was not the time or place to dwell on what happened in the river. She needed to make a plan. She needed to survive.

The time had come to cut the umbilical cord. She couldn't see a blue death wave in the dark anyway. Eventually, she'd have to restock her supplies, find out what the hell was going on, find some form of transportation, and see if anyone else survived. Why not rip off the bandage and do it now?

Would there even be a town left when she emerged from the woods? The man said there wasn't, but she needed to see for herself.

She turned to the forest. She found a meandering path—the same path the man must've taken to get to the river. Dread clung to her skin as much as the dirt. What if the other survivors were like the man? Had they destroyed the town? Would she have to kill again?

Her gut twisted more. She winced. She'd do what she had to do.

Survive first. Feel later. Her dad's warm voice coiled around her memories. He'd preached all kinds of things in his self-defence classes, but this one stuck.

The sun's light weakened, casting the forest around her in shadows. A squirrel scrambled up a nearby tree trunk. She left the bright halo of wet river rock and floral wildflowers and delved into a dark scented world of dry bark, decaying leaves and pine. Tree roots crisscrossed a trail scattered with fallen leaves and twigs.

Prickly blackberry bushes lined the path and snagged on her pant legs. At least she wouldn't accidentally wander from the path at dark. Like all the other battery-operated devices at the campsite, the flashlights hadn't worked, so she left them behind. She had a bulk supply of matches instead.

Yeah, like she'd start brandishing a torch like some

tomb-raiding crusader. She'd more likely set her hair on fire. No thank you.

Leaves rustled from a gentle breeze. Her wet shoes squeaked along the path and the wet clothes slapped against the outside of her backpack, raining droplets of cold water on her pant legs. The warm, late-summer air brushed past her, full of pine and ambivalence. She exited the path to find the road she'd driven on a few days ago—an eternity ago—when her life was filled with friends and laughter, and the exciting uncertainty of a future after graduating university.

She drew in a deep breath of pine and hemlock and...smoke.

Down the road, flickering firelight beckoned with a dim, but warm glow. A town. She scanned the buildings, but no streetlights or lighted signs illuminated them. Had the man been right? Was it all gone? Surely there had to be something left in town. Or was the problem more to do with other survivors than supplies?

A horse whinnied.

She froze.

Hoof beats thundered up the road on the other side of the hill.

Oh, hell no. She was not greeting a herd of mysterious horses alone on a dark road.

Taya dove back onto the path and jumped into a patch of salal bushes. She scrambled forward and poked her head out to see horses crest the hill and barrel toward the waiting town. Large men rode on their backs, metallic armour flashed in the fading light. Metal clanked and leather creaked as the group roared past.

Armour?

Horsemen?

Was this actually a real-life apocalypse, just not some biblical or zombie one? Fuck. She'd been joking before. The situation unfolding before her eyes looked more like one of those re-enactment scenes from the documentaries on the Middle Ages she watched in high school. What the hell was going on? Was this a foreign invasion or weapons testing gone wrong?

Part of her screamed to run back to the river. The other part knew moving right now wasn't an option— even if she could will her frozen limbs to move, she might alert the group to her presence. She had to stay where her arms and legs grew roots into the soft soil, and gather as much information as possible. Ignorance wasn't bliss.

Something crawled along her skin. She stiffened. With one little hairy leg at a time, a large spider crept across her cheek, prickling her skin. Her nose twitched.

Don't scream. Don't sneeze. Don't move.

She didn't dare make a sound as the wolf spider's fuzzy body blocked the view of her right eye.

She squeezed her eyelids shut. Her heart hammered like a piston in one of those steam engine trains. Her brother had once woken up to find one of these hairy beasts on his face. He'd been eight and

22

since that day refused to sleep unless they kept a light on. He had a dedicated bedside lamp and called it his "anti-spider" device.

Her lungs constricted. Tommy. Would she see him again? Or would she find more piles of ash when she made it home?

A sob threatened to escape her throat.

No.

She swallowed the cry down.

The spider moved on. An involuntary shudder wracked her body.

Screams from the town erupted. Some men yelled, but without binoculars or adequate light, she had no way of knowing who hurt who. She could take down an untrained river rat. Ten likely trained and powerful men on horseback in full armour? Her prospects for success were non-existent. Running into battle to help the unknown people accomplished nothing but adding her life to the death toll.

She pulled her head into the bushes and settled into the dirt. She couldn't risk running from her hiding spot now. She'd give herself away. The best plan involved staying still and waiting, painfully, for daylight.

Her limbs weighed down as if tied to cinder blocks. Her eyelids drooped. With an unknown band of medieval warriors terrorizing the survivors in a nearby town and an unaccounted for wolf spider the size of her eyeball, sleep should've alluded her. Hell, the adrenaline-laced blood pumping spastically through her veins should've been enough to keep her awake. Except it wasn't. Nothing was. The screams dwindled and the pleas of victims faded into silence. Exhaustion plowed through her body like a steamroller and turned off the lights.

CHAPTER 4

A HISTORY LESSON

Heavy hoof beats jerked Taya awake from her exhaustion-induced coma. She froze. Her stiff muscles screamed in complaint and dirt coated her tongue. Morning dew clung to the leaves and left the soil and her clothing damp. She peered through the small break in the waxy salal leaves. Luckily, the thick bush covered her well. She used to hide in similar places when she played hide and seek with her brother. She may have gotten dirty, but she usually won.

Sorrow pulled her farther into the dirt.

Her brother.

Tommy.

A procession of armoured horses ambled up the road toward her. Metal clanked. Smoke rose in the distance from the town. Among the clip clop of horseshoes on pavement came the hushed whimpering of men and women.

The leader pulled his horse to the side of the exposed road, right in front of where Taya hid and turned to watch the group. Or maybe he wished to view his destruction of a town with pride. Sunlight reflected off the warrior and horse's armour with a blinding effect, and the animal kicked up dirt and dry grass.

The procession continued. Weary men and women with tear-streaked, dirt-caked skin, shuffled behind two horsemen. Shackled to a common chain, their cuts, bruises and swollen faces spoke of a lost battle. The scene looked like something from a history book.

Taya shuddered. The leaves rustled. *Oh no. Please don't look over here.*

The leader looked over his shoulder. His ice blue eyes scanned the forest. He didn't look down at the foliage. Platinum-blonde hair, similar in colour to her own, poked out from under his helmet. His smooth white skin resembled a handsome ivory statue and remained unflushed under thick armour and the morning sunlight. He bore no signs of the struggle from last night. He didn't look tired. He looked bored.

Bastard.

Ruining lives should take a toll and come at a cost.

Another horseman drew up to the leader. "Why are we taking so many?" he growled. He spoke English with a clipped accent. Similar to her Norwegian friend, yet different somehow.

The leader turned and looked down his straight aquiline nose at the other man. "Are you questioning me?"

Red flushed the other man's cheeks. "No, sir. You put me in charge of supplies. We don't have enough to support this many for the trip home. Some will die."

The leader snorted. "I'm counting on it."

The man's heartless words ran over Taya's skin like cold hands.

"They are cattle," the man continued. "We want the best stock. The House of Jericho placed me in charge of this collection run, not you."

The second horseman nodded, but turned pale.

"You're too young to remember the early days of the last reaping. As with that other godforsaken hole we invaded, we will replenish our working class with these earthen scum and fill our houses with this planet's resources."

Taya stiffened. Reaping? Earthen? This planet? Fear squeezed her spine and locked her in place.

All this time, fear mongers warned of possible attacks from outer space. Apparently, they were attacked, but not by slimy green aliens with oversized eyes in flying saucers.

A woman in the retinue turned to glare at the soldiers. She'd heard them, too. Young and pretty with long dark hair and a curvy figure, her expression held defiance. The men ignored her. She dropped her gaze. And spotted Taya.

Crap. Taya's whole body tightened as if all her muscles seized in dread of discovery.

The woman's mouth twitched with a brief sad smile before she turned away and continued her march to an unknown fate.

Taya relaxed a little. If only she could help the woman. But what could she do? Create a diversion and release all the prisoners from their chains? She'd need lightning speed and reflexes for that. As she was now, utterly normal and bereft of any magical superpowers, she wouldn't make it five steps from the bushes.

"I'm sorry about your brother," the soldier said to the leader.

"I'm not."

The soldier hesitated. "Are you sure it's safe to leave them?"

Taya frowned and leaned forward. What did they leave behind? Soldiers? Survivors? Something more heinous?

She didn't catch the leader's whispered response, but the other man paled and quickly turned his horse to ride away.

Well, okay, then. No love lost there, apparently. With the pleasantries over, they turned their horses to follow the procession.

Taya remained lying in the dirt while her brain scrambled. How did these strange men speak the same language, especially if they were from a different planet? A different *planet*. Her brain waves shorted out.

They didn't look like aliens and not only did she understand their words, she grasped their intent. She really wished she didn't.

Taya remained prone in her salal bush hiding place for hours after the last horse and slave disappeared over the hilltop.

They didn't appear to have any plans of returning and no trailing scouts followed after them. She couldn't stay here forever with her face pressed against damp soil and spiders roaming over her body. Taya needed food, shelter, transportation and a plan. She also needed to find out how far the death wave travelled. She needed to get *home*.

Her parents and brother lived on another island on the other side of a small mountain range. She needed a boat, too. Geez. Her list was getting long.

She took a deep breath of soil, cedar and salal, and forced her tired body from the bush. She brushed off the dirt from her jeans while something crawled over her skin. She swatted the spider from her arm. Another shiver travelled through her body and she rapidly swept her hands all over her body in case the mammoth spider had any friends.

Dirt and spider free, she hauled on her backpack and stepped from the protection of the forest and onto the grassy bank on the side of the road. The land around the town was a clear, gently sloping field. Her skin tingled. The summer sun beat down on her. The trees swayed in a gentle breeze. She paused.

A long branch about an inch in diameter lay broken on the side of the road. It wasn't perfectly straight, and a little short at roughly five feet, but it would do. She bent and plucked it from the ground. Using her pocket knife, she shaved off the straggling twigs jutting out randomly from its length before standing to twirl it in her hands. Not quite long enough for a bō staff, too long for a jō or hanbō and unbalanced, the rough stick wasn't ideal as a weapon, but the familiar sensation of gripping the stick in her hands bolstered her confidence. She couldn't hide in the forest forever.

She turned to the still-smoking town and stepped onto the road.

CHAPTER 5
LEFTOVERS, ANYONE?

Taya held her breath the entire walk into town for nothing. It was deserted. Whatever the leader left in town, it wasn't people. The fires had burned out, leaving the carcasses of old buildings. Smoke and chalky dust plugged her nose and left her throat raw. Scattered ash lined the cracked sidewalks. At first, she assumed the dry flakes were residue from the fires, but then a sick realization punched her in the gut. The ash was also the remains of the victims.

The horsemen took the only survivors. No one remained.

Though a number of houses with caved-in roofs lined the street, it didn't feel right to loot them. Not yet. The inhabitants were ripped from their protective walls less than twenty-four hours ago. She'd check for a grocery store first.

When she rounded the corner and turned onto

Main Street, birds called out to each other in warning. Wings fluttered and flapped. She let out a long, pent-up breath. A grocery store sat at the end of the street. A large display window had been smashed and the door hung ajar, but it was one of the only buildings left standing relatively unscathed from the fires.

Ash and soot lined the old, unevenly paved road running through the center of town. She stepped into the store and perused the aisles. She needed high protein food, like beef jerky. Her sneakers squeaked against the hard flooring.

She exited an aisle and turned into a fist. She stumbled back. Her ears rang. What the hell? A young man lunged forward. Taya brought the staff up and V-stepped out of the way. With a twirl, she whipped the staff down and smashed it into the back of the man's head. He flailed and fell to the ground.

Blood pulsed in her veins. The man wore jeans and a ripped, black T-shirt. He wasn't an alien soldier. He was another survivor like her. Would she have to kill him, too?

"What the hell is wrong with you?" she hissed. "Haven't enough of us died?"

He groaned and rolled over. He blinked up at her, studying her clothes and weapon.

"We have a whole grocery store to share," she continued. If she missed signs of this guy in the town, had she missed others? Was it not as deserted as she thought?

He propped himself up on his elbows and frowned.

In a different time, in a different world, she would've found him attractive, and probably would've danced with him in a club if he asked.

"You look like them," he said.

"Like who?"

"I'll show you."

Like hell she'd go anywhere with this guy. She opened her mouth to tell him where to go. Glass cracked at the front of the store. She snapped her mouth shut and flinched. She turned toward the sound. No view of the entrance.

"Are there more of you?" she whispered.

"No."

Taya scrambled behind the meat freezer—the kind without doors that opened upward for passing customers to view the contents. The products had started to spoil and everything smelled slightly off. Ice flowed along her skin. She hadn't counted the number of horsemen going in and out of the town and one of the men had mentioned leaving something behind.

She had assumed because no one waved too-da-loo from the town's entrance, nor shouted vivaciously along the streets, that the big bad villains had all left together. *Stupid, stupid, stupid!*

The man joined her. He had short black hair, hazel eyes, and despite punching her in the face, he had a kind mouth.

She scowled at him. He could get his own meat freezer to hide behind.

He glared back, but didn't try to attack her again.

She slipped off her backpack, the wet clothes from the other day still tied to the outside, and clutched her staff. This hiding place sucked. As soon as the others stepped past the displays at the back of the store, they'd see her and Pretty Boy squatting beside the hunks of expired ham like pathetic ducks.

She remained crouched and waddle-walked to the edge of the freezer. The light from outside streaked in and sparkled off metal near the front of the building.

Armour.

Great.

The soldiers moved forward. They didn't mask their movement or make any attempt to hide their progress. It would've been difficult since their armour creaked with each step.

Taya eyed the swinging doors to the butcher area behind her. She hadn't gone through them before because she made a split second decision and feared the hinges would creak. She didn't want to alert the soldiers of her presence. But that was ridiculous. Of course they knew she was here. They would've heard her and Pretty Boy scuffling around and hissing at one another.

There should be an emergency exit out the back or a loading bay.

And knives.

She considered the man crouched beside her. He narrowed his eyes. She didn't owe him anything, but... but he was a survivor like her.

She jerked her head toward the swinging doors.

His gaze flicked toward her escape route and back. He shook his head. To each to their own then. At least she tried. What about her backpack? Should she take it? Though light from dwindling supplies, the sack and straps would prove cumbersome in a fight. But without it, she'd have nothing.

Decision made, she slung the bag back on and bolted for the doors.

The men didn't call out or yell for her to stop. Their heavy boots thudding against the floor grew louder, faster and closer. She charged through the swinging doors. The hinges screamed. With no electricity, she had no glaring red sign to indicate the exit. The sunlight didn't cut through the gloom this far into the building. She rushed into darkness and ran straight to the back. She slammed into the exit door. The metal bar dug into her stomach, unyielding. The air whooshed from her lungs and pain erupted in her belly.

Locked.

Goddammit.

She swore and her stomach ached.

Think. Think. *Think.* Taya rounded the butcher station and pressed against the far wall. She sucked in air. She was breathing too hard. They wouldn't need to search for her at this point. They'd just follow the sound of heavy panting.

The doors swung open again, the hinges announcing more players to the dark pit. Light momentarily reflected off knives lying on the table.

The soldiers halted inside. The doors swung shut and darkness enveloped her again.

Come on, heart. Stop thumping so loud. Footsteps travelled to the back of the room. Metal groaned as one of the men tried to push down the same metal bar on the exit door.

They knew she was still in here.

The heavy thumping of their boots separated into two distinct patterns. They'd split up. One went toward the fish section—brave soul—and the other headed toward her. The soldier's boots smacked across the cold tiles like a gut-wrenching countdown.

He'd pass her hiding spot in three, two, one...

A large shadow of a man stepped beside her. She flung up her staff, and smashed the butt of the stick into his face.

His dark head whipped back. He snarled and swung. She dropped down in a crouch and narrowly missed his giant fist. With a twist, she flung out a leg to sweep him. Her leg slapped the hard armour. Pain streaked up her leg. The soldier remained standing. He gripped her head and pulled her up by her hair. Some ripped from her scalp.

"Motherfucker."

He flashed a cruel smile that somehow managed to gleam in the dark.

She spun her staff and struck his unprotected armpit. He grunted. She struck again and again. He pinched in his arm to defend the vulnerable area and she took the opening to strike him in the face.

His nose cracked. Blood gushed from the wound.

He swore and released her. She wrapped her hands around the cold plastic handles of one of the knives on the counter and drove it into his neck. He coughed and spat blood. His eyes widened. He fell to his knees, and face-planted in front of her. Oh God. She'd killed an—

Standing directly behind him was the other soldier.

He glared at her. With no helmet, his dark hair and skin disappeared without a shiny surface for the sparse light to shine off. He pulled a sword from the scabbard on his belt.

Fuck.

Her little carving knife wasn't up for this task.

She'd beaten his buddy because he'd underestimated her abilities and planned on capturing her, not killing. From the murderous glare of Soldier Number Two glinting in the dim light, he didn't share the same plans. He stepped forward.

She backed up.

He stepped forward again.

She moved back farther and into the edge of the countertop. He'd cornered her.

Fuck, fuck, fuck, fuck, fuck.

She flipped the carving knife in her hand and threw it at the man. He batted the blade out of the air with his sword. It clattered to the floor.

Fuuuuuuuuuuuuuuuuuuck.

She readjusted her hold on her staff as Soldier Number Two advanced. He raised his sword and smiled cruelly.

She widened her stance. Engaging a battle-proven, armoured, sword-wielding warrior who watched her stab his comrade in the neck was less than ideal, but that didn't mean success was impossible. Taya wouldn't give up. She'd go down fighting like a crazy banshee.

Do the unexpected. Never give up. Her dad's voice trickled through her memory.

No, Dad. I'm not giving up.

She ran through her defensive and offensive options. It didn't look good.

The solider straightened, gurgled and fell to the side. A carving knife jutted out of his exposed neck.

Pretty Boy stood behind him with eyes wide, mouth parted to a trembling "O" and eyebrows reaching up to his hairline. Her brother had worn a similar "did I just do that?" expression when he'd accidentally tipped over Mom's china cabinet and broke every single piece of Grandma's fine china.

They looked down at the body, almost imperceptible in the dim light. This invasion had made them into killers.

"Thanks," she said.

The soldiers had walked right past Pretty Boy. He could've escaped to safety. Instead, he'd entered the dark butcher area to help her. Maybe he wasn't so bad after all.

He nodded, reached down and yanked the knife from the body. "You were right. Enough of us have died already."

She waved her hand at the dead soldiers' bodies and their shock of dark hair. "I don't look anything like either of these guys."

Pretty Boy shook his head. "Not them. The others."

She leaned on her staff. Her limbs shook.

"You look like their lords. The ones they call Tarkas."

"How are they different?" she asked.

"They wield magic."

CHAPTER 6
LIGHTNING RARELY STRIKES TWICE

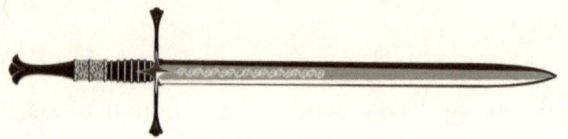

The glazed eyes of a man with long platinum hair stared at Taya from where he lay on a dead clump of charred grass next to an old road. The afternoon sunlight played with the white highlights of his hair splayed against the ground and dried blood. Of course the dead man wasn't actually looking at her, but studying his appearance and noting the uncanny resemblance to the men in her family sent shivers racing along her limbs.

"A Tarka?" She glanced at John. They'd exchanged names on the awkward walk over. He'd also told her the soldiers referred to each other as Arkavians and they'd apparently travelled to Earth through some sort of portal. She hadn't asked yet how he avoided capture when he was obviously close enough to gather this information. He probably hid somewhere and watched the entire invasion. She would've done the same—she did do the same—so the guilt probably ate at him like it did with her.

"That's what the other men called him."

The dead Tarka must've been the brother to the leader, the one the other soldier mentioned as they casually monitored the progress of their spoils of war through the dust cloud.

"If he wielded magic, how'd he die?" she asked.

"A knife."

"That's obvious." She waved at the gaping wound in the man's neck. The surrounding skin was mottled and black, and caked with dried blood.

"One of the men from town hid around the corner," John said. "He surprised him by attacking from behind. It's where...it's where I got the idea for the other guy." The colour drained from his face. Most untrained fighters would've gone for the body, regardless of the armour. Not John. He saw a murder and learned from it.

Her chest tightened as if her own cells tried to hug away the influx of memories from her recent killings. She nodded, ignored the nausea rising within her, and crouched beside the body. Apparently, these Tarkas were not all-knowing or all-powerful. They bled and they died like everyone else.

Noted.

His body gave off an odd floral smell. "What powers do they have?"

"This one moved things."

"All kinds of things?" She glanced up.

John nodded. "People, too."

"Lovely." The glimmering hilts of twin swords reflected the sunlight and caught her attention. She leaned forward.

"I wouldn't do that."

"Why not?" How'd he know what she planned to do anyway?

"Gives you a zap."

Well, he obviously survived whatever love tap the swords gave. Why should he have all the fun? She rubbed her sweaty palms on her pants before she reached out and grabbed the hilt of one. A tingling sensation ran through her arm. Not painful, but not exactly pleasant either. So far, so good. She took a deep breath and pulled, unsheathing the sword.

Flashes of blue and white light traveled in bolts of lightning from the pommel to the tip of the blade. The scent of fresh rain and loam surrounded her and a tingling energy pulled at *something* inside. Like tugging the arm of a friend to come and play on the monkey bars, the power called to her, begged her. To do what? The sword wanted something and demanded payment. She shivered when she realized what it was.

The blade wanted blood.

John whistled. "Didn't do that for me."

She sheathed the sword. The fire in her blood took a long minute to cool. She traced the intricate design stitched into the leather straps for the scabbard with her finger. "What happened?"

"When I touched them? Zapped me so bad it sent me flying back about five feet."

"Maybe the blades prefer blondes?"

He chuckled and rubbed the stubble on his jaw. "Maybe. Are you going to take them?"

Hell yeah, she'd take them. The power *still* called to her. Magical lightning blades only she could wield? She'd be a fool not to keep them. She found the clasp for the dual back scabbard. "I'm not leaving them here."

"Should I take his armour?" John pointed at the thick metal breastplate on the body and the helmet resting on the ground next to a flattened pile of ash.

"It's your decision."

"But?"

She shrugged. "I think it will be too heavy, too noisy and too big." The Tarka was twice the width of John. Her fellow survivor would look like a little boy playing dress up.

"I guess you're right." John's shoulders drooped and he eyed the metal.

"You can always come back for it or hide it somewhere."

His eyes lit up. "Yeah. We can stash it at my place along with your swords...you know, until you learn how to use them."

Until she learned to use them. Could he sound more condescending?

To be fair, most people didn't know how to use swords. It wasn't an unreasonable assumption on John's part, but his words and tone still grated on her nerves.

She unbuckled the scabbard and rolled the corpse so she could pry the weapons from the cold body. The metal armour clanked against the broken pavement. God, the Tarka's arms were huge. "No offense, but I'm not staying with you."

"What?" His head snapped back as if she punched him in the face. "Look, I'm sorry I attacked you. I think we should stick together."

"I agree, but I don't think we should stay in a town where they left two soldiers waiting for their return. The sun's going down soon, and I need to make camp."

"Camp? As in a tent?"

"Yes, princess, a tent. If it's not glamorous enough, you can stay here and welcome the Arkavians when they return for another raid."

John scowled.

"And you need your own tent and sleeping bag."

He stared at the sky and mouthed a silent prayer.

"I don't know you. I'm not going to sleep in a small, confined tent with a man I don't know." She'd sleep next to her knife anyway, but if he decided to attack her, hopefully the zipper would provide an early warning.

His shoulders relaxed. "I hadn't thought about that."

Of course he hadn't. Men didn't constantly make decisions to minimize their risks of sexual assault. Not that all men were bad or men weren't victims, but the majority of them lived life blissfully unaware of the additional precautions a lot of women had to consider to stay safe.

"I have a tent. Let me pack supplies."

She straightened, buckled the swords to her back and readjusted the straps. She hoisted her backpack on next, pinning the sheaths between her body and the bag. Luckily it worked. She'd have to practice drawing the blades with the backpack on to see if she could do it without decapitating herself, or slicing her supplies to pieces.

"We can come back and restock tomorrow. I don't want to be in town at night. That's when they arrived last time. We could make camp near the river."

He nodded toward the direction she entered town. "There's a trail—"

"No!"

He snapped his mouth shut.

"Sorry." She wrung her hands together. "Is there another one?"

He jabbed his thumb over his shoulder in the opposite direction. "Yeah. About a kilometer down the road."

"That'll do. I'm going to get a head start. I'll meet you at the head of the trail."

"Give me thirty minutes."

She nodded and headed in the direction he indicated. Even if this town of death and ash didn't unsettle her, she had no desire to follow John back to his home. Who knew what memories or loss waited for him there?

Dust kicked up from her running shoes striking the dry road and ballooned around her. The sun beat down. The safety of the trees ahead beckoned to her. Safety from the heat and safety from Arkavians *and* survivors of the blue death wave. She stepped into the shade and waited for her new companion. Whether he ended up a friend or another foe remained a big ugly question looming over her head, but if she wanted to survive, she needed allies. She needed a community. She wouldn't survive one winter without one and she'd never make the trek home to find out if her family survived. Right now, Pretty Boy with a good right hook was it.

CHAPTER 7
SACRIFICES MUST BE MADE

Taya hadn't decided whether to trust John wholeheartedly, but they'd formed an uneasy alliance over the last three days and made a plan to gather and store supplies away from town in case the Arkavians returned.

Taya whirled around at the sound of creaking wheels piercing the air and found a cloud of dust billowing around her fellow survivor. "What the fuck is that?"

John glared. "A wagon."

"Why? Do you want to announce our location?" She pointed at the road with her staff. Yeah, she had swords, but her training sessions prior to the death wave didn't focus much on blade work. At the time, playing with swords seemed so impractical and more of a novelty than a necessity. Now, she was just as likely to sever her own limb as an opponent.

"You said you left all your friends' gear at the campsite. We didn't find any additional camping supplies in town that hadn't burned along with the buildings."

Her stomach sunk, knowing where he was going with this.

His scowl softened. "I can go alone if it's easier."

"No...No. We should stick together." Though it had only been a few days since he mistook her for an Arkavian death lord and punched her in the face, she found the idea of forced solitude devastating. Besides, if John could walk around town and the charred remains of his neighbours and friends, she could suck it up and do this. A post-apocalyptic Earth was no place for wimps.

"I wish they'd left the soldier's horse along with his swords," she said, glaring at the wagon.

"I don't. Horses are noisy and need food and maintenance and love and I have no experience with those things."

"With love?"

"As it pertains to *horses*, no." He narrowed his eyes. "Is this when you tell me you're a top-ranked horse master in addition to being a Kung-Fu ninja?"

They turned toward the street leading out of town and started walking. The heat beat down on them. Thankfully, she opted for shorts and a T-shirt for the more exposed walking along the road. Silence fell between them. The creaking wagon crunched along the dirt road and tree branches swayed in the gentle breeze around them.

Even though it took Taya two days to reach the town from the campsite, she'd followed the rocky and often-winding river. Since they left during the early morning hours and took the direct route, they'd reach the destination by nightfall.

Hopefully, they didn't have to camp there.

Taya wasn't weak, but she wasn't stone, either. She mulled over John's last words. Who was this guy? He answered most of her questions earlier with one or two words. Maybe she had to give a little to get a little.

"I don't think there's such a thing as a horse master," she said.

John jumped and glared at her.

She continued. "And if there is such a thing, I'm not one. When I was really young, I wanted to be a horse."

John focused on the road ahead, frowning slightly.

"But I don't think that counts," she said. "When I realized that was never going to happen, I started asking for a horse every Christmas."

"No luck?"

"I got riding lessons."

He smirked as if she answered some unasked question. What was his problem? Besides the whole end-of-the-world thing? Yeah, she came from a middle-class family that made sacrifices to provide her with training. She still had to work three jobs to pay her way through university and took twice as long to get her English degree.

"How'd it go?" he asked.

"Good. Until it came time to put the bridle and saddle on."

"Is it hard?"

"Not really, but I didn't want to hurt the horse's ears so I couldn't get the bridle on and Dawn, the horse, had a nasty habit of pushing her stomach out so I couldn't cinch the saddle tight enough. My instructor told me to smack the horse so Dawn would release her breath and let me wrench the saddle strap tighter. I couldn't do it." Memories of Dawn's light face and flicking ears brought scents of dirt, straw bedding and wood shavings.

"What happened?"

"I lied."

John kicked a rock from his path. "How'd that work out for you?"

"Three trots into the lesson and the saddle slid to the side. I ended up eating a lot of dirt."

John chuckled and shook his head. They turned onto the gravel road leading to the campsite. The hint of campfire and hamburgers still lingered in the air and made Taya's mouth water.

"The instructor was furious. She said if I didn't have the guts to saddle a horse correctly, I had no business riding them." Though this occurred almost twenty years ago, the cruel words still cut. Her instructor had destroyed her childhood dream.

"Sounds harsh."

She nodded. "Now that I look back on it, I think she was scared. I could've been hurt and she might've lost her job."

"Still. You'd think there'd be a more humane way to get a horse to exhale."

Taya shrugged. "If there is, I don't know it. I still love horses though."

The birds grew silent around them. This wasn't right. Normally, they chirped away, mocking Taya with their care-free happiness. She stopped and flung her arm out to halt John. Her palm smacked his chest. The wagon's wheels squealed to a stop.

They shouldn't have brought that stupid wagon.

The air buzzed with tension. Taya dropped her hand from John's chest and gripped her staff. She waggled her finger back and forth at the wagon.

John nodded and set the handle down in the dirt.

They walked forward, each crunch of gravel making as much noise as an avalanche. The air continued to buzz. The sound wasn't her brain freaking out like she thought. It wasn't the cicadas, either. She followed the noise.

Bugs. Flies. Insects of all sorts swarmed close to the ground of an abandoned campsite. Despite the heat of the day, ice flowed through Taya's veins.

Bodies littered the clearing. Not piles of ash and

not decomposed enough to suggest they'd been here prior to the death wave. The smell of spoiled meat and churned barbeque surrounded them. *Oh God*. The hamburger smell.

"Oh my God," John whispered, echoing her unspoken words. He lurched to the side and puked violently.

She gulped down her rising stomach contents and stepped farther into the campsite. If she let the nausea overwhelm her now, she'd hunch over beside John.

The bodies weren't as disorderly as she first thought. They lined the large campsite in one giant circle. In the middle sat the charred remains of a campfire.

"Are they...gutted?" John asked and heaved again.

They were.

With blank stares gazing at the exposed blue sky, mouths gaping, arms and legs thrown to the sides, the bodies resembled cadavers from the forensic investigation shows she watched on television.

She wiped her sweaty palms on her shorts and stepped closer to one of the bodies. Blow flies coated the woman. When the gravel crunched under Taya's feet, the flies dispersed to reveal an empty body cavity. No guts, no heart or liver. Just an open rib cage like some alien burst out after devouring everything on the inside.

Her head grew light.

Something or someone had removed all the internal organs.

What had they done with all of it?

The cooked meat smell still clinging in the air burned her nose. Stomach acid bubbled up her throat. Did they...eat it?

Nausea surged. She swallowed and she glanced at the woman's face and her horrified expression. Her final moments must've been awful.

A memory flashed. The woman from the slave line. The one who'd turned to glare at the leader and spotted Taya hiding in the bushes. The pretty woman who kept quiet. The woman Taya couldn't save without risking her own safety.

Her stomach wrenched. She turned, doubled over, and spewed on the bushes lining the campsite. She continued again and again until nothing remained.

Nothing left.

Like their insides.

Nausea rose again.

John walked over, his feet shuffling along the gravel and kicking up dust. "Fuck. That's Kaydence."

Taya turned away from the bushes. John stood over the woman she'd recognized, his face pale.

"She worked at the post office," he said. "We had a date at the river."

Taya placed a hand on his bare arm, his skin cold and clammy. He shrugged it off and went to the next body. "I recognize him, too." John pointed to another body. "And that's Tony." His mouth flattened. "These were the survivors from town. The ones the Arkavians took with them."

Taya nodded.

"Do you think..." John shuddered. "Do you think this is their plan for us?"

She shook her head and forced her gaze away from Kaydence's horrified expression. "I don't think so. I overheard two of them talking and they made it sound as though they intended to use us as slaves, not food or sacrifices."

"Something interrupted their plans." He walked around some of the bodies and paused by one of the men. "Is this one of them?"

Taya joined him, carefully skirting the pools of dried blood. Too many. Too many faces and bodies to take in. They blurred together. She swallowed and forced her eyes open to study the body John indicated. Sure enough, he'd identified one of the Arkavian soldiers. "He's the one who spoke to the leader."

What the hell happened to them? What else had come through the portal with the magic wielders? Monsters? If magic was possible, what else existed on this other planet?

A cloud passed over the clearing, casting them in dampened light. She glanced up. They had at least four more hours of daylight, but not enough time to stock up and make it back to their camp by the town. Her vision swam as she scanned the area again.

"I don't want to sleep near here," she said.

John cast her an incredulous look as if she were evil for even entertaining the idea.

She flung her arm out and pointed toward the river. "The campsite I shared with my fri...the campsite is a few plots over by the water. Let's strip it. Rebottle and get the hell out of here in case whatever it is that did this comes back."

"I'm surprised these bodies haven't drawn predators already," John said.

"That's another happy thought." All the more reason to run. "Should we dig them graves?"

"The two of us? We'll be shoveling for days in the heat. As much as I hate to leave them like this, we have to be practical."

"I know, but—"

"They're dead. They don't care." He picked his way around the bodies and walked toward her. "And I don't want to camp at all. I say we grab the supplies and keep moving through the night."

She sighed. He'd suggested they travel at night to get here, too. Although she agreed with him about the graves, she didn't with this. "I don't want to get caught on the road at night. We won't see the attack coming and that squeaky wagon will draw attention and lead anyone looking right to us."

John glared at her.

Fine. Glare all he liked, she wasn't budging once the sun went down.

He squeezed his hands into fists. "Fine."

She didn't wait for him to sort through his feelings. Maybe she was wrong and he was right, but she didn't see any benefit to travelling at night except to get back to another site of pain and loss sooner. She spun on her heel and marched out of the death camp. Cold pricked at her exposed back as if evil still lingered and watched her leave.

She walked straight to her old campsite. If she stopped and thought about how she looted her dead friends' possessions meters from a massacre after a magical death wave from another world obliterated almost every human and left her with a grumpy pretty boy who hated how she had an opinion, she might break.

And if there was one thing Taya learned about this new world, it was it had no time for anything other than survival.

Her father raised a warrior. She'd battle this weird, alien apocalypse. She'd persevere and live on so the memories of her friends and family would survive with her.

CHAPTER 8
A FRIEND IN NEED

Taya stepped from her tent and stretched in the early morning sun. The tent beside hers rustled and John crawled out, zipping up the flap behind him. The birds chattered in the nearby trees and the river burbled a few feet away. John had relented and they'd made camp for the night.

Not that she slept much.

Her thoughts had filled with images from the clearing with the circle of dead bodies and memories of her dead friends. The nightmares wouldn't let her rest.

Taya's skin rippled with unease. The birds had gone quiet.

"What are—" John stopped speaking when she snapped her hand up. He narrowed his eyes and curled his lip to show his teeth.

A branch snapped, then another.

"Who's there?" Taya called out.

John stiffened.

A woman stepped from the bushes lining the forest. She looked around Taya's age, maybe a little older, and wore a sweater and khaki shorts. Her clothing was dirty and scratches crisscrossed her toned legs. Even at this distance, even with the amber brown tone of her skin, bruises stood out, decorating her exposed skin. She'd tied her loosely coiled hair into a high ponytail. A few twigs stuck out from the black mass. Whomever this woman was, the last few days had been rough.

Then again, it had been rough for all of them. Taya and John probably looked the same.

"You're not one of them?" the woman asked.

Taya sighed and put her knife away. The strange men who'd led the attacks had white hair like her. Gauging from this woman's reaction, and John's, it wasn't just a fluke coincidence. "No, I'm not."

"Oh, thank God." The woman let out a long breath and her shoulders slumped.

John chose this moment to step around his tent and join Taya. "Who are you?"

"Chantelle." She stepped farther away from the forest. "You're not the first survivors I've come across, but the others..." She rubbed her arms. "The others stole my stuff and threatened to kill me. I have nothing. Can I...Can I join you?"

No.

How could they possibly trust this woman?

What if she planned to do the same thing to them?

Taya looked over at John. He shook his head. He didn't like the idea any more than she did, and Taya's first experience with a survivor hadn't been great, either.

"How do we know you won't do the same thing?" Taya asked. Worse things could happen than their food being stolen.

Chantelle flinched, her bottom lip trembling. If she'd been an actress in a former life, she would've been phenomenal. "I'll promise? Please. I've been travelling ever since...ever since it happened. I know there's a town nearby. Maybe there are more survivors. Maybe we can travel to the town together and find them."

Taya and John shared a look. His most definitely said no.

Chantelle studied them, her lip quivering, her shoulders sagging down. "The town is empty, isn't it?"

John grunted.

"There are more farther south," Chantelle said. "Maybe we could travel to those. That blue stuff couldn't have gone on forever." She licked her lips. "Please. I don't want to be alone."

Taya's brain told her to dump the extra baggage and run, but she couldn't survive on her own, either, and the weather would only hold for so long.

"Taya..." John reached out to grip her elbow gently. "We can't."

She sighed and shook her head. Leaning close, she

whispered to him. "We need more people if we're going to survive the winter. There's safety in numbers."

"And more mouths to feed," John snapped back.

And more opportunity for betrayal. He wasn't wrong, but they had to start trusting someone.

"I can cook," Chantelle called out. "I know a lot about herbs and medicine as well. I was practicing to be an herbalist before...well, before."

Taya nodded at Chantelle to acknowledge she'd heard her but focused on John. "We can't keep wandering around and scavenging. We need to make a plan. Those...people...might come back."

"They already have," Chantelle piped in.

Taya froze before slowly turning to the newcomer. "What?"

"After the survivors stole from me, I ended up finding them again. They had been slaughtered. I heard horses, so I hid. There were more warriors, and the leaders looked like you. They had rounded up a group of survivors. They also had carts full of food and another towing fabric and what looked like bedding."

"They're raiding for supplies," John said.

Taya nodded again. "Now we really need to make a plan."

John groaned, obviously reading Taya's decision on her face before she spoke.

"You can join us," Taya said.

CHAPTER 9
KNOW WHEN TO FOLD THEM

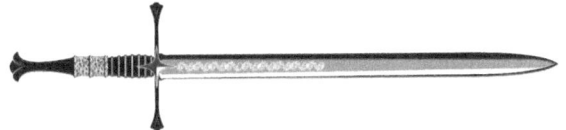

Taya rolled the chunk of fresh snow in her mouth to cool her breath and prevent condensed air from rising above her like a giant "I'm here" sign for the approaching Arkavian supply cart. She waited, crouched in the treeline, shielded by bushes and shrubs. The cold ground pressed into her shin and the snow melted under her legs and soaked through her pants. The creak and groan of wooden wheels grew louder.

After Taya and John left the slaughter site at the campground four months ago and met Chantelle, the Arkavians returned en-masse. The soldiers wiped out the remaining food from the town where they'd met, and travelled farther south, hitting town after town for supplies and leaving nothing but ruin and waste in their wake.

Taya, John and Chantelle followed, stealing from

the Arkavian's unguarded food and picked up more survivors like them. Apparently, Arkavia wasn't an alien planet from her own reality; instead, the world existed in an alternate universe and they travelled here through a magical portal.

Fuck, we shouldn't be out here.

The Arkavians caught on to their scheme of attacking supply carts and the gravy train dried up. Now if Taya and her group wanted food, they had to scavenge for themselves or fight for it. Normally, they succeeded at both. Taya carefully selected supply carts with minimal guards, but it only took one Tarka to travel with the Arkavian group for utter disaster to occur.

Taya shouldn't be out here, none of them should, not so soon after their last haul. With their growing numbers, though, they needed supplies constantly.

The wheels groaned and a horse snorted. Two guards flanked the wagon on restless horses. The young gazes of the soldiers darting erratically. For all the death-wielding might of the Arkavians, they struggled to find skilled and experienced employees for their supply chains.

Just two guards? She had ten fighters in her group. Sure, not all of them were trained from birth to wield a sword or fight like her, but she made them practice daily. She drew from her experience of helping out with classes at her dad's dojo.

John turned out to have phenomenal bow skills.

Apparently, he used to go hunting with his uncles a lot before Arkavia. They'd plucked a bow and arrow set from a house in one of the abandoned towns.

One target for John and one for her. Yet... Something *felt* wrong.

She withheld giving the attack signal.

John's head snapped to her. He frowned so hard his eyebrows might attack his nose. He still hated taking directions from her, as if her ideas chafed his skin. Since he found the bow and demonstrated his hunting prowess, he argued with her more and more and openly challenged her in front of the group.

Honestly, she'd let him lead if he had good ideas, but he was hotheaded and impulsive. Her leadership bothered him. Her skills as a fighter bothered him. Her existence bothered him. But as far as she could tell, the only reason those things dug under his skin and grated his nerves was her possession of girly bits. If she'd been a dick with a dick, he'd probably fall in line.

She shook her head. After winter, she'd leave the group to his questionable leadership and take off to the south to find her family. She'd already delayed the trek to her parents' place through forest and across the island's mountain range. The trip was long and dangerous by herself, and she needed supplies and skills to survive the journey. After this winter, she'd hopefully have enough of both to go home and discover what remained.

John glared and jerked his head after the supply cart.

She shook her head again. They'd taken out three supply carts in the last four months. Their boldness hadn't gone unnoticed. The Arkavians sent a Tarka with the last one. Taya noticed him right away.

How could she not see him? A beautiful beast of a man with features more likely cut from stone than a living person. His stillness set him apart from the rest of the soldiers before she identified his platinum-blond hair. He matched the snow surrounding them. Even his silver and black armour with white leather lining differentiated him from the rest.

Taya shivered from the memory. More lethal and devastating to behold than the first lord she'd seen months ago, his sharp gray eyes still haunted her dreams. After spotting him, she'd given her team the signal to withdraw.

Here she was again, hesitating. Flicking her hand quickly in the air, she gave the signal to stalk the supply wagon but not engage.

She wanted more information. If everything checked out, she'd use the bird call and her team could attack the wagon without her. That would make John happy. He'd have his chance to shine and prove himself as a leader.

George, their scout, had made the owl call an hour ago that the cart was on its way, giving them time to assemble and take their positions. Time to visit the boy.

She pulled her hood up and tightened the drawstrings to keep the material in place and the cold out.

She picked her way through the pine and fir trees lining the forest, the sharp smell of their needles a calming familiarity, and made her way to George's position at the top of the hill. He had a complete view of the valley below from his lookout.

Carefully skirting branches and twigs littering the cold ground, she kept her footing as flat and even as possible until she found the tree George liked to climb. His footsteps surrounded the base.

She peered up the tall conifer. George was nearly invisible from the road unless you knew where to look along the wet bark and dense moss. She knew where to look and she didn't see any sign of him.

Where had he gone?

She studied the tracks. Fresh ones led away from the tree. She gripped her staff and followed until they met the road and crossed. She peered up and down the road. No tracks other than the supply wagon and George.

Why the hell would he cross the road? She told him not to do that. She wasn't the only one who read tracks.

She took a deep breath and crouched low. As she took three steps on the road, the opposite tree foliage became clear. What the hell was—?

A shoe?

The sole of a shoe poked out from under the bush. Taya froze.

George's shoe. Attached to George's leg. Attached to his body under a bush.

"He's not dead." A deep voice spoke behind her.

She whirled around.

A Tarka.

The Tarka.

She'd recognize the beautiful beast from the supply cart anywhere. He stood well over six intimidating feet with a powerful build from a lifetime of training. Where the hell had he come from?

"I don't make a habit of killing children." The Tarka held perfectly still, gray gaze flashing, platinum-blond hair shining under the setting sun. He looked like a warrior angel sent to Earth to smite the pest-like humans.

She clutched her staff and brought it up with numb fingers.

He raised a dark eyebrow. "You plan to fight me with a stick?"

"I can hand it over and tell you what to do with it, if you promise to follow directions." She moved the stick slowly. Not fast enough to give away her skill, but enough to warm her wrists and get blood flowing back into her limbs.

"I'll take option number one, thank you," he said.

"Fine with me. I'd prefer anything to becoming your next sacrifice." They'd never confirmed the Arkavians were responsible for the bloody sacrifice they'd stumbled on, but no crazy magical beasts had roamed the forest since the portal opened, so they made an assumption. The Arkavians had to be responsible for that, too. She glanced behind her at the trees and George's exposed foot. What the hell had the Tarka done to him?

"He's incapacitated. You won't get any help from him."

Taya snarled while her mind raced. The man hadn't used any magic yet. Maybe he didn't have any. Maybe only some of the blondes had power. Could she outrun him? She wasn't fast, but he was bulky with muscle, and wore lightweight armour and a heavy cloak to stave off the damp cold.

Where would she run? She couldn't lead him to the others, and she couldn't survive long in the woods without supplies.

The man cocked his head, studying her and probably reading every thought screaming through her head. "Sacrifice? Exactly what kind of fantasies have your kind concocted about us?"

"I would hardly call them fantasies."

"What would you call them, then?"

"Nightmares." Duh.

He nodded. "Is this where you tell me my evil ways are done?"

"I'm not sure. Is this where you make some grand speech about ridding the world of my kind or do you plan to preach about the superiority of your race and how you deserve to suck our planet dry?"

"I'm waiting for you to finish warming up so we can get on with it."

She fumbled and almost dropped the staff.

His smile was scary, a flash of teeth. He stepped forward. "I plan to take you with me."

Ice froze along her spine. "You sure about that? Dead bodies stink pretty badly."

"Alive."

"I'm not going anywhere with you." Why the hell were they having a conversation like they sat at some sort of warped tea party?

"Are you ready, yet? Can we get to the fun stuff?"

"Fun stuff?"

"The part where we fight and I win." Metal rang as he unsheathed one of his swords. It glowed like a bright, white star and emitted a buzz that rose every hair on her body.

Don't overthink.

She gripped her staff and attacked. Caught off guard, the Tarka's eyebrows shot up. He flicked his sword up to block her staff, but instead of swinging down like an axe, she shoved the forward end of the stick under his guard and into his face. His perfect nose crunched. He grunted.

His hand gripped her wrist and spun her around. She drove her elbow back. Her heartbeat thudded in her ears. He slipped to the side and avoided the blow.

He flicked his wrist and chopped her staff in half with one short swing of his vibrating blade, before ducking behind her again.

She stared at the cut ends of her staff.

"What will you do now?" he asked, his breath whispering behind her. She gripped the shortened sticks and slammed them back. They met a wall of muscle.

The Tarka chuckled and shoved her away. Taya stumbled a few steps, dropped the sticks and unsheathed her blades. Her fingers gripped the smooth leather wound around the hilts. The power vibrated along her skin. The electrifying blue energy danced along the shafts and whined, begging for blood. She whirled around and her hood fell back. The wind pushed her hair across her face.

The Tarka remained expressionless and drew his second sword. He now wielded two blades like her. "Ah. Now we see the true you."

She lunged. He parried. The power of the swords pulled at her. She fused with them, merging into one, as if the blades became extensions of her arms as she danced. The light reflected off the metal and she became a flurry of sharp edges. Each slash propelled her faster and she spun, transforming into a whirlwind of blades. Her father called it the *Makani*, and it was only taught to family members.

The Tarka moved with her, ducking, slipping, side-stepping, the antithesis of her attack. They kicked up snow and frozen rocks from the road. Their swords screamed and clashed, sending sparks flying. The blades hummed and whistled with each sweep and strike, only to scream again with the next contact. Lightning flung around them.

"A whirlwind attack," he said. "A unique tactic." He spoke normally with no panting or rushed words, as though he sat across a table from her and asked about the weather while he poured her a cup of tea.

Grrrr.

He was better than her. But running wasn't an option, nor was becoming a sacrificial lamb with no guts.

If you have nothing left, fight with heart. It's the only thing they can't take from you, her dad's voice guided her.

Now was not the time to think about what they did to the internal organs of the sacrifice victims. *I'll see you soon, Dad.*

Taya continued to strike and dodge, nipping in and out. He neatly avoided, deflected or blocked each attack. Sweat poured down her face. She narrowly dodged a counter strike.

The Tarka stepped in, did something with his blade along hers and suddenly one of her swords flew in the air. The lightning energy cut off.

"No!" Pain lanced through her arm as though he'd severed it, but her hand appeared normal. And attached. She stepped to the side and flicked up her second sword.

The Tarka dodged in time, barely. A thin red line ran along his porcelain cheek. A drop of blood pebbled on his skin. He smiled. He fucking smiled and his gray gaze danced. "What a nice surprise."

She stepped back. She knew he toyed with her, like a cat playing with its food, but this took it to a whole new condescending level.

Screams travelled down the road. Her team!

John.

That rat bastard had attacked despite her orders. He couldn't wait to flex his leader muscle and walked the rest of the group into a trap. Her shoulders slumped. Nicks and bruises decorated her skin. Her fallen sword lay on the other side of the Tarka. Its raw power called to her like a lost child—*Pick me up. Don't leave me.*

The river ran behind her, a soft musical accompaniment to her tragic end.

The river.

For whatever reason, the Arkavians avoided crossing rivers and every one of the death wave survivors had been in running water when the blue magic swept the Earth.

She needed to get to the river.

She spun and bolted.

And froze.

An invisible force lifted her in the air. No hands

held her. The Tarka hadn't caught her. At least not physically. The magic slowly turned her in the air until she faced the Tarka once again. He stood with a wide stance, one arm flung in front of him with his hand open and palm facing out. He had sheathed the swords. His cheek scratch and broken nose no longer bled, but his tussled hair and heaving chest indicated he had to put some effort into fighting her after all.

Yippee for her.

George groaned in the bushes. His shoe twitched.

The Tarka's attention remained trained on her, potent, powerful and full of an emotion she couldn't read.

"Spare him. He's just a boy."

The Tarka frowned, dark brows slicing into his statuesque face. "I did. He lives."

"Then spare him from your sacrifice ring. You'll have enough of us for your perverted magic."

He frowned harder. "Why would we sacrifice earthens?"

"Power?"

"We have enough already."

"Then what do you want with us?"

His expression brightened. "Ah, now you ask the good questions. I don't want anything from your comrades. They are nothing to me. You, on the other hand..." He floated Taya closer with his magic. "I have plans for you."

72

CHAPTER 10

OFF TO THE SLAUGHTER

Taya woke up with a crick in her neck and covered with a light dusting of snow. Hog-tied and gagged, she bounced with each jostle of the wagon. The dirt and oil on the rough cloth rubbed on her tongue. Her cheek pressed against the cold, coarse wooden slats.

At least she wasn't marching in a slave chain behind a horse. She'd conserve energy this way.

Horses snorted, multiple horses. A man coughed. A low conversation trailed behind the wagon. A stream of morning light bathed her face and the birds chirped like happy little lovebirds. Perhaps she was wrong to hate birds, yet she did anyway. Why the hell were they so happy when she was so miserable? And it was winter, goddammit. They should be miserable, too.

The wagon lurched to a stop. She tumbled forward and smacked her head against the wooden slats. *Ouch.*

A man vaulted over the far side of the wagon and landed near her feet. His footing, though agile, jostled the floorboards. He blocked the sun with his giant body and cast her in darkness.

The Tarka.

He crouched beside her, a large and looming shadow, bringing with him scents of the forest and horses.

"I'm glad you're awake. Your luxurious ride has ended," he said. "You have a choice. You can continue the rest of the way on foot, glaring at my horse's fat ass while I pull you along on a rope, or you can ride on the horse with me. One hint of any mischief and you'll hit the snow and no longer have a choice. What will it be?"

He reached forward and tugged the gag away from her mouth. She wanted to bite his fingers. Her shoulders screamed from the hog-tied position.

"Why?" she asked.

"It's faster for you to ride with me, but if you're going to get feisty about it, we may as well start with you on the ground."

"Why can't the wagon go farther?" Where were they? The view of the surrounding tree tops laden with heavy snow told her nothing. How long had she been out?

"There's no road access to the gate from this point."

Chills ran through her body. The gate? Other soldiers talked about the portal connecting their two worlds. The same portal that emitted the lethal blue wave.

Then she processed his words. Cold seeped into her skin and stabbed at her heart. He planned to take her to Arkavia? Through that magical door?

Oh, hell no. She had to escape before he took her through that gate. "I'll ride with you."

He smirked as if he plucked her intentions from her mind and looked forward to the challenge.

Light flashed off metal and a dagger appeared in his hand. He leaned over her with his gargantuan body, and cut the rope. Instant relief flowed through her, followed by pixilated pain as blood flow improved. Her arms and legs flopped to the floor. She rotated her wrists and gently rolled into a sitting position. Her vision swam. Her arms prickled from increased circulation.

"Are you thirsty?" he asked.

Yes. Her dry throat screamed for water. "No."

The Tarka chuckled and held up a canteen of water. He wore a huge ring. Sunlight reflected off a giant white stone embedded in the intricate metalwork. Opal? The stone looked like someone plucked the glowing moon from the night sky and set it in silver. She ignored the pretty jewel and focused on the canteen. He wouldn't poison her now after carting her all this way. He also had plenty of opportunity to murder her a thousand different ways while she lay vulnerable and unconscious.

She snatched the container from his hand and chugged the cold water. Some ran down her chin. The faint citrus taste washed away the dirt and grime from the gag.

The man watched, fixated with the movement of her throat.

Whatever. As long as he looked with his eyes and not with his hands.

"I'm Thane," he said. "From the House of Jericho."

What now? She'd heard that name before. Was it from one of the Arkavians or was she getting it mixed up with one of the beaches she visited in Vancouver? She handed back the now-empty canteen and wiped her mouth with her dirty sleeve. She returned his stare.

"Shall I make up a name for you? Or would you like to have a say in that?"

"Taya."

He smiled, flashing even white teeth and stood. He held his hand out.

She stared at his calloused palm. Would his skin zap hers? Did he offer his hand as some sort of magical trap? Why would she voluntarily touch him? An Arkavian Tarka who came to her planet to steal and kill.

He sighed.

What the hell did he expect? He might act nice and accommodating, but that didn't make them besties.

She scrambled to her feet and brushed the dirt and snow from her clothes. Her pants were soaked and a chill rippled through her body. She ignored his outreached hand and glanced at her surroundings. Three battle-hardened warriors sat on giant horses and studied her with flat expressions. None of these guys resembled the shifty, newly trained guards on the supply wagons.

One of the men sported a black eye, and another had a split lip, but otherwise, they appeared fresh and ready to pillage the next village. A fuzzy memory of a fight flittered through her mind and flew off before she could grab hold of it.

If she'd seen any of these men, Thane included, anywhere near the Arkavian supplies, she would've run in the opposite direction.

Wait. Where was everyone else? Where was her team? She scanned the surrounding forest and snow covered, gravel road.

"Did you kill them all?" she asked. Their faces streaked through her mind like a movie film. *Please say no.*

"Some were injured when they attacked the supply wagon, but I spared them, as requested."

An invisible weight lifted from her shoulders. Well, at least there was that. She glanced back at Thane. He'd dropped his hand and stood at the edge of the wagon, waiting. The sun danced along his platinum-blond hair and his armour.

"Why are you doing this?"

"You might be a prisoner, but that doesn't mean I have to be uncivil."

"Not that. Why me? Why did you take me?"

His gaze turned hard. He clenched his mouth shut and a jaw muscle popped out. "You interest me."

That sounded ominous. Yet something in his scowl contradicted his statement of idle curiosity. Maybe she did *interest* him. Whatever the hell that meant and implied, but that wasn't the only reason Thane nabbed her.

He hopped off the cart. The wooden slats creaked and wobbled. "Come on, princess. We're losing the sun."

Taya originally agreed to ride with Thane so she could plan her escape and reserve her energy. After viewing their company and getting bombarded by recurring memories of how Thane's magic rendered her helpless, she should've gone with the other option. Walking would slow their progress and delay her departure from the realm of Earth.

She knew better than to hope John mounted some rescue mission. He wouldn't come after her. Why would he? There was nothing in it for him except regaining a leader he didn't want or value. For once, his selfish behaviour was a good thing. Attacking these battled-hardened soldiers would be suicide.

Thane led her to a giant black stallion with a flaxen mane and tail. No, wait. The horse wasn't black, but rather a rich dark brown. She had no idea what an actual warhorse looked like or what made one horse qualify for the label and another not, but the majestic beast standing two feet away from her was definitely a fucking warhorse.

The horse turned his massive head and snorted in her face. Her hair whipped back. She held out her hand, palm out.

Someone snickered. Thane's glare cut to somewhere over her right shoulder and the laughter stopped.

He turned back to Taya. "They're just pissy because you got a couple shots in when you came out of the stupor early."

Ah. That explained the hazy memory of fighting.

"I don't get pissy," one of the men growled.

She rolled her eyes and turned. "Let me guess. You just get even?"

The man with the black eye snapped his mouth shut.

The horse leaned forward, sniffed her hand and turned away disinterested. Maybe she should've waited until she had food to offer before she held her hand out like some wannabe horse-whisperer.

"He likes you," Thane said.

"How can you tell?"

"He didn't head butt you."

Peachy. She ran her hand along the horse's neck and walked to his side.

"His name is Hades," Thane said.

Apparently, Arkavians also had Greek mythology. Or was it a reality for them? The unusual name couldn't be a coincidence. What else did the two worlds share? "And what would happen if he didn't like me? Other than head butting?"

"He'd carry you anyway because that's his job."

Taya nodded and fumbled for the saddle horn. She wasn't short, but she wasn't an Amazon, either. Standing at his side, she could just see over the horse's withers.

"Would you like a boost?"

"Fuck off." Abandoning the horn, she gripped the side of the saddle, placed a foot in the stirrup and hoisted her body higher. Once up, she gripped the horn with ease and swung her other leg around the horse's broad back. She ran a hand through the coarse hair.

Where were her swords? Would she ever see them again? Did Thane leave them on the ground like unwanted trash as the other Arkavian lord had?

Before she could dwell more on her lost weapons, Thane swung into the saddle behind her and Hades pranced in the snow. Suddenly the Tarka was all around her, smelling of fresh soil, pine and metal. His armour pressed into her back. One vambrace-covered arm reached around her and clamped her body tightly against his while his free hand picked up the reins.

He clucked and Hades stepped forward.

She hadn't thought about the physical proximity with her captor when she chose this option.

Big mistake.

"Why are you holding your breath?"

Because you smell too good.

Why did she have to notice something like that? What a totally inappropriate observation. And why did she like how strong he felt behind her? She should be scared. She should be planning when to drive a dagger through his chest.

Take a deep breath.

She forced the air from her lungs through her teeth and wrapped her hand in Hades' flaxen mane.

Thane's chest rumbled against her back like a giant massage. Why was she suddenly hyper aware of him? This would end up being the longest ride known to man.

CHAPTER II

NOT AGAIN...

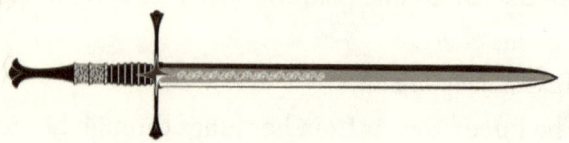

Taya gave up trying to hold herself ramrod straight in the saddle to avoid touching Thane and sagged against his brick-hard armour-plated chest.

They moved along a narrow snow-packed trail in the woods, the horses quietly picking their footing over broken branches and overgrown brush. The late afternoon sun streaked through the canopy, but offered no warmth. Instead, the rays of light illuminated the path and reflected off armour, distorted only by the clouds of air escaping the horses and soldiers. The clinking of armour, the crunch of snow under hooves and the occasional snapping branch broke the otherwise eerie silence hanging over the evergreen forest.

A man in worn leathers stepped in front of them without a sound. He had long brown hair and flat, dark eyes.

Taya jerked back in the saddle. Thane's arm tightened around her waist.

"Bruno." He didn't sound surprised to see the man appear out of nowhere without warning.

"There's something you should see." The man had a raspy voice that reminded her of a snake somehow. His dark gaze flicked to her. He frowned.

"Lead on."

"It's easier on foot." Bruno frowned at her. "And not for the eyes of a lady."

One of the other men—Axel, from what the other men called him—snorted. "She's earthen."

Well, thank you very much, asshole. Last time she checked, being one didn't exclude the other. Maybe she could give him a second black eye to match his first. She always hated the "earthen" label. It made her think of dirt. Like she and her fellow survivors were the filth beneath Arkavian boots and not worthy of further contemplation or some cool sci-fi nickname like "terran."

Bruno's eyebrows shot up. He grinned and this time his gaze held entitlement and contempt.

Ewwwww. No. Taya's skin crawled as if it wanted to slough off to escape Bruno's attention.

"Fine." Thane released her, leaving an imprint of his gauntlet on her waist, and slipped from the saddle. He left her back cold and exposed.

"I'll be back." Thane turned to the group. "Bruno and Axel with me. The rest stay with Taya. Lokni, you're in charge." He pointed at the large warrior with a scar running down his cheek.

She gathered and clutched the reins. She scanned the forest and the tree branches weighed down by thick clumps of snow and ice. If she clucked like Thane and dug in her heels, would Hades run for her? Could she escape the men?

The warrior with the split lip shook his head at her in warning.

Okay, then. Maybe these guys read minds, or maybe she was super obvious with her plans. Damn it.

Lokni pinned her with his violet gaze. "Don't even think about it." It's the first time he'd spoken to her. He had one of those deep, almost growly voices. They all did. They sounded like how she imagined an alien warrior race wielding swords and riding demon-like horses would sound—like grizzly bears could talk.

"Can you all read minds?"

He shook his head. "No, but we don't need to with you. You give away everything with your face."

"Don't ever play cards," Split Lip said. Taya didn't know his name yet.

"I'm fucking awesome at cards."

The men smirked in unison. With exception to Lokni's scar, they looked a lot alike. Brothers? "Twins?"

"Has anyone ever complimented you on your powers of observation?" Lokni asked.

"No."

He smirked, the scar dimpling his cheek. "There's a reason for that."

Oh, ha, ha, Asshole.

Split Lip opened his mouth to say more, but froze at the sound of movement through the trees. Branches shook snow onto the forest floors. *Plop, plop, thud.*

Thane stepped onto the path. The air moved around him, crackling with power. Every time she tried to focus on his magic, though, she saw nothing. Like the waves coming off heated pavement in the summer, or an illusion in a desert, the power was there, but not visible.

One thing was clear, though. Thane was pissed.

He stalked up to his horse, grabbed her wrist and tugged. He didn't pull hard enough to make her fall to the ground, but enough to make her scramble to pull her leg over the saddle before she slipped off the horse.

"Come with me." The steel in his voice told her this was not the time to test boundaries.

He pulled her through the forest on a worn deer path. His calloused hand became a warm clamp on her wrist. Snow crunched under their boots and no one made any effort to cover their progress. The air bit at her face, too cold to offer any comforting smells. Her toe caught on a branch and she tumbled forward.

Thane's iron-clad grip kept her upright. He didn't pause and kept stalking forward as he held her up and she found her footing. A memory of her mom hauling her brother through the mall mid-tantrum rushed up and pierced her heart.

What the hell was going on? Why was he so angry? She hadn't done anything. Not recently, at least. Was this it? Had his promises of a sacrifice-free existence all been a lie?

Then the smell hit her.

Death.

Decay.

The putrid smells cut through the cold and attempted to gouge her nose out. She dug her heels in. Backpedaling brought up frozen dirt and snow. Thane tugged her through the brush as if her resistance had zero impact, and stopped in a clearing.

Axel, the warrior with the black eye, marched into the death camp, nonplused, and Bruno waited on the trail.

Her stomach rolled. Snow-dusted, decomposing bodies lined the small clearing in a circle. Frozen body cavities ripped open. Her memories from a similar circle swirled in her head.

She lurched to the side and heaved the entire contents of her stomach into the brush.

Thane let her go, his solid presence unmistakable behind her.

She straightened and wiped her mouth with her sleeve. Ugh. She needed a change of clothes. The material stunk.

Instead of turning to view the massacre, she faced

the forest and Bruno's smirking face. Her vision swam. Her world careened to the side. Thane stepped around her and inserted his gargantuan body into her field of view and steadied her with his warm iron-clad grip on her arm.

Her head stopped spinning and Taya focused on the warrior.

"When we first met, you said you didn't want to be my next sacrifice." He released her arm.

She nodded. How could she forget? Her midsection clenched. Images bombarded her mind. The blood. The flies. The birds silently watching instead of making incessant noise. How long ago was that? Over four months now?

"Is this what you meant?" he growled.

What else could she have possibly meant?

He took a menacing step forward, invading her personal space with the bulk of his giant armoured body, muscles tense, fists clenched.

She flinched.

Thane froze. He rocked back on his heels and visibly shook himself. He relaxed his hands. "Have you seen this before?"

"Yes," she hissed.

Thane clamped his mouth shut. His jaw clenched and unclenched. His cheeks turned red for an instant before clearing to pale porcelain. "Is this what you thought I was capable of doing?"

Why the fuck was he angry at her? "Of course it's

what I thought. Why wouldn't I? You obliterated us and then rounded up the survivors to haul off as slaves or to massacre in some weird sacrifice circle."

His gaze blazed silvery white. Energy vibrated around him, tingling along her skin. "How many?"

She stepped back. "What?"

"How many sacrifices like this have you seen?"

"Only one and it was...fresher."

Bruno shifted on the path, visibly apprehensive with the scene.

Thane pointed to the dead, mutilated bodies. "This is not what we do."

She shrugged. "If you say so."

Thane glowered.

They stood in silence. Even the birds shut up.

"We should move." Axel walked up to Thane's side and leaned in. "What do you want to do with the bodies?"

"Leave them," Thane said. "We need to make camp soon and I don't want to be near here."

At least they agreed on that. "So it's not some crazy Arkavian monster that slipped through the gate to kill these people? We were right? It's a who, not a what?"

He nodded, grimly. "I need to know more about the other sacrifice you saw."

Cold shimmied along her skin. She rubbed her arms through her shirt sleeves, but they remained frozen. "Fine. Can we discuss it later? Away from here?" And in full daylight without the lurking shadows of the trees where the sun could scare away her nightmares.

Thane's stern expression softened, appearing less like a granite statue and more like an actual living person. He stepped back and waved at the path. "After you."

CHAPTER 12
I'LL TAKE MY CHANCES

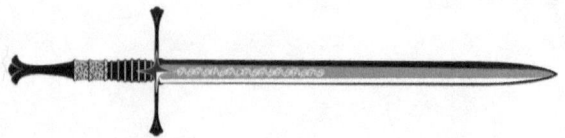

The campfire crackled and metal clanked as the men pulled off their armour and set up camp while Taya watched from Hades' back. The arrogant bastards left her, perched on the warhorse and turned their unconcerned backs to her to get to work.

Her wet pants had dried and the chill seeping into her bones had fled. This was her chance. She had to go now.

No amount of nudging or soft whispering encouraged Hades to take a step, let alone go for a walk. He tossed his flaxen mane at her before sniffing the frozen ground. She had to slip off this beast unnoticed and keep to the thick woods so their horses wouldn't be an advantage. She waited. She gripped the leather reins in her hands and squeezed.

The men continued to mill around her and the

90

campsite. They didn't look at her once. Why were they so unconcerned about her escape? Were they that arrogant they believed her already an obedient, good little slave?

Split Lip called out and the men moved to set up a large tent.

Now!

She swung her leg over and slipped off Hades into a patch of soft snow. Without a glance back, she picked her way into the trees. Her heart thudded so hard, surely it would give her away—a biological alarm. She sped up. Cold sweat broke out along her hairline. She weaved around the trees and pushed forward on numb toes.

Ten minutes into the woods, a man yelled out.

No! Too soon! She didn't have much of a lead. With the snow, they'd track her easily. Branches snapped behind her. She dropped her chin and surged forward. The cold air raked her throat and burned her lungs.

Faster!

Farther!

Go!

Wood snapped under her feet. Snow sprayed up behind her. She broke through the forest and nearly stumbled at the sight greeting her.

The ocean curled into a long bay. Gaze wild, she scanned the treeline. It would take at least an hour to go around the frozen sea. The other side of the bay beckoned her over the glistening shards of ice, reflecting the last rays of the day. The temperature had dropped so low, the salt water had formed large chunks of ice over the surface. The bay must be very shallow.

The men emerged from the forest as her feet took their first steps onto the ice.

"Stop," a deep voice boomed.

Taya whirled around to face them. The three men. No sign of Thane.

They stalked toward her. She backed onto the ice farther. She stepped over a large crack. The sheet of ice groaned but held. The smaller piece she now stood on rocked. The dark marine water moved underneath, taunting her with a lethal promise. If she fell into the icy depths, she'd die of hypothermia.

"We'll find you," Axel snarled. "He'll never let you go."

Split Lip stepped onto the icy surface. The small ice floes creaked and cracked under his weight. He glared at her.

Taya lifted her chin, turned, and ran. If she kept running, the cold couldn't get her. They couldn't get her. She'd be free. She slipped and slid and crashed onto the ice. Her face scraped the cold, rough surface.

Keep going!

She pulled herself up, licked the blood from her bleeding lip and charged forward again, bounding from one floe to the next. Each sheet of ice swayed under her weight. Though the floes were tightly packed, some freezing together to form larger sheets of ice, one wrong step, one tumble, and she'd slip into the ocean. The far shore beckoned and grew closer and closer with each thumping stride. Her chest heaved. Cold air sheered its way through her body and burned her lungs. Her muscles ached.

Her foot hit solid ground. She sprawled onto the snowy bank and panted. She'd made it. They were at least an hour behind her.

She might just die here. It would be so easy. Giving up required no further action besides letting the cold get her. She could take the path of least resistance.

Taya got up with snow caked to her body and stumbled farther up the beach to where waves had pushed snow crusted driftwood before it iced over.

Thane stepped from the forest. The last shards of daylight streaked across the bay and illuminated the chiseled perfection of his features.

Her scalp prickled as if an invisible beast gripped her head in his hand. What the hell? How'd he get here so fast?

"That was an impressive run," he said.

"I should say the same," she wheezed. Why did he look so fresh? Had he taken Hades for a leisurely jaunt around the bay while his men chased her? Or had he used his magical powers to somehow teleport himself here.

"I take it you will not come willingly?"

Taya snarled. He might have powers, but he didn't

have his armour or sword. Maybe if she got a surprise attack in, or bolted before he could blast her with his magic, she'd make it to freedom. She refused to cower or bow to this man. She still had a chance.

"And if I promised no harm will come to you?"

She backed away and glanced behind her. One of his men, Lokni, the one with violet eyes and face scar, precariously made his way across the broken sheet of ice covering the bay. His scowl was clear, even at a distance.

Damn it!

She changed course and edged toward the trees.

Thane moved with her and his smile broadened, revealing perfect, white teeth.

Taya reached to the edge of the forest where the trees protected the forest floor from the majority of the snow. With her feet on firm ground, her confidence bolstered and her mind raced through possibilities. She'd never outrun him. She sucked at jogging on the best days and she was already exhausted. Even with her extensive training, she probably wouldn't best him in hand-to-hand combat, either.

She curled her hands into fists. No! She wouldn't yield. If he wanted her to go with him, he'd have to fight for it.

She didn't give him the warning of squaring off. She turned and kicked snow into his face, before slamming the side of her foot into his jaw.

He grunted and leaned back.

She dashed for the trees. He snagged her damp sweater with his hand. The material ripped and sent her sprawling forward. She braced for the impact with her hands. Her teeth clamped together and rattled. Pain jarred its way up her arms. She grabbed a rock near her head and hurled it at Thane's face. He swore.

She stumbled to her feet and raced into the woods. Weapon? Where's a weapon? She needed a stick. A rock. *Something.*

Thane hurtled through the brush after her. Branches cracked and snapped. Taya dove on a large stick and managed to straighten before he reached her. She whipped around with it, aiming for his head. He blocked it, brushing it aside.

"This again?" he sneered.

The stick was too heavy for her to use. It wasn't like her staff. It took him no time or effort to disarm her. He changed tactics.

Up until then, he'd defended. Now he attacked.

Taya managed to partially block his first blow. His fist glanced off her skull and left her ear ringing. They went back and forth with a fury of blows, each met with blocks rendering them ineffective.

He didn't strike with full force. He moved with swift accuracy, but his strikes had the relaxed ease of someone sparring or shadow boxing. He toyed with her like a cat facing a bird with a broken wing.

Grrrr.

Taya stepped back and slipped. Thane followed

her, catching her in the most unladylike position. A smile spread across his face as he looked down at her. She quickly brought her leg up and around his head, slamming his face and smug grin into the snow. As her leg came down, she captured his neck between her legs. She squeezed and watched his face turn red. She squeezed harder. If he didn't have the neck of a bull, she might have a chance of breaking it.

He splayed his hand on her stomach and zapped her—the bolt of energy knocked the air from her lungs. Her legs slackened their death grip. Before he attacked again, she shoved him away with her foot on his face. She scrambled to stand and took two steps when a bulldozer slammed into her.

Thane sent them flying through the air and onto the frozen path. He pinned her to the forest floor.

"Asshole!" She punched out her arms and thrashed her legs. Cold metal slid around her neck and a link snapped shut.

She stilled.

No!

The prickling sensation returned. The urge to hit a non-existent rewind button overcame her. This couldn't happen. This wasn't happening. When would she wake up and find out this had all been an awful dream?

He locked the slave collar around her neck and leaned over, his breath brushing her cheek. "You're mine."

CHAPTER 13
ME, TOO

Taya startled awake. A fire crackled in the distance, but sent little warmth to her numb body. With the thin bedroll protecting her from the frozen ground, a threadbare blanket covering her from the chill of the night, and the rattle of the chain binding her hands together and latching her to a nearby tree with her slave collar, her circumstances hadn't changed...except a dirty hand clamped on her mouth.

She tensed. The chains clanked.

"Don't scream and I won't hurt you," a low voice hissed in her ear.

Her vision adjusted to make out the dark shape cast in shadow from the muted light of the low burning campfire. Bruno, the scout, crouched over her. His rough hand smelled of horse and bark. His other hand shoved her manacled arms over her head and pinned them down to the cold dirt. He let go of her mouth and dragged his hand down her body.

Her breathing hitched. Her heartbeat thudded. *No. Not this. He couldn't do this. Not here. Not this way. Not this man. No.*

As suddenly as his weight pushed her into the thin bed mat over the frozen dirt, it vanished.

Bruno's body disappeared and landed with a thump a few feet away from her.

Taya sat up and blinked. Her head swam and she panted to catch her breath. Sweat ran down her face.

Thane stood at the base of her bed roll, statue-still and the air crackled with power around him.

"You don't understand." Bruno scrambled to his feet and scurried over to Thane.

"Try me." His expression gave nothing away, but his cold detached voice sent ice down Taya's back and he wasn't speaking to her.

"She looks like them. Like a royal house member."

"So?"

"I'm not like you. A guy like me would never have a chance with a noblewoman."

"And this way you can? It didn't matter that she's not willing or that I explicitly told everyone to keep their hands off her."

"She was into it."

Thane narrowed his eyes. "There's only three reasons that could be true. Either, she planned to seduce you to escape. Or she's a scared hostage who believed she had no choice because saying no would result in bad things happening, or..." Thane paused to scowl. "Or you're a piece of shit, too absorbed in your own satisfaction to recognize what no looks like."

Thane unsheathed one of his white-glowing swords and in one fluid motion drove the blade forward to skewer Bruno.

The scout sagged on the blade, his surprised expression illuminated by the blazing weapon. Thane twisted the sword.

Bruno gurgled.

Thane turned to the watching men. "I don't care what or who you think she looks like. If you can't follow orders, you will die." He pushed Bruno off the blade with his foot. The body flopped to the ground with a wet thump. Blood dripped from the sword a few feet from her face.

Thane crouched and used Bruno's shirt to clean his weapon. He didn't glance her way once. When he straightened, he sheathed the sword and pointed to the body with his forefinger. "Get rid of this."

The men grunted and moved with quick efficiency to follow his order.

Thane finally turned to her, expression hard. "Are you okay?"

She hugged her knees to her chest and looked away. "Just peachy. You didn't have to kill one of your soldier boys on my account." She said the words, but she meant none of them. She must harbour an evil demon inside because she reveled in the scout's death. He got what he deserved. She was only sorry she hadn't been the one to end his life.

What concerned her was whether Thane thought this bought him some sort of brownie points or made him think she owed him for his magnanimous efforts. Oh hell, no. This asshole zapped her in the stomach and clamped a slave collar around her neck. Even if he was gloriously beautiful, he'd captured her like some rare stag on a hunt.

Snow crunched as two of the men walked over, grabbed Bruno's body and hoisted him off the ground.

"I didn't kill him for you."

She frowned and turned back.

His expression had softened, but his eyes still flashed. "The man directly defied an order. If I can't trust him, he's of no use."

Branches snapped as the other men made their way through the forest to dispose of the body.

"You could've sent him away." Wait, what? Why suggest alternatives? She didn't want to owe Thane, but not enough to wish Bruno got a lighter sentence.

"Perhaps." He rubbed the platinum stubble on his chin. "But I never liked him. A man who doesn't hesitate to take advantage of a powerless woman has no honour."

If only she could trust all Arkavians to have an honour code.

"The other men won't touch you," Thane continued. "You have my promise on that."

He said nothing about his own intentions.

Taya pulled the blanket up, the chains latching her to the nearby tree rattled. Her hands shook. Was it the frigid temperature or her nerves? Did it matter?

Thane studied her for a minute and hesitated. "I'd like you to move closer to the fire. I don't like how cold you appear."

She pursed her lips. It was the middle of winter and they camped in the open on cold ground at the north tip of Vancouver Island. They'd given her only a thin mat and a thinner blanket to curl up with. Of course she was cold. Maybe Arkavians didn't feel the cold like she did.

She slipped from the bedding, picked up the materials and waited for Thane to move the chains.

She had to choose her battles. This was not one of them.

Besides, the light of the fire might burn away the feel of Bruno's unwanted hands on her body.

One Arkavian down...how many more to go?

CHAPTER 14
AN OFFER YOU CAN'T REFUSE

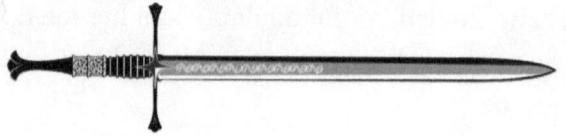

Taya stood ankle deep in fresh snow in front of a wave of death-blue crystallized air in the shape of an oval as large as a two-storey house and froze. Sunlight streaked through the forest and made the gate to Arkavia glow. Her spine straightened as if the vertebrae fused together. The air buzzed with magic so potent she tasted metal.

"I can't walk through that," she said.

Multiple paths led to the small clearing in front of the portal to the alternate realm of Arkavia. Horses and boots had trampled the ground, killing any type of greenery and leaving the exposed dirt to freeze with divots and ripples. Exactly how many supply routes did they have? How far did their influence and power reach?

"You can and you will," Thane growled behind her.

"The death wave looked exactly the same and it annihilated my friends while I watched from the river. This field of magic, or whatever you call it, is lethal to people from Earth."

"You see the visible boundary between our realms. Other earthen slaves have passed through unscathed. It's not lethal. It's the effect caused by the magic from Arkavia bordering the magic-less atmosphere of Earth, its anathema. This space is like a semipermeable membrane that allows Arkavia's magic to slowly cross over. When the gate opened, the first wave raced out, obliterating technology to lay a dusting of magic over the entire planet. Now we have this membrane in place to slow the rest of the transition."

"That speech did absolutely nothing to assure me of my likely survival."

"The magic wave also included a death curse purposefully included to kill earthens and lessen the resistance of our takeover. This portal contains none of that death magic."

She glared at him. He spoke about the Earth's extinction so matter-of-fact. Like his actions were somehow justifiable.

He returned her glare and waited, giant arms folded over his broad, armoured chest.

"I'm not going in there," she repeated.

"You don't have a choice."

She crossed her arms and mirrored his posture.

"I will carry you if I have to."

"Why not kill me now?" She really needed to think through her responses before speaking.

Thane sighed and looked at the sky. He dropped his arms and he relaxed into his stance.

Uh-oh. This couldn't be good.

"I don't wish to kill or harm you."

"Then let me go."

Thane clenched his jaw, took two giant steps forward and bent to catch her by the middle. When he straightened, he threw her over his shoulder. His gauntlet armoured fingers dug into her thighs. His swords' hilts stared back at her, tempting and teasing. Her fingers itched to wrap around the smooth leather and yank one from its sheath.

If you're going down, go down fighting, her dad's life motto played in her memory.

If only her hands weren't bound. Instead, she flopped uselessly as Thane strode toward the gate. His shoulder dug into her stomach and her face smacked against the cold metal back plate of his black armour. She had a perfect view of his ass. Fitting since he acted like one.

What did she expect? She wasn't any different than any of the other slaves brought through this portal. Expecting preferential treatment would be futile.

Thane walked unhindered through the thick air. The blue haze cleared. The buzzing stopped.

She wasn't dead.

Thane pulled her down from his shoulder and set her on her feet in the snow in front of him. Over his shoulder, the other men walked through the gate leading the horses.

Cool air brushed her skin. The winter breeze contained exotic scents of Arkavia, smelling of pine, but different, more floral.

Thane watched her expectantly.

"I may have overreacted," she said.

He raised a dark brow.

"This isn't so—"

Searing hot invisible hands clawed at her body and gripped her head in a vise-like grip. Pain stabbed her skin. She crumpled to the powdered ground as the raw power of Arkavia attacked her and attempted to shred her flesh from her bones. She flailed on the ground, flinging and kicking up snow. As fast as the attack happened, another power, cold and ice-like wrapped around her like a protective salve. The other magic beat at the wall, but the ice magic held, keeping it at bay.

Someone picked her up and held her to their body. Armour. Metal. Thane. He carried her away from the gate and the world turned black.

TAYA BLINKED and waited for her fuzzy vision to clear. Tent. Inside. Candlelight. Arkavian air. She took a deep breath of floral forest, fresh dirt and candle wax, and wiggled her toes. They moved. She scraped her tongue with her teeth to rub the stale taste of dirt from her mouth. Ugh. Breath mint, please.

At least she was alive and well, despite whatever had happened. The now-familiar cold sheath of magic still coated her, holding the volatile energy away.

Why was she suddenly so aware of magic, power, and energy? Before, the vision of magic alluded her, now she saw the ribbon-like bands and hazy clouds like puffs of smoke all around her in different hues, temperatures and strengths.

The tent rustled and Thane stepped through the flap. The low murmur of men's voices and the crackle of a large fire trailed after him. The flap settled back in place and cut off the trickle of sounds from outside, leaving her alone and in silence with a giant, magic wielding alien. His presence shrank the tent even though it could house the mammoth warrior as he stood straight. A cotton shirt stretched over his body. Without his armour, he still managed to loom, intimidating and just as inhuman.

"You're awake," he said.

"You're perceptive."

He pressed his lips together. Instead of replying, he unbuckled his sword belts.

Taya's eyebrows rose. He'd made a pretty speech

earlier about not wanting to kill or harm her. What the hell was he doing now?

The phantom hands of Bruno ran along her skin.

She shuddered.

Thane placed his swords against the breastplate sitting upright on its own near the cot. The metal reflected the flickering candlelight. On the other side of the breastplate, two familiar blades rested. Her blades. Hope rose instantaneously and spread through her like a wild brush fire.

No. She couldn't hope. It would only hurt more later. She'd never wield those swords again, and the sooner she accepted that cold, hard fact, the less the loss would sting. God, she missed them. She wanted to reach out and wrap her hands around their familiar hilts.

Thane crouched by the cot. His boots creaked. He reached over and plucked a canteen from the ground and held it out to her. "You need water."

She pushed the canteen away from her face. "I need an explanation."

Thane sighed, his minty-fresh breath brushing over her.

Where the heck did he get a mint?

Focus!

Thane placed the canteen on the ground beside him. He shifted his weight back on his heels. "You had a reaction to Arkavian magic."

"I thought Earth already had a *light dusting*. Why didn't I react to that?"

"I think you did."

She blinked.

"I think you already possessed the innate ability to wield magic. Arkavia is an alternate universe. There are infinite realms, but at one time, we shared an existence until something split our realities and we branched out. You retained the biological ability to access magic from our common ancestors."

She blinked again. She wasn't dumb, but how did this evolution of reality explain what happened? Did this mean she couldn't refer to Thane as an alien anymore?

Thane's expression softened becoming less granite and more human-looking. "Think of your magic as a separate entity, housed inside of you and fast asleep. When the portal opened, it nudged your magic, so it started to wake up, slowly. When we went through the portal, the Arkavian atmosphere violently shook your magic awake."

"So now my magic is freaking out?" Could she tell her power to calm the fuck down?

"Exactly, and you're not trained to control it."

Taya paused and re-evaluated the giant hulk of muscle beside her. He took all her questions and took the time to explain his answers. He'd saved her from a would-be rapist and placed his protection over her. But he'd also captured her and snapped a slave collar around her neck. "Did you know? About the magic?"

"I suspected."

"How?"

He grinned, a wicked flash of white teeth. "You could wield the twin blades of House Raiden. Elias could hold them, but struggled to control their magic. His brother didn't have enough power to touch them at all. It was a point of contention between the brothers. Elias' brother hated those swords. They represented his greatest failure."

That explained why the leader of the slave procession had left the swords with his dead brother. Not that they would've done him any good where he ended up. The sacrifice circle flashed in her memory. She shuddered.

"Do most of the survivors have magic?" she asked. John didn't. The blades hurled him through the air when he tried to touch them.

Thane shrugged. "Your world was devoid of magic prior to us opening the portal gate. That's why your... technology..." He said the word as if it tasted bad in his mouth. "Reacted so violently against it. Our reality has replaced yours."

Did that mean they could rediscover electricity and reinvent technology somehow, or had magic fundamentally changed how things worked at the subatomic level? But wasn't all life biochemical reactions? How were they still alive? Still breathing? Still functioning?

Did magic keep them going somehow? But why would—

A headache bloomed behind her eyes.

She might never understand how this technological apocalypse worked and it didn't really matter, not right now. Understanding wouldn't change her current circumstances.

"What are your plans for me?" He certainly didn't treat her like a slave. She took that as permission not to act like one.

"I'd like to make you an offer."

She sat up and pulled the rough wool sheet with her. Even fully clothed, the cold seeped in.

"Your fate as a free earthen raiding Arkavian supply chains doesn't have a bright future."

Ugh. Again with that word. "Can you not use that term?"

"What term?"

"*Earthen*," she said.

"Earthen is from our shared language and refers to something characteristic of the earth. You are from Earth. How is this a bad term?"

"You're calling me dirt."

He frowned.

She waited.

"There are more important things for you to be concerned about right now," he said, shaking his head. "They sent me to neutralize you. If I let you go, and you return to your previous ways, they'll send more and the others won't spare you. If you managed to avoid slaughter, winter is here. Resources are low and you're starving."

Okay, he had a point about focusing on more pressing matters. A label was a label, and she could live with this one. As for his assessment, he wasn't wrong. Things were getting bad with her group's increasing numbers, but not that bad. Not yet.

"As a slave in my world, your future prospects are also grim. There's manual labour and housekeeping, but with your looks, you'd most likely end up in a whore house."

She balked.

"You're beautiful and Bruno wasn't the only man who'd like a woman who resembles Arkavian aristocracy."

The phantom hands of Bruno returned. She brushed off her shirt and rubbed her arms.

Thane narrowed his eyes, but didn't comment. He relaxed into his crouch and leaned back. "As my captive, you'll be spared those fates. You have a choice. I can send you off with a slave collar to my steward. He'll assign you a role in my house. This role will most likely involve cleaning or stable work, but you'll be fed, clothed and housed, and any violence or unwanted attention toward you will not be tolerated. That's reciprocal though. Any attempt on your part to escape or harm someone in my house will result in your swift execution. You'll live a long, boring life of hard manual labour."

He hesitated.

The wait ate at her nerves. There had to be a fourth option. *Please, please, please be an "or."* He hadn't made an offer yet. Not really. "Or?"

He smiled, but it didn't reach his sad eyes. "It's not lost on me that a woman with beauty, combat skills, and raw power could be an asset to my house."

How? She stopped rubbing her arms. Her fingers longed to dig into the soft fabric of his shirt and throttle him for answers.

"I'm proposing a year of service. You will train with my men and carry out my orders like the others. I will teach you to control your power and use your swords."

She clenched her teeth. She already knew how to use her swords. "What's the catch?"

"No catch. You will be a soldier. My soldier. You will be bound to my service. You will train for me. You will kill. You will likely bleed and you may die. This life is not for everyone and I don't make this offer lightly."

"Earthens?"

"Pardon?"

"Will I kill other *earthens*?"

He shook his head. "It's unlikely any of your fellow survivors will be used as guards, so no. Your targets will be Arkavian."

The weight of her promise to her dead friends

lifted from her shoulders. Picking off untrained supply cart guards hadn't eased the ache of her loss or the compulsion to avenge them. Maybe this would. Maybe this deal would satisfy her debt for surviving. "I have no chance against trained, fully grown Arkavian males. You guys are beasts."

She didn't say it as a compliment, but he smiled. "Not in direct combat, you're right."

"So you're suggesting...indirect combat?" What the hell was that? How could she indirectly kill—Oh! "You want to train me as an assassin?"

His grin was wicked.

She didn't need to ask why he needed an assassin. What little information she'd gleaned over the last few months painted a picture of an almost medieval society with ruthless lords constantly vying for power. Assassins fit with her assessment of Arkavians.

Thane might've phrased the offer like she had a choice, and in essence, she did. But in reality, when faced with the alternatives, only one of the options appealed to her. Only one might relieve the burning need to wring out justice from the blood of dead Arkavians.

"What happens at the end of the year?" she asked.

"You will be given another choice."

She snorted. *No catch my ass.*

"If you survive this year, you will have to decide whether you want to leave or if you want to stay."

"Is that so? You're just going to let me walk away with all that knowledge and training?"

"I think a year will be long enough to show you why leaving won't be in your best interests. Not because I'll do anything to prevent it, but because your world is changing drastically. Earth will become a barren husk. Arkavia will suck it dry and you'll have no home to return to. If you want to survive, you need to make a life on Arkavia. The surest way of survival in my world is to align yourself with a powerful house. My house."

"The House of Jericho?"

"This year will give you time to acclimatize and make an informed decision."

What was in the fine print? He didn't make this offer to her comrades and some of them could fight. Sort of. Okay, maybe not as well as her, but was this offer solely because she looked like an Arkavian or was there something more going on here? Something he wasn't telling her?

"And you're going to take my word for it? I promise to be good, we shake hands and that's it? You're going to trust me not to run off at the first chance or slit your throats while you sleep?"

His face hardened. "Ah, well. I guess this is the part you might consider the catch."

She fucking knew it.

"Instead of a slave collar, I will use a non-permanent bond to ensure your honourable service. I will always know where you are and it will prevent you from disobeying my orders, one of which will be not to harm any of my house unless training, in self-defence or ordered."

Surely she could work around an order and its wording. Was a perceived threat enough to justify self-defence? "What does this bond involve?"

"Consent. Which is why I'm making this an offer in the first place instead of demanding compliance. I can't force you to be a good little assassin for me with a slave collar. Training an unwilling participant is futile. To be the house asset I want you to be, you have to agree to this and willingly accept the magical bond. You have to want this life."

His expression told her he braced for rejection. He didn't expect her to agree.

"You didn't answer my question. What does the actual bonding process entail?" A handshake? A blood pact. A horizontal mambo? What was she willing to pay for her freedom, or at least the promise of it? What was she willing to give to avenge her dead?

Anything.

He narrowed his eyes. "Nothing physical. My magic is already wrapped around you. To bond, it will go inside and make a little house for itself."

He planned to penetrate her with his power. Awesome.

She lifted her chin and met Thane's intense, storm-filled gaze. "Let's do this."

CHAPTER 15
BONDAGE 101

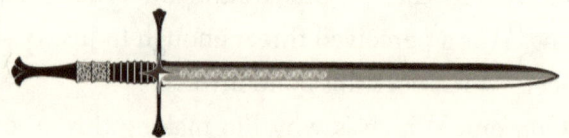

Taya sat under the scratchy blanket and waited for the bonding-mojo to begin. One of the men outside said something and they erupted in laughter. A draft of cold air snuck through the tent flap and Thane continued to study her, firelight flickering against his skin. "You need to be sure."

"I am."

His eyebrows pinched in. "I know my reasons for making the offer, but I'd like to know yours for accepting without any apparent reflection."

"I don't need to reflect." And she didn't owe him any answers.

"You can't stab me in the back."

"I don't want to stab you." Not at the moment, anyway.

"Working in my house will be safer and more

secure." The firelight played with the serious contours of his face.

Why was he trying to talk her out of his own offer? She leaned forward. "I promised my friends after the death wave reduced them to piles of ash that I'd avenge them if I could. My own family is likely dead as well. You said I'd get to kill Arkavians. Accepting your offer is the closest I'll get to keeping my promise to them."

His expression closed off. The crystalline gray of his eyes clouded over again as if a thunderstorm raged in his vision. He shifted from his crouch to kneel beside the bed. His large body cut off the candle-light and cast his face in shadows. He leaned over her, bringing with him the exotic, floral scent from outside and his own pine and metal.

"Close your eyes."

She glared. He was too close. This was too inti-mate. Maybe she should stab him.

"It's easier if you close your eyes instead of staring daggers at me."

She scowled.

"You can't stab me," he reminded her.

"So you've said." She closed her eyes.

Thane's leather-scented hand pressed against her forehead. The cold sheath of magic coating her body stirred. While maintaining the barrier against the angry magic on the outside, Thane's energy expanded and pressed against her skin. The magic pushed inside her, inch by inch, with undulating waves. Her body vibrated with need, wanting to draw the power in faster, wanting more, wanting to consume Thane's magic.

He sucked in a breath, but said nothing. His magic pressed forward.

Her heart raced. She forced her body to relax and took deep breaths of candle wax and Thane. As if this signalled her permission, the power flowed in, cascading along her nerves and making them sing. Energy spread to her brain and suddenly a memory flared up, vivid and real.

The hinges groaned and creaked. The cell door slammed shut with a clank. Surrounded by the smell of damp earth, death and mould, I spun to face Father.

Julian stood at his side, arms folded and smile smug.

"Father, please," I begged.

Water dripped somewhere farther down the cell block. A prisoner groaned a few cells over.

"You need to learn your place, boy," Father snarled, his ruddy face in shadows. Without another word, he turned and walked away, heavy boots slapping against wet stone.

Julian peered over his shoulder and sneered. I'd find no help from my brother.

Why did they hate me so much? What did I do this time? Why couldn't I make them happy?

I turned to study the cell. A worn cot lay in the corner. A ripped, dirty blanket lay strewn over the exposed mattress, part of it spilling onto the damp floor.

Cobwebs lined the edges of the room and dirt caked the rough stone walls. A single beam of sunlight shot into the room from a small open slit less than half a face width wide and illuminated the dust motes floating in the air.

A dark shape scurried along the uneven floor and hid under another cot on the opposite side of the cell. Someone lay huddled under the threadbare blanket.

"Hey." I walked over.

The man didn't move. He remained still as if expecting a beating.

"Hey." I reached out and shook his shoulder.

Something snapped, like breaking a stick in two for the fireplace. The man rolled over. Blank eyes stared back at me. Master Rami. The sunken cheeks and gaping mouth made him almost unrecognizable, but the birth mark on his stubbled chin was unmistakable.

My Tarka instructor. The one who said I was talented and intervened when Father tried to beat me for being what I was supposed to be.

Father said Master Rami left without a word a month ago. He lied. My instructor had been here the whole time...starving to death.

A large black spider crawled out of Rami's mouth.

I stumbled back, tripped on a bowl and fell over.

The memory fled as fast as it arrived only to have another slam into its place.

I huddled under the bed, wrapped in a soft blanket. Father grabbed Mom by her white hair and shook her violently. Something ripped. I cowered farther into the shadows.

She sobbed. "Not in front of him. Please."

"Tell me the truth," Father demanded.

"There's nothing to tell."

Father snarled and threw her across the room. Her body thumped on impact. "You lying whore."

I pulled the blanket over my body and shook.

Mom screamed and begged for mercy.

The pounding of my father's fist hitting Mom's soft skin rebounded off the walls.

A coward. That's what I was. A worthless coward, just like Father said. I couldn't even protect Mom and now he beat her.

Because of me.

A.

Worthless.

Coward.

The memory snapped away and suddenly Taya was back in the tent, on the cot, staring into Thane's gray eyes. A storm raged on his face. He breathed heavily. His platinum-blond hair no longer behaved and stuck out at different angles.

"What the hell was that?" Her voice came out hoarse, like she'd been screaming karaoke all night on a bender. Did those memories belong to him?

He tugged at the hem of his cotton shirt. "Sometimes the bonding lets me see memories. They tend to be ones from intense moments, which can be upsetting...or embarrassing."

Huh? So he saw her memories while she saw his? He didn't mention it worked both ways. Did he know she got glimpses of his past?

Wait.

He saw her memories? *Oh, no.*

"What did you see?" she asked.

His intense gaze cut away. "I saw you kill for the first time."

Her skin crawled. The homeless man's face still haunted her nightmares. His lifeless body, sagged in the river, while the water carried away his blood.

"I also saw your friends."

She stiffened.

"I'm sorry. You obviously cared for them very much."

Yes. Yes, she did. The beginning of the camping trip was the last fun memory she had of them, but she couldn't look back on it without the taint of the blue death wave ruining the moment.

"What else?" she asked. Please, please, please, don't let it be her break-up with that douchebag cheater. He deserved it, but she wasn't proud of her actions.

"Me."

"Huh?"

He leaned down, unbearably close. "I saw me through your eyes."

Nope. That didn't sound ominous at all.

The tent rustled. Axel flung the flap to the side and stomped into the room. "Thane?"

The Arkavian lord glanced at her, some unrecognizable emotion flashing through his gaze too fast to read and stood to face the other warrior. "Yes?"

"A messenger from your father has arrived. He must've been watching the gate. Your Daddy Dearest wants a progress report." Axel's gaze cut to Taya.

"Tell him the cargo threat has been eliminated."

"And our hostage?"

They both stared at her now. She tried really hard not to squirm in the cot. And failed.

"We don't have a hostage. We have a new recruit to the team that we picked up on the way."

"Welcome to the team, Taya." Axel flashed teeth at them. Was that a smile?

"Fuck you."

His smile widened. He turned to Thane. "She'll fit right in."

"My thoughts as well."

"What story will we give them? You know he'll ask." Axel's growl spoke more than his words.

Thane stretched his neck side to side. "Found in the forest by the gate. She has unknown parentage and no education. If he or anyone else wants more, you know nothing. Send them to me."

"Got it." Axel winked his non-black eye at her and left.

She frowned.

"What is it?"

"You just told him an *earthen* woman was joining your sausage party."

"And?"

"He took it well." More than well. Had Thane picked up helpless slave girls before? Was this a regular occurrence? And why did that thought make her more nervous instead of reassured?

"He watched us fight before I used my power to control you," Thane interrupted her thoughts. "It was an impressive demonstration of skill. You also fought him when you were delirious and half restrained and you still managed to give him a black eye and Soka a split lip. My men aren't stupid. They know you'll add dimension and skill to the team."

"Oh."

"They also know my magic will prevent you from betraying us, they can overpower you, and if you pose a threat, they can eliminate you with ease."

He just had to keep talking.

CHAPTER 16
EXPECT THE UNEXPECTED

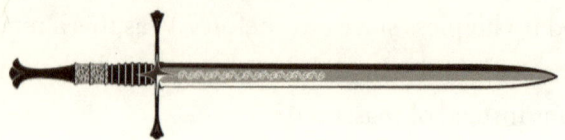

With her swords strapped to her back and her own horse under her, Taya couldn't shake the unease twisting her stomach in a knot.

They'd passed through the portal two days ago.

Two days since she accepted Thane's deal and he listed a number of commands designed to prevent her from betraying him and his team. Each order settled on her shoulders, one lead blanket after another, enforced by the power of the bond.

Thane announced her decision to the rest of the group that night. No one acted surprised, but afterward, they treated her more like a person and less like cumbersome, unwanted baggage left on the carousel at a busy airport.

Her horse was a beautiful mare named Skygge, pronounced something like "sheee-gyah" but after

124

attempting to repeat Thane, she gave up and called her Sugar. She had a silvery, dark coat, black legs, mane and tail and a black face. A few black specs, patches, and lines marred her body.

"She's a warhorse," Thane said as an explanation when she asked about her gray horse. "And she's not gray."

Yeah, okay. Like that made sense. Sugar looked gray to her.

She ran her hands along Sugar's withers and patted her neck. Maybe she looked gray, but up close, an even mixture of white and black hairs covered most of her body. Is that what Thane meant?

Axel—the large beast of a man she gave a black eye —rode beside her like a giant lumberjack bodyguard. The clip-clop of the horses' hooves over the dirt road punctuated the silence. They'd descended from the mountainous region and the air grew warmer and the snow disappeared. Still cold, but not I-can't-feel-my-face cold. His gaze kept shifting to her. Not wariness, not pervy interest like Bruno, but something else.

"What?" she asked.

Axel scowled and looked away. His broad shoulders hunched forward. "You remind me of someone."

If she rolled her eyes any harder, she'd fall off Sugar. "I'm not Arkavian, so you need to rein in that imagination."

He shrugged and nudged his horse forward. Apparently, their bonding moment had ended.

Soka passed her on the other side, his dark hair and violet gaze shining under the winter sunlight. His breath condensed as he clicked his tongue at her and moved on.

"Want another split lip?"

Soka chuckled and shook his head.

"Have you always been this good at making friends?" Thane asked, bringing Hades up beside her.

The horses plodded along the wide dirt road lined with thick forest on each side. They passed tree after floral-scented tree. She reached forward and ran her hand under the plated armour covering Sugar's neck and patted her soft coat.

"I had friends. They're dust. It took my whole life to find them."

Thane nodded.

"Why does Axel think I look like someone? He knows I'm earthen."

Thane glanced at her, gaze calculating.

She sat back in the saddle and tightened her grip on the reins. Her inner thighs ached as if someone took a mallet to them and they'd transformed into one giant bruise.

He chuckled. "What?"

"You have the same look my parents always gave me when they debated how much to tell me." Like during the recession when enrollment to Dad's classes dropped and the business was in danger. "Since I jumped in with two feet, I'd suggest dishing."

"Dishing? What does food have to do with this?"

She clenched her teeth. "I would like you to tell me everything. Please." See? She had manners. And she could use them, too.

He relaxed into the saddle. His armour creaked. "The blue death wave didn't signal the first gate opening to your realm."

"Oh." Wait. What?

"About a hundred years ago, your realm was discovered by the Tee-oh."

"The what?"

"T-O. The Tarkavian Order."

Of course they had a preposterous name. She traced the intricate patterns carved into the leather of Sugar's reins with her thumb. Thane had said his house was a powerful one. What exactly would she find at the end of this rainbow?

"One of their most talented disciples opened a gate," Thane continued his story. "When he traveled across, the portal closed behind him and he never returned."

"Why not open another gate to go get him?"

"The Tarka's notes on Earth's specific ethereal location and how to form the gate to the magic-less land went missing."

Silence filled in the blanks. She traced the black lines in Sugar's coat. Why would the Tarka's record disappear? Unless... "He took his notes with him."

"That's the common belief. Most Tarkas are

intensely protective of their spells and the full extent of their abilities."

Hades huffed.

"But not you."

"Especially me."

The memory of his dead tutor's face flared up. Cold sweat broke across her forehead.

"Everyone figured the scout was lost. He was the last son of his house and it died with his disappearance. They call it the Ghost House, now," Thane continued. "But what if he didn't disappear altogether? What if he found a lovely woman and made a family and life in your world? What if his house lives on?"

She ignored his side-eye and dissected his words. "I thought you said I was a descendent of a common ancestor?"

"Also possible."

They continued to pass evergreen trees, Thane evidently content to let her stew in silence. Was this the reason he offered her the deal? "You think I'm the descendent of some long lost Arkavian Tarka scout from a Ghost House."

"It would explain a lot."

"There are plenty of people from my realm with blond hair and gray eyes. Even if this Tarka created a new life on Earth, he couldn't have been the only source of blond genetics."

"If you say so." He opened his mouth to say more when Lokni's warning called out from the trees.

Thane turned toward the cry.

Thunk.

An arrow sank into his broad chest. Right side. Not the heart. He grunted and fell between their horses. His body thumped against the cold, hard ground. A sheen of glittering green magic coated his body.

Taya leapt off her horse to join him and used the large animals as shields. She stood over Thane. "Stay down."

Not that he looked like he'd get up anytime soon.

Fast and fluid, Lokni notched and released an arrow. A man cried out from the forest. His shriek cut-off with a gargle.

Lokni slung his bow over his shoulders and slipped down the tree trunk with a finesse only a chimpanzee should have.

What the hell? Why was he putting the bow away?

He winked at her over his shoulder.

Taya stiffened behind Hades' dark flank and peered over the saddle. Five men ran through the forest toward them. Armour and swords flashing in the sunlight. Crap. She couldn't use her magic yet and these guys carried their weapons with skill. Should she run?

"Form a line," Axel barked.

She ducked from the horses and unsheathed her swords. Raw, potent energy thrummed through her veins. She let the magic course through her and over-power her shaking nerves. The blades shrieked with delight, primed and ready for battle. She glanced at the road behind her. The bond tugged her close to Thane. Running wasn't an option. Fighting to secure her place and meet her end of the deal was. She'd promised to train, bleed, kill, and possibly die for Thane.

The men bellowed and thrashed through the underbrush to close the distance. Five against four. Not only were they outnumbered, but Taya couldn't hold her own yet.

Thane's men looked unconcerned, though. Instead, their expressions were...giddy?

Axel yelled back at the attackers and stepped in front of Taya to take on two of the fighters at once. Soka did the same on her other side while his twin, Lokni ran to join them.

Taya stood behind the wall of fighting warriors with her swords drawn and waited.

Her vision cleared. Time slowed. The skilled fighters danced, sunlight glinting off their swords. Her own blades hummed with anticipation and an unseen force pulled her toward the fight.

One of the attackers stepped through the line.

Before he drove his sword into Soka's back, Taya darted in and deflected the thrust to the ground, her blade's hilt rotating smoothly in her hand. The man snarled and whirled toward her. Already injured and tired from fighting, his first swings were weak. She side-stepped and slashed at his midsection. He dodged and lunged. They exchanged a flurry of blows. Each strike she deflected and redirected. He was too strong, even injured, for her to meet head-on. Sweat broke out across her face. She had to be quick and smart. She had to slip, dodge, and weave.

The power of her blades vibrated in her blood. It called to her. She drank it in, fusing with the raw energy. The swords' shrieking grew louder. She spun in a whirlwind attack, batting away her opponent's strikes and blocks until she ducked inside his guard and slashed open his chest. Blood sprayed across her body and face. The thick red fluid plastered her hair against her face. The man flopped to the ground beside Thane's prone body.

Taya straightened, her chest heaved as she fought to control her breathing and racing heart. No more swords clashed. She turned to find Axel, Soka and Lokni studying her, their opponents dead at their feet.

Axel nodded. "Like I said. You'll fit right in."

He smacked Soka on the back.

She ignored him and glared at Lokni. "Why did you put your bow away? You could've picked them off before they reached us."

He shrugged. "This was more fun."

"Fun?"

Soka nodded. "We were promised epic battles against savage earthens and instead, we got stuck with babysitting a scrawny girl."

The leather of her blades' hilts creaked as she gripped them tightly and squeezed. She pointed the tip of a sword at Thane. Blood dripped from the blade's tip onto the gravel road beside his face. "What about him?"

Lokni's expression grew grim. "They must've shot him with a Tarkavian dart."

"Looks like an arrow to me."

"It is, but if it carries the poison that neutralizes his power, it's called a Tarkavian dart. Nothing else would knock him out like this. We need to take it out and get him to a healer."

She knelt by Thane's side and examined the arrow embedded in his chest. What happened if he died? Would she be released from her promises and set free? Or would she be treated like a possession and transferred to one of those other, less desirable life paths?

Soka crouched beside her, shuffling dirt and crunching pebbles. "It missed his heart and his breathing is fine. It must've missed his lungs, too."

He reached forward and yanked the arrow from Thane's chest. Blood spurted from the wound.

Geez! She pulled the shirt from the dead guy beside them. The rough material tore and snagged. She tugged. The body flopped. She gave the shirt a hard jerk. It ripped free and she toppled back on her ass. "A little warning would be nice."

Soka chuckled.

She balled up the cloth, slapped it over Thane's wound and applied pressure. "You should've left the arrow in. It prevented him from bleeding out."

Soka shook his head. "We need the poison out."

This guy hadn't taken a first aid course in his life and it showed. She pressed her fingers against Thane's neck to find his pulse. The second her hand contacted his skin, her mind spiraled into a memory.

Julian halted, the slap of his boots echoing down the empty hall faded. Dimly lit, this wing of the fortress had belonged to our mother. Now it only housed stale air.

Julian turned to me and sneered. "Why do you think father hates you? He doesn't know if you're his."

"Of course I'm his. Why wouldn't I be?" I gripped the hilt of my sword and squeezed. I'd killed the last man who called me a bastard.

"Your power is different."

"Different? Different how? You and Father are powerful Tarkas. Why is it so unbelievable that I am, too?"

Julian scowled. Instead of answering, he walked away and left me with the fading sounds of his boots hitting the hard tile.

Taya bolted upright in a cot. Same cot, same tent, same wool blanket smelling of horse and Thane. Candle wax and a metallic tang filled the air. The low murmur of male voices outside trickled in.

What the hell?

"You passed out." Thane spoke at her side. She twisted to find him sitting beside the cot with his shirt off. A thick bandage wrapped around his enormous chest. The center tinged red where the blood had soaked through. His weapons rested against his discarded breastplate next to hers. He looked tired. And angry.

"Soka never should've let you touch me," he growled. Even with no armour and sitting in a vulnerable position, he was huge and imposing. His smooth skin rippled with movement. The bandage and lack of a shirt made him look a little more human, though.

"It obviously didn't kill you." Nope. He looked just fine. A little too fine. And too close.

"But it hurt you."

"What happened?"

His dark brows bunched. "My magic latched onto yours and used your power to expel the poison."

"I don't remember any of that."

"I drained your energy." He grimaced as though saying the words tasted bad.

That didn't sound good.

"It's not permanent and it wasn't intentional."

Those words sounded like an apology. So he drained her to the point of unconsciousness, felt bad about it, and carried her off to his man cave for her to recuperate.

"Why didn't you drain one of the men? Soka touched you first."

His lip twitched. "Not skin to skin he didn't. But it wouldn't have mattered. None of the men have Tarka power to drain."

Huh. That explained a little bit of what happened.

Thane's motives for keeping her around crystallized some more as well. "So you want me on the team to use as a battery pack?"

Thane frowned. "A what?"

"Never mind." Did it really matter? He hadn't hurt her and he'd kept his word so far. He seemed legit. If the first lord she came across had captured her, she would've ended up in that sacrifice circle with the other survivors from John's town. Could she trust an Arkavian, though, when his society purposefully caused the demise of her world and enslaved the other survivors from Earth? Trust, no. Work for and use for continued existence, yes.

"Why did those men attack us?" she asked.

"You didn't leave any alive for me to ask." He shrugged, the movement emphasizing his large chest and broad shoulders. He was a gigantic man with muscles built from a lifetime of sword practice and fighting. Fine-lined scars ran along his torso and shoulders.

"What's the most likely reason, then?"

"Food and money." He didn't hesitate answering. "They saw a small group with one Tarka and thought they could overpower us after incapacitating me."

"Does this happen often?" What kind of world was this? Earth had its own problems, sure, but it sounded like Arkavia was far from Utopia.

"It can. Arkavia is not a safe world. You should never travel alone."

"Already preparing your end-of-year pitch?"

He leaned forward and smiled. The sight of his even white teeth breaking his regularly-stern expression had a staggering effect. "Is it working?"

Her heart pounded in answer, traitorous thing. Why was he so close? Why did he have this effect on her?

"Jason was an asshole," he said.

What? How did he know her douchebag ex-boyfriend's name? *Oh no. No, no, no, no...* Heat flooded her face. "Another vision?"

Thane grinned. "I like how this one ended."

"He deserved it." She crossed her arms.

Thane nodded. "Are you hungry?"

Her stomach growled.

"I'll take that as a yes." He stood and winced.

She cursed her body, not because her stomach needed food, but because another hunger stirred within Thane's proximity. A hunger her body had no right to feel or have. She would fulfill her end of the bargain for Thane. She'd train. She'd kill. But she refused to lust after an Arkavian Lord.

CHAPTER 17
HOME SWEET HOME

The House of Jericho.

Taya stood at the edge of the embankment and studied their destination, a fucking castle. Complete with watch towers, turrets, crenellations along parapets and arrow loops, the building sprawled along a rocky shore with the ocean behind it and a long flat field in front. A few beams of afternoon sunlight broke through the gray cloud cover and illuminated the exposed path to the front gates.

Unless someone could scale walls from a rowboat, it would be almost impossible to sneak up on the inhabitants. Seabirds that resembled a cross between seagulls and crows swarmed the outer edges of the fortress and swooped down to the gray ocean. They sounded exactly as expected.

Axel told her "Jericho" was Old Arkavian for

"moon." The black and silver armour lined with white leather made more sense now—house colours. The warriors identified strongly with the night sky.

"This is your new home." Thane stopped his warhorse beside hers. Hades played with the bit, his lips smacking on the metal. "Do not discuss where you're from. If anyone asks, you don't want to talk about it."

Well, that wasn't much of a stretch. She nodded. She didn't need Thane to tell her it would be less than ideal for others to learn she was a dirty earthen. One memory of Bruno's hands on her body squashed any urge to dish her secrets.

"What about the others?" She glanced over her shoulder where the men waited.

"They will keep quiet. They are loyal to me." He hesitated. "Be careful around my father and brother. They are the only two I can't protect you from."

And just when she was getting all warm and fuzzy inside he had to keep going. She narrowed her eyes. He said she'd be safe here.

"They rarely concern themselves with what I do. You should be fine," he said.

Great. She muffled a groan. She was totally not going to be fine.

"My ass is numb," Axel barked. "Can we go?"

Thane smirked and nudged Hades. The horse stopped lipping the bit and surged forward. "Let's go."

The horses galloped across the long exposed expanse, hooves thundering against the frozen ground. Taya clutched the reins and gave Sugar control. Heck, despite her childhood lessons, she had no idea how to control this beast.

Sugar's black mane flung back, lashing Taya's face with the long, coarse strands. She leaned forward and held onto the hard leather of the saddle horn for her life. Her teeth rattled. The seat slapped against her butt. Her bruised thighs screamed in agony. Her knees ached from all the riding threatening to snap. The faster Sugar ran, the more Taya's legs smacked the horse's sides. The mare snorted and tossed her mane.

She wasn't making any friends, not even with her horse.

Taya started to bounce to the side. Each saddle ass slap sent her farther off-balance. *Oh no!* She was going over. Taya clutched the horn and hauled her flailing body upright, butt squarely back in the saddle.

Slap, slap, slap.

Ow, ow, ow.

How long was this field? It went on forever. Each thundering hoof striking the hardened soil jostled her already knotted stomach.

Men bellowed from the ramparts. Metal groaned. Wood creaked. A drawbridge rumbled to life and lowered. It landed in time for their party to cross without breaking stride. Instead of stopping in the main courtyard, Thane slowed his horse and took a right down a wide cobble road.

"He has his own section of the fortress." Lokni drew up beside her and waggled his eyebrows as if that was supposed to impress her somehow.

"But not his own entrance."

Lokni frowned. "There are other ways in, but this is the fastest method to announce his return to his family without having to talk to them."

He spoke as if she should know this already. If they hosted an Arkavian 101 tutorial, she missed it. With Lokni's statement and Thane's memories, she had zero desire to meet Thane's fucked up family.

Lokni shrugged and scanned the crowd. His shoulders slumped after he made a complete circuit with his violet gaze. He was searching for something or someone. *Interesting.*

They drew to a stop in a small courtyard near the outer edge of the fortress. Swords clanked and the air smelled of coal, metal and leather. And sweaty men. A whole lot of sweaty men. Said men put down their weapons and walked over to meet them.

"Welcome back." A large man with a long scar running down his entire face and into his thick, black beard approached Thane's horse.

Hmm... Lokni had a similar scar, but it was smaller. Different cheek, thickness and angle, too. The old wounds didn't appear to be some badge of honour or weird Arkavian hazing ritual.

"Any problems?" Scarface asked.

"None." Thane slid off his horse and clasped the man's forearm.

He neglected to mention the sacrifice circle, Bruno's betrayal or the ambush attack. If those counted as nothing, what the hell did he consider something?

"And here?" Thane asked.

"Boring as a nun's nancy."

What the hell was a nancy?

Lokni snorted. "A nancy is never boring. You're not doing it right."

Oh. A nancy must be a... She tried to swallow her laughter and ended up coughing.

Scarface scowled and turned to her. His eyes widened.

She pursed her lips and returned his stare unflinching. The conversations in the courtyard also died down as everyone slowly turned to see what Scarface glowered at, including Thane.

"We have a new recruit," Thane said.

"So I see." He looked unimpressed. Instead, he appeared as though he had a compelling need to fell a tree and hack it into tiny pieces for firewood and kindling.

"She needs a room," Thane said.

"Barracks?"

Thane glanced at the burly man. "House."

Yup. Everyone stared at her now. Great. Something significant had happened and she had no idea what it was or what it meant. Was she overanalyzing? Maybe their wary glances had more to do with her presence alone than the exchange between Thane and his man. A gentle wind filled with the scents of baked goods and cooked meat slipped over her shoulders. Taya's mouth watered.

"Taya, this is Bertrand." Thane nodded at Scarface. "My steward."

Her eyebrows rose. This man looked more like a human battle-axe than the caretaker for Thane's domestic needs.

She nodded in greeting. A finger wave was probably not a good idea right now.

Bertrand grunted and scanned the group again. "Where's the cocksucker?"

"Bruno couldn't follow orders."

Bertrand chuckled. "Julian's going to be pissed."

Soka leapt from his horse. "Then he needs to send better spies."

Yup. A whole lot more going on than she knew. No wonder Thane didn't have a problem skewering one of his men. Bruno wasn't his.

I didn't kill him for you.

Taya shivered.

The team dismounted and the weight of their attention fell on her again. She was the only one remaining on a horse. She swung her leg over the saddle and slipped from Sugar's back. Her inner thighs trembled with a deep ache and her legs threatened to collapse. She gave the horse a pat on the neck. Dirt billowed from her coat. Sugar turned her massive head and bumped her muzzle against Taya's arm.

"More pats later. Promise," she whispered. It wasn't Sugar's fault she wouldn't walk properly for days. Weeks. Maybe fucking years. God, this hurt. How did the men do it? Did they have any nerve endings left down there?

"Thane!" a man bellowed.

Lokni leaned in. "Here we go."

Taya peered around the horse. Her hand froze on Sugar's sleek chest. A man resembling Thane's identical twin stomped down stone steps to enter the small courtyard. His lips curled into a cruel sneer and his steel gaze flashed. Thane's brother. She recognized him from the memories. Three thug-looking barbarians trailed behind Julian like sluggish shadows with muscles.

"Don't make eye contact," Lokni whispered.

She turned and glared.

He shrugged and jerked his chin toward the scene unfolding in the courtyard. Guess this was the Arkavian equivalent of daytime television drama. They just needed popcorn.

"Where's Bruno?" the man demanded.

"Thank you for the warm welcome home, Julian. I'm fine. Thank you for asking." Though Thane spoke with nice enough words, his voice contained ice.

"Cut the bullshit. Where's Bruno?"

"He met an unfortunate end while neutralizing the supply chain marauders."

Julian snarled.

The men in the courtyard shifted. Hands drifted to sword hilts. Julian's guards stepped forward. Thane's smile grew cold and vicious. "He fought valiantly against the evil earthen scum and died a hero's death."

Julian vibrated. His cheeks flushed red. He took a deep breath and looked away from his brother.

Uh-oh. Too late. Before she could duck behind Sugar, Julian's glare landed on her. "Who's this?"

Thane ignored her as if she was some peasant he passed on the street and had as little interest in her as he did the lint in his pocket.

Okay, then.

She straightened and stepped from the safety of the horses to face Thane's cruel brother. Her legs wobbled. She gripped Sugar's bridle for support.

"This is Taya," Thane said.

Julian's mouth turned down. "House?"

Thane faced off with his brother, staring him down. "Undetermined."

"Don't you have enough women skulking about your team?"

"Oh, come now, cuzzie, I don't skulk." A lithe woman with straight, platinum hair cropped to her shoulders and a honeyed voice sauntered down the stairs and walked over to the men. She stepped up onto a wooden bench and slung her arm around Thane's shoulder.

Lokni sucked in a breath.

Honestly, until he started mouth breathing, she'd forgotten he stood behind her.

"Why is she here?" Julian seethed.

"You're as privy to Adrianna's motivations as I am, brother, but our cousin is always welcome here."

"Not her." Julian snapped his arm out and jutted a pointed finger at Taya's face. "That one."

"She's a part of my team."

Julian's brows shot up. He looked so much like Thane, yet completely different at the same time. "Father will want to meet her."

Oh goody.

"Undoubtedly."

Julian finally turned to his brother again. "You would do well not to antagonize him."

Thane's false smile disappeared. Apparently, their terrible act of civility was over. "My existence antagonizes him. What do you want, Julian? You don't usually grace me with your presence to welcome me home."

Julian straightened and brushed non-existent dirt off his shirt. "Father wants a full report."

"I already sent a report ahead of our arrival." He obviously left out Taya's presence.

"Yes. He wants to know more about Earth's energy

and the possibility of bringing in more earthen slaves." Julian turned to leave. "I suggest bringing the girl."

Girl? Who the hell was he calling a girl?

"Did he request to see her?" Thane asked.

"How could he if he doesn't know of her existence yet?" Julian's voice dripped with sarcasm.

"Then I'll attend our father once I've cleaned up. Alone."

Power snapped around Julian, dark and ugly. Gnarled streaks of black and gray wound around him like barbed wire. As quickly as they appeared, the powerful bands dissipated, leaving Julian visibly more relaxed. He flung a non-committal gloved hand in the air, half-wave, half-salute, and walked away. His three goons trailed close behind him.

Taya repressed a shudder. Her muscles tensed and her feet itched to run away. What the hell was wrong with that guy? Taya had no idea, but this was not the place to show how much Julian's quick display of potent power scared the crap out of her.

Had Thane mentioned cleaning up? She couldn't wait to pull on clean clothes instead of stepping into pants roughened by tears and grime. Or soak her legs in a hot bath for days. Bathing would be a nice distraction from the unease broiling in her gut. She turned to Thane once his brother was out of earshot.

A soft smile tugged at Thane's lips. He was apparently unaffected by his brothers magical temper tantrum.

"It's about time you brought in some actual muscle." Adrianna punched Thane in the shoulder.

Taya winced. The other woman's form was terrible.

Adrianna brought her hand back and shook it, glaring at her cousin.

He shrugged.

Adrianna hopped off the bench and beamed at Taya. "When you're done with these dumb lugs, find me and I'll give you a proper Jericho welcome."

"Um..."

"Don't worry, I'll take good care of you." The woman winked at her and bounced up the stairs after Julian, most likely to make more mischief. Thane's cousin reminded Taya of a playful cat following an unraveling ball of yarn. The question was what sort of destruction would she inflict when it came time to pounce?

"I should be fine?" she repeated Thane's earlier assurance.

"Absolutely." Thane turned to Bertrand. "Get her a room, give her a tour, and drill her on the schedule. I expect everyone at training tonight."

Lokni and Soka groaned in unison. Her inner thighs wailed in protest.

Bertrand nodded, his dark gaze flicking to her, his expression unreadable.

"She's not to be harmed," Thane added.

Axel stepped up beside Taya. "She's one of the team, Thane. We'll look after her."

Lokni and Soka grunted in agreement, but the rest of the men either looked unsure, wary, or completely unconvinced.

Only time would tell whether they'd end up friends or foes.

PART TWO
REBORN

Arkavian Upper Houses

Jericho
House of the Moon

Lane, Head of House
Julian
Thane
Adrianna

Raiden
House of Lightning

Corentine (deceased)
Gale, Head of House
Elias (deceased)

Auroris
House of the Sun

Ayden (deceased)
Aries, Head of House
Alexis

Draco
House of Constellations

Edur
House of Snow

Maris (deceased)

Ramiel
House of Thunder

Ghost
The Ghost House

Aello (deceased)
Izar (deceased)

CHAPTER 18

WAX ON, WAX OFF

JANUARY, FIVE MONTHS AFTER ARKAVIA (AA)

Three weeks had passed since her arrival at the House of Jericho. Training sessions proved brutal and confirmed how much weaker and less trained she was at pretty much everything compared to the battle-hardened warriors. Instead of earning their derision, though, her consistent failure and persistence seemed to earn her a little respect.

"Grapple day!" Thane announced as he walked into the large room. He appeared unaffected by the early hour and cool morning air. For once he wore no armour, and the black shirt and loose fitting pants did little to hide the solid muscle beneath.

They stood in a room probably intended as a ball-room for the second son of Jericho to hold court.

Natural light streamed through large stained-glass windows. Sweat, metal, and citrus clung to the air instead of perfumed powder like the grand hall, though, because Thane had converted the large space to a medieval-style gym.

The men groaned at his proclamation.

Taya perked up a little despite the early hour and lack of caffeine. Finally, a day without swords, daggers or knives. Although she yearned to wield the lightning blades of Raiden, Thane had forbidden their use in practice. The heavier, dull practice swords she used in their place swung awkwardly and made her arm muscles scream.

Today, though... Today she would show off a little of her training.

Lokni swatted her butt as he passed. "I'll spar with you first. How would you like that, baby?"

She rolled her eyes at the giant. He couldn't help himself with the flirting. She'd seen him interact with the women around the castle. From barely legal to hobbling with a cane, Lokni laid on the charm with everyone except Adrianna. He became a blithering mess around Thane's cousin.

Taya followed Lokni to a free space and squared off.

Among various martial arts, her father raised her to fight in a style more gritty than Kung Fu. It was a style all its own and something he referred to as their "house style." She couldn't use half the moves in tournaments or when she trained with world-level MMA fighters. But even the times she wore protective gear and fought all out with her father, nothing prepared her for the reality of fighting a grown man intent on killing her.

At least that's what it seemed like Lokni tried to do.

"What's the matter? Didn't get any last night?" She panted.

"I get plenty."

"Just not the right one."

He growled.

She scrambled out of his hold, spun and thrust her leg back. Her foot made contact. Lokni wheezed and doubled over. He swatted at her, like a pesky fly. She ducked, stepped to the side and leapt onto his broad back. With her legs wrapped around his waist, she squeezed out whatever breath he had left in his lungs. She snaked her arm under his neck and locked it with her other arm in a classic figure four.

Rear naked-choke. She pulled into his body, panting in his ear. "How do you like that, baby?"

Lokni flung his weight back. They sailed through the air.

Taya curled her body into his, protecting her head and neck, but she took the brunt of the impact and his weight. Her back slammed against the hard ground. Her breath escaped. Her sore muscles protested and her lungs screamed for air.

Not today.

She tightened the clamp on Lokni's neck and

arched her back to apply more pressure. God, he was heavy. Her arms shook.

Lokni gurgled and tapped her shoulder.

She released him and remained on the ground, panting, while Lokni scrambled to his feet. He turned to her, cheeks still flushed.

"Vicious beast." He walked off to find another partner.

Too winded from the fall to make some sort of witty response, she remained on the ground to recuperate.

"Impressive," Thane said.

She twisted on the floor to find the warrior standing behind her, arms crossed.

"Lokni is one of our best grapplers," Thane said.

One of? Interesting. Who were the rest? She had a hunch the men she first met with Thane—Axel, Lokni and Soka—were the best on his team. He'd taken his elite crew to travel to Earth. Because of her? Or something else? Surely an earthen pest didn't require that much display of force.

She got to her feet, hoping she appeared confident and not slow because of a hurt back.

"There's not much use for grappling in a dance with swords," she said.

Thane smiled. "You're right. The fight doesn't often last long enough to go to the ground when sharp edges are involved, but it's still a valuable skill and you need to hone these skills more than the others." *And become the best.* His unspoken words hung in the cool air.

"Stop talking and let me hone." That sounded wrong.

Thane grinned, his expression turning predatory.

Her survival instincts shrieked and the small hairs on the back of her neck stood up. *Uh-oh.*

He went from amiable instructor to deadly Arkavian warrior standing a foot away as if he simply flicked a light switch. And he didn't even know what that was. For all of Arkavia's power and realm conquering, they lived a medieval existence in a lot of ways.

"You need a partner to...hone," he said.

Yeah...she'd hoped the reference wouldn't translate to Arkavian. Apparently, the evolution of language from the two realms was freakishly similar. It hurt her brain trying to figure out how that was possible.

She stretched side to side. Her back cracked. "Let me guess. You're the best?"

His smile answered her question.

Lovely. This was going to hurt.

So FAR, Thane's tactics involved tackling her to the ground and smothering her with the weight of his giant body until she gassed out and left herself vulnerable to a submission. And fuck, it was working.

Normally, she excelled at wrestling and won high school and university championships. Taya found the down to earth grit and honesty of the sport a nice offset to the more traditional martial arts.

Usually.

Today, she found it exhausting and discouraging. It reminded her of when she started training in jujitsu, another humbling experience. She didn't want to be humbled. She wanted to kick ass.

She needed to change her approach and focus on her take-down defence and alter this fight to her advantage. Easier said than done when a freight train barrelled toward her at a speed faster than she could dodge.

Thane caught her again and they flew to the ground. She wrapped her legs around his waist and locked her ankles together to prevent him from shifting to a full mount position. She raised her arms to protect her neck. His hot breath fanned her neck and his pine scent surrounded her.

"Thane!" Julian called out from across the room.

Thane grabbed her arms and pinned them to the floor. His chest rose with each heavy breath and a light sheen of sweat broke out across his forehead. He looked as fresh as a daisy compared to her.

"Thane!" Julian bellowed, clearly wanting an immediate answer.

Thane peered down at her. His face unbearably close, the striking silver accents of his stormy gray gaze mesmerized her. As if someone snapped their fingers, she was now intensely aware of their intimate position, and how his hard body pressed her into the floor.

A sudden image of him naked on top of her flared to life. Thane grinding and moving his strong body against hers, flexing his hips. She clung onto his muscled arms and threw her head back as he pumped into her.

Heat flushed her skin.

She couldn't think like this.

The more she tried to stop the X-rated images, though, the more carried away her imagination got.

Thane leaned closer, gaze wild. "Do you submit?"

She lifted her chin. "Never."

Heavy boots pounded the mats laid over stone. "Will you get off your play thing and answer me?"

Thane winked at her.

Winked.

Rat bastard.

She unlocked her ankles and released him. He stood up and held out his hand. When she placed hers in his, he hoisted her to her feet as if she weighed less than a sack of potatoes. Sweat poured off her skin.

Julian studied them with open disgust. "Father wants to see you. Both of you."

"Are you Father's personal messenger now?" Thane jerked his head at the three men standing behind his brother. "Why not send one of your thugs?"

Julian snarled. He ignored Thane and raked her

body with his scalding gaze. "You better clean her first. Why is she so sweaty?"

Taya grinned and blew him a kiss. Sweat dripped from her nose.

Julian jerked back as if she slapped him. Thane's men chuckled. Julian spun to glare at them, but he found only passive, schooled expressions.

"We'll come right away." Thane placed a hand at the small of her back and nudged her forward. "Seems urgent."

Dread crept along her spine. The infamous father. She had no wish to meet the man who locked his own child in a jail cell with the dead body of his favourite instructor to "teach him his place." Hard pass, thank you.

Julian gave a dismissive sneer over his shoulder and led the way out of the training room. His guards trailed behind him as if competing with each other to see who could get closer without stepping on his heels. With Thane at her back, she had little choice but to follow— sweat and all.

CHAPTER 19
YOU CAN'T CHOOSE
YOUR FAMILY

T he door shut behind them with a deafening
click. Another mammoth of a man lounged
in an armchair by a roaring fire. He
continued to stare at the flames instead of turning to
greet them. Maybe his morning coffee hadn't kicked in
yet. Taya heard enough stories about Lane, Lord and
Leader of House Jericho, and his epic fits of rage, to
know she needed to exercise extreme caution in his
presence. Hell, Thane's memories provided enough
warning without the men's gossip.

Leather and soft musk laced together as a subtle
perfume in the room. And the crow-seagull freaks of
nature shrieked outside with wild abandon. A slender
woman with platinum-blond hair cascading in soft
waves down her back stood beside the Lord of Jericho
in a beam of sunlight shooting through a large window.
She had lush red lips and black arched brows over large

161

doe-like gray eyes. Her gown's full skirt billowed down to the floor to brush against the stonework and intricate lace decorated the tight bodice. She looked like a real-life version of a doll, the kind that came perfectly dressed and positioned in a display-case styled box. When Taya was a little girl, she used to play with them and use the dolls as target practice for her military figurines. Where was Ken?

On cue, Julian crossed the room, the plush rug muffling the thud of his boots on the stone flooring.

"My love." Julian held out his hands and grasped the woman's. After studying her face, he turned to Thane. "Have you heard the news, brother?"

Thane stiffened where he stood beside Taya. "I have not had the pleasure."

"Lady Alexis and I are betrothed."

"Congratulations," Thane said, voice hollow.

"I'll join you later, Alexis. We have house business to discuss." He patted the woman's hands.

Ugh. So patronizing.

The woman smiled sweetly, but her gaze flashed with irritation. "Of course."

She nodded toward Thane's unmoving father and sashayed across the room to stop in front of Thane. "I hope you can find happiness for us. I don't wish for things to become awkward, given our history."

Too late for that, lady. A whole lot of awkward just lit up this room. Taya shifted her weight on her feet. Her sweat had cooled and dried, leaving her skin itchy.

Alexis side-eyed her before batting her long lashes at Thane expectantly.

"It's a little late for that," Thane said, repeating her own thoughts. "But I'm thankful you found someone deserving of your affections."

Oh, burn.

Alexis' cheeks reddened. She smiled, but the action looked more like a wince. She slipped past Thane to leave the room and a wake of floral air trailed behind her.

"Do you have to be an asshole?" Julian asked after the door shut behind his betrothed. "Or does it come naturally to you?"

Thane shrugged. "Must be hereditary."

Julian scowled. "Listen, you—"

"Enough." Lane, the head of House Jericho cast a dismissive look at his eldest son before turning toward her and Thane. His cold blue gaze settled on her.

All three men shared the chiseled, cut-from-stone features, straight nose and full lips. Where Thane looked strong and intimidating like a Norse god sent to the mortal realm to reap vengeance on mortals, and Julian looked cruel and condescending, their father resembled an ice king. Cold, detached and slightly off. The magic in the room stirred and brushed against her, the energy dark and twisted.

"Bring the girl here," Lane snarled.

She walked ahead of Thane before he had to

choose between hauling her to his father or defying him to spare her feelings.

She stood by the fire and faced Lane. Her movement brought a waft of her own body odour to her nose. *Oh, wow.*

Lane's nose wrinkled and he scowled. His platinum-blond hair had lost all the blond tones, and the firelight reflecting off his hair and pale face did little to add warmth to his appearance.

His brow creased and continued to study her. "Did you think to keep the girl from me?"

The girl stood right in front of him and bit her tongue. Now was not the time for her snark to tumble out. She'd already pushed it by blowing Julian a kiss.

"I thought my team was beneath you, Father."

Lane scowled. "What house is she?"

"Undetermined. She doesn't know her ancestry. She was practically raised by wolves. We found her in the forest near the gate."

Taya swallowed a laugh. Not a "ha, ha" kind of laugh. The nervous kind of giggle that erupted at the most inopportune times. Interesting how well Thane skirted the truth. He didn't say she was actually raised by wolves and they *had* found her in a forest near the portal. He just left out which side of the gate.

Lane continued to scan her, cold and calculating. "What are your plans for her?"

"Personal bodyguard," Thane answered.

Her muscles twitched. She wanted to spin around

and look at his face. A bodyguard? That's not what he told her. Who did he lie to? His father or her?

Lane's white brows shot up, exposing a fine line scar running diagonally across his forehead, "Why would you need a sweaty girl to guard you? Have you grown that weak?"

"I always take at least one guard."

"Axel and one of the morons. They are more formidable than this scrawny thing."

Taya curled her hands into fists and dug her fingernails into her palms. She'd grown up with a lot of privilege, mainly being treated like a fucking human being. No one had ever spoken over her like this and it grated her nerves like a rough pumice stone.

"More formidable, yes. I want someone unassuming who can guard me day *and* night."

She took long, deep breaths. Okay. That made sense. She doubted he'd want Axel in the same room as him, sawing logs while he tried to sleep. She'd travelled with Axel. That man could snore. Even in a separate tent, he'd kept her up. If she was Thane, she'd choose to sleep with her, too.

Wait. What?

Don't look. Don't look.

She tensed and straightened, pulling her shoulders back.

Lane rubbed non-existent stubble on his smooth chin. "Having a female Tarka as a personal bodyguard that you can also fuck does hold a certain appeal."

Oh no.

"It will raise your status in society." Julian didn't sound so pleased at the idea.

"I don't want to raise my stature. I want to avoid getting assassinated like Ayden," Thane said.

She needed a play book with a list of all the players. This was like watching a game of tennis with all the volleying between everyone.

"I wasn't talking about you," Julian said.

Lane nodded at his eldest son.

Oh, fuck no. Her muscles tensed. If only she could run from the room. Maybe she could dive out the window? And survive the five story fall? Maybe the crow-gulls would swoop in to save her?

"I want her." Lane's smug smile spread like that fake cheese in a jar, and looked just as gross.

"No," Thane said. His mouth tightened.

Lane waved his hand as if to swat away a non-existent fly. "You can keep fucking her. I don't want her for that."

Taya visualized thrusting her sword through Lane's throat. Would his eyes bug out? Would he snarl or whimper? She clutched the loose fabric of her sparring pants. If only she had her swords. She might stand a chance if she had them with her.

Lane finally turned his upper body to fully face his youngest son. "This isn't a request."

"I'm aware. The answer is still no." He moved his weight onto his toes, subtly. Training with him for the last three weeks, though, taught her some of his tells. This was one of them. He couldn't move that gargantuan bulk of muscle without her noticing.

The men scowled.

Of course they'd recognize his tells, too.

"You will give her to me."

"I bonded her," Thane said, voice flat.

Julian hissed.

Lane recoiled. "You idiot."

Thane remained still and let their reactions flow over him without flinching.

What the hell? What was the big fuss? Thane bonded all his team. And it was reversible...wasn't it?

"Leave us." Lane rubbed the bridge of his nose and flapped his other hand at the door. "Take this street rat with you and bathe her."

Street rat? According to Thane's fabricated story, she hailed from the forest. The insult didn't even make sense.

Thane wrapped his giant calloused hand around her arm and tugged her toward the door. She didn't need any encouragement. They left the room and didn't speak until they exited the main section of the fortress and entered Thane's wing. The hallway was empty. Like the barren corridors of a high school at night, the sound of their feet hitting the tiles rebounded down the stark walls ahead of them. They stopped in front of the door to her room.

"I thought you couldn't protect me from them," she said.

"I didn't want to reveal the bond."

"But you did."

He nodded, lips turning down. "I did."

To protect her.

She stared at the Arkavian warrior. Her chest expanded with a weird fuzzy feeling, like someone inflated a fur-lined balloon inside. She should hate him for what his people did to hers, but he'd given her a choice, a home, and protected her. Now he studied her as if he wanted to say or do more, but he clenched his jaw and remained silent instead. He held something back.

"Who were you lying to?" she asked.

"What do you mean?"

"You told your father you planned to use me as a bodyguard. You told me something different."

"Ah." He straightened. "I didn't lie to either of you. I don't wish for my father to know all my plans." Nor did he wish for her to know everything as well. Noted. She'd figured as much already.

"Offer the crust so he misses the whole slice of bread?" she guessed.

"Exactly."

"When do my new duties start?" she asked.

"Right away."

"Like, right now?" She scanned the empty hallway.

Surely he didn't mean for her to follow him to his room and guard him tonight.

"Tomorrow. One of the scouts came back from Earth and reported another sacrifice ring. He met a mysterious end before I could question him, but luckily, he'd already sent the report to me."

Cold crept along her skin. "Another circle?"

He nodded.

"What do you think is the purpose of the circles?"

His thunderous expression showed how much he hated this topic. "That's what I intend to find out."

CHAPTER 20
COUNTRY ROAD

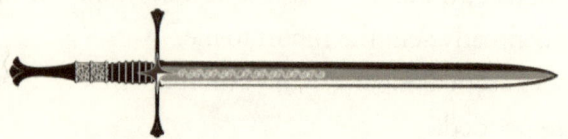

Taya stepped through the blue haze and took a deep breath of air filled with cedar and fir. The dew covered needles on low hanging branches glistened in the morning light. The remaining mist clung to the rolling landscape as if begging the mossy trunks and ferns to save it from the sun. It must've rained sometime during the three weeks she was away. Only small patches of snow littered the ground.

Home.

The familiar scents of the Canadian forest surrounded her like an invisible hug. Instead of running off into the damp underbrush, she remained on Sugar trying to soak it all in through her eyeballs and plumes of air escaping her mouth and nose.

"This way." Thane nudged his horse past hers and

led them down a path. This wasn't the same narrow trail they'd travelled before.

Sugar ambled forward, her smooth gait gently swaying Taya in the saddle. Taya's thighs still hadn't fully recovered from their last ride, but the ache wasn't as deep and her muscles not as tender.

Taya's lightning blades pressed against her back and offered comfort with tiny zaps of energy through their sheaths. Out of the entire team, she was the only one not wearing heavy metal armour. She was also not the size of a fully grown grizzly bear, or trained from birth to wield battle axes and broadswords. Her leather riding pants allowed a more comfortable ride and protected her from the damp cold currently biting at her face and trying to sink into her bones.

Taya leaned forward and patted Sugar's neck. The horse rumbled with approval. Despite the soreness of her legs, Taya rode Sugar every day. She'd learned her horse was called a blue roan, not a gray, and the black marks lining her body were caused from rubbing or injury.

Taya also learned Arkavians, despite all their flashy armour and extraordinary magical capabilities, were suborn mules. From her limited experience, mares and geldings seemed easier to handle and just as hard working, but the warriors from the House of Jericho rode stallions...because stallions. They equated the virility of their mounts to the potency of their manhood.

Well, she had no manhood to prove. Hopefully,

Thane would let her keep riding this mare. She patted Sugar's neck again.

Thane sat rigidly on Hades, back straight and expression closed. He'd hardly spoken to any of them this morning. She let him get ahead before following.

"Don't take it personally," Soka whispered.

"Huh?"

Lokni leaned in from the other side. "He's been in a foul mood all morning."

"Because of the sacrifice?" she asked.

Lokni grumbled and looked away. Their horses picked their way over dead branches and exposed gnarled roots.

Soka waved his brother away. "Because he learned the woman who spurned him and cancelled their engagement is now planning to marry his brother."

Oh. That. No wonder the meeting last night was tense.

"Now he'll never be rid of her," Soka said.

"Did she call it off because she wants to marry the heir instead of a second son?"

Soka glanced at Thane who'd placed more distance between them. "No."

"Then what."

Soka appeared to visually calculate the distance separating them from Thane again.

Oh, for fuck's sake. What was the big deal? "Come on. You all know except me." A thought hit her. "Or does the bond with Thane prevent you from sharing?"

Soka straightened in his saddle. "He laid a geas over the team."

Oh. Bond. Geas. They were probably the same thing.

"A geas isn't the same thing as a bond."

Fuck.

"Did he bond you?" Soka leaned in.

Uh-oh. Thane didn't tell his team about the bond and he hadn't wanted to disclose the little fact with his family either. She probably shouldn't be talking about it. Whatever "it" was.

"That would explain why he brought her." Lokni spoke to his brother over his head. The brothers exchanged a knowing look. "She's not exactly up to standard."

"Hey!"

He shrugged. "It's true. You're more of a liability right now."

Her brain was too rattled to make any further protest. What the hell did Lokni mean with his first comment? Did Thane have to keep her close because of the bond?

The men waited.

"Fuck if I know what he did," she said. *School your face. School your face. You're a rock.* Why did these twins have to be so perceptive? "Your Arkavian magic voodoo crap is all the same to me. Now are you going to tell me the story or not?"

"Alexis heard the rumours," Soka said, eyes still

173

narrowed in her direction.

She hadn't fooled him at all. Her deflection failed.

Wait, what did he say? Taya sat up in her saddle. "What rumours?"

"That's enough Sokanon," Thane bellowed over his shoulder.

Did he have super hearing? And...Sokanon?

Soka clamped his mouth shut. Red tinged his cheeks. He flashed an apologetic smile before dropping back to the rear of their procession.

She turned to Lokni. The twin shook his head and joined his brother.

Taya blew some errant strands of platinum hair out of her face and clucked at Sugar. The roan picked up her pace, her dark coat rippling under the weak sun.

When she pulled up alongside Thane, he scowled at her. "What are you doing?"

"I'm your bodyguard."

"And?"

"And I need to be close to your body to guard it." That came out wrong. She winced.

Thane's grip tightened on the reins. "You shouldn't listen to gossip."

"No. I shouldn't believe gossip. I should still be aware of it, especially if it creates bitter ex-fiancés or other hazardous materials."

Thane took a deep breath. His armour rose and fell with his chest. "My father believed my mother was unfaithful. He beat her to death when I was eight."

The memory surfaced, loud and vivid. The sick sounds of Lane's fists hitting Thane's mother over and over again. Her heart ached. He'd been the same age as her brother when he had the spider incident. One of those childhood experiences was normal, the other wasn't remotely close.

"Many believe he was right," Thane said.

"To beat her or believe she cheated?"

"Both."

Pressure squeezed her chest as if an invisible giant wrapped Taya in his massive hand.

"There are rumours I'm an illegitimate child of this scandalous union."

The other memories flooded in. His father and brother were truly horrible people. What other childhood wonders had they destroyed for Thane?

"It only takes one look at you with your father and brother to see the resemblance," she said.

He nodded. "Yet the rumours persist."

She sat back in her saddle and willed the memories away. They ignored her, flooding her senses with smells of dark, damp jail cells and the sounds of Thane's mother screaming.

"I sometimes wish they were true," Thane whispered, watching the road.

"Because then you wouldn't be like them?"

His stormy gaze settled on her, flashing like lightning. "I'm already nothing like them."

She nodded like she understood, but she didn't. He

sounded both proud and upset. Maybe he was just as confused.

"What do you think the sacrifice circles are for?" she asked and winced. She'd already asked him that question, but she said the first thing that sprang into her mind to change the topic.

"If I knew, we wouldn't be here."

Geez, she was trying to be nice. Help her out, buddy. "What do you think is going on?"

"Do you know why Arkavians invaded your world?" Thane asked instead.

His abrupt change in topic startled her. Like an older-model car with a misfiring cylinder, she stumbled to catch up. An explanation for all her pain and suffering? Yes, please. All she'd gathered over the last few weeks was the general impression of greed. Maybe she should've asked outright, but she'd been more concerned about her fate among the Arkavians. *Why* Arkavians invaded Earth would never change *what* they did or *how* they devastated her entire world.

"Take a guess," Thane continued.

Okay, she'd play. "A sadistic overlord fetish fantasy?"

He hesitated. "That's actually not far off."

"Lovely."

"Our society is a parasite. We use other worlds as energy sources. We take and take until all the natural resources are depleted and the natural power of the land is drained."

Even more lovely. Arkavians were a civilization of good-looking locusts. "I thought Earth didn't have magic."

"It didn't have magic in its atmosphere. Every planet has a natural essence that can be extracted or drained."

How fortunate for Earth. If Thane represented all of Arkavia right now, she'd punch him in the face.

Large dark clouds moved in and cast them in shadow. Winter sunshine rarely lasted long on the coast. They should make camp before the rain set in.

He glanced at her. "It wasn't always this way. Arkavia used to be a thriving, self-sufficient world. We sill reaped other realms, but more for..."

"Fun?" God, she hated Arkavians.

He grunted.

"Validation? Feed the superiority complex?"

He winced. "Is your world's history so squeaky clean? Does it not contain stories of one group trying to conquer or take over another?"

Taya turned away and bit her lip.

"I thought as much," Thane said. "Human nature mixed with power can be a despicable thing. My ancestors raided other realms for all the reasons you mentioned. Mostly for power. But something changed. Instead of reaping for status, we began to reap out of need. Necessity."

"What happened?" she asked. "Plastics?"

"What?"

"Never mind. Please continue."

He gripped the leather reins hard. They creaked under the pressure of his gauntlets. "No one knows. I suspect dark magic. Normally, power is a renewable resource. Like water, once used, it returns to its natural lifecycle. I believe someone leached magic from Arkavia and disrupted the balance."

"Leaching?"

"Yes."

"And this has the same effect as cutting holes in a bucket?"

"Exactly. No matter how much we refill the system, it keeps leaking and never stays full because someone keeps draining it. What else can explain why Arkavia no longer retains any of its magical resources?"

"But you said the first gate opened years ago. This can't be one person." She paused. "Unless you guys also have freakishly long lifespans in addition to height."

Thane straightened in his saddle. "We live as long as you. I suspect this has been going on for generations and one of the major houses is involved. Someone has to know something."

"And these sacrifice circles?"

Sugar danced a little in her step. Taya patted her neck again.

"I think the leechers found a way to funnel energy directly from Earth instead of using Arkavia as an intermediary. These circles might be an anchor of some kind," Thane said.

Taya ran her hand through the coarse black and white hairs of Sugar's coat. "Sounds like you already have a lot figured out. Why are we even going to this one?"

"I need to see a fresh site. The last one was too old for me to read the magical signatures and figure out how the spells were constructed or carried out. If I find a new circle, I might figure out how it all works, and more importantly, how to reverse or at least stop the leaching."

"What if you can't?"

"Then I'll find who's responsible."

Taya smiled. She might not gain the ability to reverse time and prevent the reaping from obliterating Earth and leaving only a small number of humans alive like some sort of mathemagical remainder, but if she stuck with Thane, she might help him stop the leaching. She might save her home world from becoming a barren wasteland.

"Uh...guys?" Axel called out from behind them. "Smell that?"

Taya sniffed the cold air. Her stomach turned. Decay.

Sugar's ears pinged back and she lowered her head as if someone might jump out of the trees and smack her on the head.

They entered the clearing surrounded by moss

covered trees. The moisture clinging to dangling strands of lichen refracted the diminishing light to illuminate a ring of corpses.

Luckily, the well-trained horses didn't bolt. They had more courage than Taya. She wanted to run.

Thane stomped around the flattened, frost-encrusted grass. His breath escaped in angry billows of air as if he housed a pissed off dragon.

She stilled.

No. Not possible. Surely she'd know by now if Arkavians secretly shifted into dragons. She eyed the giant warriors, all wearing grim expressions and surveying the area for threats. If they were supernatural were-creatures, their beasts would be bears, not overgrown lizards.

She glanced at the badly decomposed bodies and immediately wished she hadn't. *Think of a big Thane teddy bear with a jar of honey. Thane-bear with honey.*

Nope. Not working.

"I'm not an expert, but these bodies look about the same as the ones we saw three weeks ago," she whispered.

Thane glared.

Okay, then. At least she knew she was right.

"The snow and ice slowed decomposition significantly, which is why these look similar to the ones we saw earlier. They're about five months old," Lokni confirmed. "This places their deaths around the time of the portal opening."

"Why does this site and the last one look less organized than the one I saw?" she asked.

"Scavengers," Lokni and Soka answered in unison.

She shivered. The image of a raccoon scurrying away with a dismembered arm and wolves gnawing on exposed rib bones made her stomach drop and her lungs feel too small.

"Mount up. We'll find a place to camp away from here." Thane grabbed Hades' reins.

"We're not heading back?" Axel asked.

"No. I want Taya to show me the first site's location. Maybe the position will give us some clues."

She had zero interest in returning to the campground of her friends' demise a third time, but maybe it would provide her with an opportunity to either help or escape. Three times a charm, right?

She mounted Sugar and grabbed the reins. Did she really want to escape now? In the dead of winter, she had no supplies or shelter. With Thane, she had food, clothes and a warm place to sleep. It certainly beat living in the woods.

Thane said he could use the bond to find her anywhere. Running now wouldn't achieve anything except wasting time and damaging her acceptance in this group.

She directed Sugar to follow the group away from the massacre while her mind spun.

Guilt stabbed at her chest. Guilt for surviving. Guilt for living among the enemy and not trying to slit their necks at every opportunity. Guilt for actually liking the men on Thane's team and guilt for...guilt for Thane.

Survive first, feel later. Her dad's words hugged her brain.

Well, that's what she did. She survived. And she'd keep surviving. The backlash of feels she'd suffer one day scared her. The emotions might prove her undoing.

If Thane spoke truthfully, and the Arkavians planned to suck Earth dry of its essence and resources, even if she evaded Thane with the bond in place, she had finite time to exist on this side of the gate anyway. Much better to serve Thane and hopefully find a way to either stop the leaching from continuing or save whatever survivors remained.

She watched the men ride ahead, their backs broad, their bodies strong, and their armour glinting in random bands of sunlight as it streaked through the cloud cover and forest canopy.

And if all else failed, she'd serve out her year and then she was free to kill as many Arkavians as she could.

CHAPTER 21

THREE TIMES A CHARM

T aya sat by the flowing water and threw the smooth river rock. It skipped twice before sinking. The dark clouds dumped a short deluge of rain on them before the foul weather moved on. The sun set and cast them in eerie moonlight.

"You've been lost in thought," Thane said. He sat down on the boulder beside her. "Is it hard to visit this side again?"

She nodded. "Too soon." Sure it had been over five months since the blue death wave rolled through her life and she'd had time to come to terms with the devastation and loss, but stepping into the familiar air, surrounded by a familiar forest and sounds, brought all the intense emotions rushing back.

He picked up a rock and whipped it at the river. Instead of skipping, it hit the water with a loud plunk and sank. *Glug, glug, glug.*

Someone snickered. The small campsite offered no privacy. The twins bickered around the fire and Axel grumbled about his numb ass.

"I'm sorry the sacrifice wasn't fresh," Taya said and cringed. She'd have to add that to the list of phrases she never thought she'd say.

"It's not your fault."

"I wish there was a way for you to see what I saw at the first site. Then we wouldn't have to tramp through this forest during winter." And she wouldn't have to visit the location of her friends' death a third time.

Silence answered her. Thane studied her. The men behind them stilled. The bickering stopped.

"Leave us," Thane said.

Boots scuffed against river rock as the men left the clearing without a word. Branches snapped and leaves swished as they travelled into the woods.

Maybe she could run after the rest of the team.

"There is a way," Thane said.

"But?"

His lips flattened into a straight line. "It can be...intrusive."

"More intrusive than the bond?" Her body warmed at the memory of his power pressing into her.

He nodded. "For the bond, I placed my magic within your mind. Using the bond to sift through your memories involves me moving my magic inside you."

Heat flushed her skin. "Why does this sound sexual?"

"Because, in a way, it is. It's an intensely intimate thing. To continue with your analogy, forming the bond is penetration and memory sifting is the actual fucking."

So he wanted to fuck her brains out. Literally. Her heart pounded. Part of her liked the idea. And that part could shut the hell up.

"I'll be gentle," Thane offered.

She laughed. That's not the first time a man said those words to her.

"It's your choice," he said.

"Is it though?" He was her master, after all.

He frowned. "Of course. Memory sifting is not something I would impose on anyone. Forcing a sift can be incredibly damaging and painful, much like rape."

Okay. Only consensual mind-fucking here, then.

"It won't be unpleasant. Married Tarkas often merge their magic during sex." He looked away.

She wrung her hands together. If she said no, they'd continue searching for more sacrifice circles while some dark magic leaching douchebag continued to defile her world. The alternative was to let Thane move his magic inside her and risk getting off on it.

"Okay." She squeezed her eyes shut. Heat flooded her body. She'd like to think the first reason was the motivation for her decision, but she tried not to make a habit of lying to herself.

"We should move away from the water. It can distort magic."

She knew it! Of course she knew water messed with Tarka power, but it was nice to have it officially confirmed.

Thane stood and held his hand out, much like he had in training the other day. She let him haul her to her feet, her boots scuffing the rock.

"Where are the men?" she asked.

Thane led her to his tent and held the flap back. "They'll guard our campsite from the perimeter."

She stepped into the enclosed area and the walls of the tent closed in. Instantly, the space shrank.

Thane dropped his sword belt and it clattered against the hard ground. "Get comfortable. We need to lay down and touch."

She unclasped her double sword scabbard and rested the sheaths against Thane's. "I bet you say that to all the girls."

"Only the lucky ones." He removed his armour. The metal clanked where he set it down, and his pine scent intensified.

She stumbled. With an extra step, she landed on the bed roll. Hopefully, that appeared intentional.

Thane chuckled.

Okay, maybe it didn't.

Thane stretched out beside her and gathered her in his arms. She tensed, rigid as a plank. With jolted motion, she rested her hand on his chest, solid under the wool shirt. Her palm hit him with a small thump.

"You need to relax," he said.

Yup. Not the first guy to tell her that, either. She released a bunch of pent up air. "Easy for you to say."

His breath fanned the top of her head and his thumb stroked her arm through the cloth. "Shhhh. You're ruining the moment."

Nervous laughter bubbled up her throat. Before it could spill out, Thane's magic slid inside her head and her mind spiraled into memories.

First, she relived the glimpses into Thane's past—the painful ones she'd already seen. The screams of his mother while he cowered under a blanket frozen in a fear no child should ever experience. Then Thane flipped over his dead tutor. Then he demanded answers and support from his brother and got neither. As fast as the memories appeared, they flickered away.

Thane sucked in a breath. His hands dug into her arm and side where he held her to his hard body.

Next, they stood in a clearing together, John off to one side. Bodies no more than three days old lay exposed to the afternoon sun. They walked through the scene again, slowly, reliving Taya's memory as if she stood in the summer heat surrounded by buzzing insects and death all over again.

Something flickered under the sunlight.

"Do you think..." John shuddered. "Do you think this is their plan for us?"

She shook her head and forced her gaze away from Kaydence's horrified expression. "I don't think so. I overheard two of them talking and they made it sound as though they intended to use us as slaves, not food or sacrifices."

"Something interrupted their plans." He walked around some of the bodies and paused by one of the men. "Is this one of them?"

Taya joined him, carefully skirting the pools of dried blood. Too many. Too many faces and bodies to take in. They blurred together. She swallowed and forced her eyes open to study the body John indicated. Sure enough, he'd identified one of the Arkavian soldiers. "He's the one who spoke to the leader."

The memory rewound. Thane moved his magic within her mind, back and forth as he replayed that moment, looking for something. Finally, his power slid away and the memory carried on until it ended with her and John leaving to raid the other campsite.

Instead of rousing from their shared memory, her mind spiraled forward to a more recent time. Suddenly Thane was there, naked and pinning her to the ground, his hard shaft pushing into her. The fantasy from grappling practice played out in exquisite detail.

Oh no. Please don't let Thane see this memory. Her mind scrambled and shoved Thane's magic away. Instead of sending Thane's power out, her mind catapulted into a different memory. Thane's memory. He had her pinned to a bed. She panted, hair wild, gaze heated and sweat glistening on her naked skin as he pressed her into the soft covers and pumped into her heat.

The memory snapped away and everything went black.

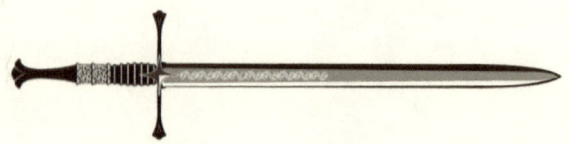

Deep voices bickering outside brought Taya out of her haze. Her lashes fluttered against the rough material of Thane's shirt.

Thane.

Bed.

Sex.

She froze.

They still lay together on his bedroll, fully clothed, in his tent. The campfire outside cast a warm orange glow through the tent fabric. The distant heat staved off some of the frost in the winter air, but Taya wasn't cold. Nope. She burned with need.

Thane held her to his warm chest with his strong arms the size of small tree trunks. His even breath teased her hair and his potent scent wound around her.

He'd fantasized about her.

And now he knew she fantasized about him.

She needed to get out of here. Her cheeks burned. She pushed away.

Thane's arms tightened around her.

"Do you always cuddle afterward?" she asked.

"Do you always talk when you're uncomfortable?" he countered.

Damn it. She clamped her mouth shut.

"You saw my memories," he said.

"Yes." Apparently, they weren't going to talk about that other stuff.

"I'm sorry," he said.

Awkward as hell didn't begin to convey how she felt right now. She shifted her weight to sit up. "That's okay."

"It's probably best that we stay like this for a bit."

"Why?" Was he a masochist? Did he enjoy prolonging uncomfortable situations? She took a deep breath of pine, wool and candle wax.

"Using the bond to memory sift can have lingering effects."

"Like what?" He never mentioned any side effects before. Then again, she didn't ask.

"Like the need for proximity. Both our minds are weak and vulnerable from the experience. Keeping close and in contact helps them recuperate."

She squeezed her eyes shut. Why was her body ablaze with need instead of spiraling into a void of self-loathing? "Did you get what you needed?"

"I think so, and I know the area you were in when

you found the circle. I visited the nearby town before we met."

"And?"

"And the locations make a triangle around the gate. The empty body cavities and the lingering dark magic indicate the wielder ate some of the internal organs and travelled back to Arkavia with the rest to anchor the leaching spell. I don't know how to break the spell. We need to locate the spell caster and eliminate him or her."

Memories of burnt hamburger swamped her senses. *Nope. Don't go there. Don't think about someone hauling a sack of bloody organs through the portal.* She recoiled. Her cheek rubbed against his shirt and stirred scents of trees, metal and man. She needed to focus on something else. "Why did you bond me instead of using a geas like you did with the men?"

He sighed. "You have Tarka power and a geas wouldn't be enough to contain or help you control it."

That made sense. "Lucky bet on which earthen slave to keep, huh?"

"I knew you had magic the second I laid eyes on you."

Oh.

"Power radiates off you."

Oh.

He cleared his throat. "While we're here, we need to talk about that other stuff."

"What other stuff?"

"We can never be together, Taya."

Oh. *That stuff.*

"We need to have a relationship before you can break up with me," she said.

He chuckled, his chest rumbling under her ear. "We share a mutual attraction. I want to be clear it can never become more than that."

"I'll try not to pine for you too hard." Geez. Ego, much? Just because he planned to sit and mope over his botched betrothal didn't mean she had to do something similar. The first thing she needed to do was rid herself of this aching need for the enemy.

"I'm serious," he said.

"So am I." She pushed away. Her brain didn't seize up. "Looks like our refractory period is over."

"Our what?"

She clambered to her feet and brushed off her clothes. Her stiff muscles complained like unfed cats. "Never mind."

"You're always saying that."

She shrugged. "Science analogy."

Thane stood swiftly without any signs of soreness. He towered over her. "We should talk about this."

"About the loss of science?" And logic and everything else that made sense in her world.

He shook his head. "You know what I'm talking about."

She flung her hands into the air. "There's nothing to talk about. I get it. You can't be with a dirty earthen, and I can't be with a murdering Arkavian. We're good, homeboy. I'm not going to boil your bunnies or plot your demise." The stabbing sensation overtaking her heart said otherwise.

"Homeboy?" He frowned. "And why would you boil..." He shook his head again. "That's not it. At least not for me."

She might not need to agonize in excruciating detail over the reasons for his rejection, but evidently he did. She folded her arms and waited.

"You've never been an earthen slave to me, and you never will be. But right now, I'm your leader and you're serving me for a year. A relationship alone would make things complicated. A relationship with a bond in place would be disastrous."

"If I pretend to understand what you're yammering about, can we end this conversation?" She eyed the tent flap. She could make it in three long strides. Maybe four.

Thane growled.

She squeezed her arms and waited for more.

He took a step closer. Less than a foot separated them. His chest rose with each angry breath and his silvery gaze flashed. "I don't want a relationship with someone who can't say no because she might view it as *her job*."

"Oh."

He gripped her face and leaned down. "When your year is up, and you're free, we'll revisit this conversation and your little fantasy about me in the grappling room."

Little? There was nothing little about it.

Thane leaned forward, so close the heat of his minty breath caressed her face. What would he taste like? Would he kiss her gently or would he take her hard with all the pent up need radiating off him? Would he consume her? Would there be anything left of her after he was through?

Thane cast a longing look at her lips, and released her face. Without a word, he stalked from the tent. A burst of voices and firelight filled the tent before the flap rustled closed. Just as well he left quickly. He wasn't present to see her wobble like a newborn filly.

His promise hung heavy in the air and no amount of mental self-chiding could rid the heat thrumming in her veins.

CHAPTER 23

A SAD GOODBYE

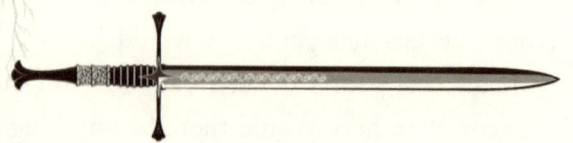

The horses ambled along the frozen path toward the portal. The air buzzed against Taya's skin with energy. She hadn't sensed the power before, but with each clip clop of Sugar's hooves on the path, the gate's presence loomed closer.

None of the men spoke to her since she stepped from Thane's tent, hair mussed, clothes dishevelled, and glaring at all of them. The reprieve was nice. Her mind still scrambled from the sift and invisible pressure tugged her toward Thane. The distance from him physically hurt and made her bones ache.

She ground her teeth and pulled back. To hell if she'd clamber back to him to appease some needy love bond. Her brain needed to hurry the fuck up and heal. This was down-right embarrassing.

Did he feel the pull at all?

"If you don't stop glowering at him, I'll assume he wronged you somehow." Axel leaned over to stage whisper.

Taya sighed. So much for silence.

"And then I'll have to pick a fight with him and I'll lose."

She glanced over at him.

"I can't afford to damage this pretty face." He ran the back of his fingertips over his weather-roughened cheek.

"He didn't wrong me. Your face is safe," she said. "Why would you fight your leader over an earthen's hurt feelings anyway? You've known me for three weeks."

Axel frowned, his thick black eyebrows digging into his scarred forehead. "You're a part of our team, Taya. Whether it's for one week or a decade, no one messes with you without a fist in their face."

"Unless you're Julian's spy," Lokni called out.

"Yeah," Soka said. "Then you get the fist."

"That sounds so wrong," she said.

"Only if you have a dirty mind," Axel said.

Thane ignored them, and continued to stare straight ahead at the path as if their banter flowed right over him.

Sugar snorted and shook her head. Her bridle rattled.

"Well," Axel said. "You—"

A piercing war cry cut off the warrior's words. A man leapt from the trees and lunged at Soka. More cries spread through the forest as people poured from the forest in all directions. An ambush. They were surrounded.

A woman screamed and swung a rusty sword toward her. Taya gripped the saddle, leaned back and kicked the woman in the face. The woman fell to the ground with an ear-splitting cry.

Taya unsheathed her swords, swung her leg over the saddle and hopped off Sugar. The warhorse danced out of the way and kicked a man running up to them. Bones cracked. The man's head whipped back and he crumpled to the ground. Dead.

Good. Sugar was fine and she wouldn't have to worry about accidentally clipping the beast with her swords. Thane's training hadn't covered horseback fighting yet and she knew enough to figure out how useless she'd be mounted.

"Taya!" Thane growled. "Get back on the fucking horse!"

Whatever. She blocked the screaming woman's attack and slid her sword under her guard to slash open her midsection. Adrenaline pumped in her veins. Her swords cried for more blood.

She needed space.

As if a giant neon sign appeared above her head, the attackers diverted and came at her in a giant surge.

Her blades rang through the air. The high pitch

whining of lightning trilled in her blood. The energy inside her fused with the weapons as they ripped through the air and slashed through bodies. She ducked, whirled and spun, slicing the attackers and deflecting their weak strikes.

A man stepped over her last attacker as he slumped to the ground.

John.

What the hell?

She hesitated.

He snarled and lunged forward. She turned at the last second, but too late. His weapon sliced the side of her waist. Her stomach burned.

John flicked his wrist and followed his initial attack with a slash. She blocked the sword and diverted the weapon to the side.

"What are you doing?" she hissed. Her vision wavered.

Another attacker cut in from the side, swiping at her. She spun with the motion, blocked the strike with one sword and drove the other into the belly of the unknown man. He sagged to the ground, releasing her weapon with a wet slap.

She flicked the blood from her swords and faced John. She didn't recognize any of the other earthens who attacked them. Where was Chantelle? George?

"Traitor!" He attacked again.

Metal rang as their blades met. John growled at her like a rabid dog. She spun and struck out with her elbow. He grunted and stumbled forward.

"I knew you were one of them." He rushed forward.

She V-stepped around the strike and drove her blade forward. At the last second, she brought the tip up so the sword sank into his shoulder instead of his heart. She held him as he gasped and sagged forward.

With his face only inches from hers, his wild gaze burned. "Traitor."

"You attacked me," she said. "Where are the others?"

He growled and pushed away. "They left."

She staggered back. Her blade withdrew from his body with a sickening wet sound. The power of the blades whined.

"They left because they preferred you as a leader," he said. "You might've fooled them, but not me. You need to be exterminated."

"Stop it."

"No!" He swung again.

Kill or be killed, apparently. He wouldn't rest until he drove his rusted weapon through her. She never liked John, or trusted him, and she instinctively knew they'd eventually part ways—and not amicably—but not like this. Never like this. They'd survived the first few months together. They'd saved each other's lives.

Her chest tightened. *Not like this.*

He attacked her again. She countered and sunk her blade into his throat, just like he had the Arkavian warrior to save her life months ago. John's eyes widened. He slumped forward. She pulled her sword out, spraying blood across her face.

John's weight pulled her down and she lowered him to the frozen ground. His gaze grew distant. More blood trickled from his mouth and dripped down the side of his face. She reached out and touched his warm face. Why did he have to attack her? Why couldn't he let them go? Her memory flashed to John crouching beside her behind those stupid meat coolers in the grocery store. He'd killed an Arkavian soldier to save her when he could have run.

And now he was dead.

Why, John?

Her limbs shook and she swallowed a sob. She knew the answer. Because she looked like *them*. He associated her appearance with all the pain and loss he'd suffered since the blue death wave bowled through the forest.

If there was an afterlife, hopefully John would find Kaydence and finish their river date. Or maybe he could hunt again with his uncles in lush forests.

A shiver ran through her, cold and heart-numbing. When she straightened and turned, she found the clearing still. No one else attacked. Earthen bodies lay scattered across the glade while the Arkavian warriors remained in their saddles, bloody swords still drawn and watched her. Blood spatter decorated the metal plates of their armour.

These were survivors, like her. She recognized some of them, but John had collected more followers. She never wanted to harm anyone from Earth, yet here she was, standing amidst their bodies with her hands coated in their blood.

Hooves stomped the ground. Hades approached, stopped inches from her face and snorted.

Thane growled down from his saddle. "Why the hell did you dismount?"

"I don't know how to fight on horseback," she said, numbly. She rubbed her arms.

He shut his mouth and glowered. After realizing his death glare didn't harm her, his gaze cut to the body at her feet. He jerked his chin at John. "Friend of yours?"

She looked down again and regretted it. She lurched to the side of the path and threw up.

"Stop being an asshole," Axel grumbled somewhere behind her.

"The sooner she realizes her own people are as much of a threat to her as Arkavians, and setting up a home here will be fatal, the better. Once she draws this inevitable conclusion, I'll stop being a dick."

She wiped her mouth with her leather gauntlet and turned back to the men. "Promise?"

Thane gripped the reins and pulled back. "Yes."

"Message received."

He nodded and turned Hades toward the gate.

The warhorse flicked his flaxen tail. "Mount up. Let's get out of here."

She nodded and stepped forward. The world spun and tilted. Her body smacked the cold, bloody ground. She lay on her back and stared at the blue sky. It was so clear for a west coast winter. Where did the dark clouds go? Her side burned.

Warm hands pressed against her stomach. Someone peeled her wet shirt from her skin.

"She's bleeding," Soka said. "That last cunt must've grazed her."

"Stand back." Thane's face suddenly blocked her view.

"No," she said, limbs growing numb.

"I have to heal you. You're bleeding out."

"I don't want the memories." Her mind was still too raw from the memory sift.

His expression softened. "I'll try to shield you."

His magic coated her. Instead of falling into his world of painful memories, she floated on a cloud. Surrounded by moments of love and happiness. Images of her father, mother and brother wrapped around her and carried her off as Thane healed her body.

A tear fell from her eye and tickled her skin as it travelled down her face. This was so much worse. Why did he have to show her this? Eventually, she'd have to let go and wake up to her harsh new reality. A reality without those she loved most. She didn't want to say goodbye. She didn't want to lose them all over again.

Her dad's crinkled face loomed in front of her. "Survive first."

Feel later. "I know, Dad. I will."

CHAPTER 24
DANCE WITH THE DEVIL

Taya drew her swords and ran the last length toward Thane, gaining momentum. He stepped to the side, taking a position to stop her flight.

Not today, Satan.

She jumped to the side, out of the reach of his swords, their sharp edges dangerously close to making contact. In the air, she spun and struck out. Only to find he'd anticipated her attack.

Again.

They moved back and forth in a flurry of attacks, blocks and counters, their swords clashing in the early morning spring hours. Their breath condensed around them and plumed in the air.

It had been months since their trip to Earth and she had to kill John in self-defence. Time might've passed, but John still visited her nightmares. To escape the dreams, she poured everything into her training.

Taya knew with the first few exchanges that Thane still surpassed her own skills. He always would. And he also could've ended this sparring match multiple times, but chose to prolong it. He probably savoured her futile attempt at victory. Sick bastard.

Taya would normally continue these games, but she was tired. She'd had enough.

Faking a strike to the body, she stepped to the side to appear off-balance. Thane didn't take the bait.

He didn't need to.

He wasn't supposed to.

She dropped her off-hand sword to unsheathe her dagger in a quick, fluid transition. With a flick of her wrist, she brought the dagger under Thane's guard.

Not bothering to hide her smile, she pressed the sharp edge into Thane's pretty throat.

"About time," he grumbled.

Her smile faltered. "W...what?"

"I was getting hungry."

She dropped the arm holding the dagger. "You're an ass."

"No." He leaned in, his face unbearably close. "I'm Thane, the second son from the House of Jericho."

She rolled her eyes and sheathed her dagger. "Can we train with the bō staff after lunch?"

"Why do you like those sticks so much?" He raised his eyebrows and waited for her response.

She chose to ignore the double entendre and answered him truthfully. "In my world, nobody walked around with swords. I always thought my father's fascination with them was misplaced, even though I enjoyed the practice. The bō was always more practical."

He raised an eyebrow.

"Slightly more practical," she amended, scooping up her dropped sword. "Even if someone had a sword on Earth, they likely wouldn't know how to use it."

"I have skill with using both."

Ugh. She raised her eyes to the sky but no divine intervention would save her from this man. He either planned to kill her with his ego, or innuendo. Instead of coming up with something witty to say, she glared at Thane.

"Oh, good," Julian's voice broke their staring contest. "You haven't finished training yet."

Thane pulled away from her to face his brother. "What do you want?"

Taya also looked over and froze. Julian stood beside his father. They both had their swords drawn.

"To test your new merchandise," Lane said.

Taya scowled but remained silent. She valued her head attached to her shoulders and now was not the time to talk back. She'd been at the house for months. Was she still considered new?

"Taya isn't some purchased item to be reviewed, father," Thane said.

"Yet, you own her," Lane said.

Thane stiffened.

Yeah, she didn't want to examine the accuracy of that statement too much, either.

Before Thane found his voice, Julian and Lane launched in a coordinated attack. Thane had the choice to defend her or step back.

He grimaced and moved out of the way.

Okay, then.

He either didn't care to defy his father or he trusted her abilities enough to let her stand on her own.

Taya didn't have a chance to think more about his motivations. Instead, she focused on deflecting Julian and Lane's attack.

They danced around her, their blades flashing in the weak rays of sunlight. Dance wasn't appropriate—it felt too fancy for something so deadly. They didn't seek to kill her, purposefully pulling away from deadly openings. They truly just wanted to spar and test her mettle.

Instead of letting fear rule her, she loosened her limbs and met their attacks with her own. This reminded her of practicing with her dad and brother.

Her stomach dropped. She swallowed the unexpected grief and pressed on. She used to spar with her dad and brother for hours, only pausing to go over mistakes. The crunch of dirt and snap of peeled arbutus bark would fill the air along with the ring of metal. The cool air would burn her lungs in the fall and winter, while the sun would burn her shoulders in the summer. The world around them would go through the seasons, but they would remain constant, practicing sword work in the yard for hours and hours until Mom yelled at them to come in for dinner.

And they were gone.

Dark energy curled around her, seeping into her skin and mind. Her vision became cloudy, her mind fuzzy. She stumbled and received a hard blow to the stomach. She spun around and someone's fist connected with her face.

She pulled on her own magic. It sparked and sputtered out, slipping from her grasp. One of her assailants gripped her arm and threw her to the ground.

Her back smacked against the dirt, air forced from her lungs.

The dark energy receded like the grime was suctioned from her skin. Julian and Lane's magic felt nothing like Thane's and the touch of their magic left her feeling dirty.

Her vision cleared to find all three men standing over her.

"Sword work isn't bad," Julian conceded.

"Need work on her magical defence," Lane stated the obvious.

Thane grumbled in agreement.

CHAPTER 25

THE PEN IS MIGHTIER THAN THE SWORD

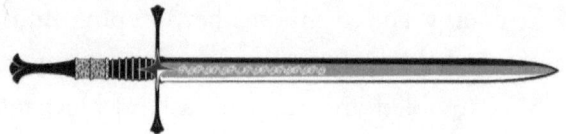

A gust of air travelled through the room and tussled Taya's hair. She was no longer alone in the library. She spent her time training during the day and laying exhausted on her bed at night, but sometimes, during the time in between, she either snuck off to the library or spent time with Adrianna.

Taya quelled the instincts to bolt. Arkavians would view such an act as a weakness and if the late-night visitor was Thane's father or brother, the last thing she wanted to do was make herself look more like prey.

Instead, she straightened in her seat and turned slowly to the door. At the same time, she drifted her hand to the hilt of her dagger.

Thane leaned against the door frame, arms crossed. He didn't wear armour or court clothes for once, instead, he wore the leather pants Arkavian royals favoured and a loose, long-sleeved shirt. With slightly-messed white hair and sleepy eyes, his appearance gave her the impression he'd tried to sleep and failed.

Tired and agitated, Thane wasn't guarding his expression like he normally did. Instead of stone, his open gaze drew her in and threatened to drown her. Something tugged on the magical bond connecting them.

Thane in off-mode was mesmerizing. He seduced her without even trying.

And she hated herself for her weakness.

"What are you doing?" he asked.

"Looking up Arkavian history."

"I thought Adrianna was helping you with that."

Taya closed the old leather-bound book in front of her and pushed the heavy wooden chair back so she could face Thane better. "Adrianna is filling me in on all the latest court gossip, house affiliations and their history, in addition to the Old Arkavian dialect."

"Swear words and pick up lines?"

Taya shrugged. "She says they're the easiest way to remember and a good place to start."

"She's not wrong."

Taya pushed off her seat to stand.

Thane swiftly stepped into the room and wave his hand up and down. "Sit. I'll join you." He pulled out a chair and slid onto the wooden seat as she sat back down. "Is there any part of our illustrious past that you find particularly interesting?"

She pushed the old book across the polished wood.

He glanced down, gaze scanning the title. "Reapings?"

"Yeah, reapings," she said. "How well do you know the process for creating the portal between realms?"

He shifted on his feet. "Enough."

Taya tapped the book. "There's a lot of information about how to forge a connection from one realm to another."

"Yes..."

"None of them mention sacrifice circles."

"That's because they're not involved in the forging process." His tone was dry, mocking.

Ugh. "Yet, the sacrifice circles are located around the portal, so that were created shortly after the connection was made. You said reapings weren't always this way. Maybe something in the process changes to allow the Tarka to set up the leaching spell." She pulled the dusty old book back, opened to the marked page she'd been reading and scanned the words.

"And they use the portal as the funnel." Thane scratched the stubble along his jaw. "There's nothing in the process that I'm aware of that allows for the leaching."

"*That you're aware of.* It might be something

hidden in the magic incantations. If we can figure out how the portal allows or funnels the leaching, we might be able to track the magic somehow to the Tarka responsible."

Thane closed his mouth, pressing his lips together firmly. His jaw muscles popped out and he glowered at the book in front of him.

"Is there anyone we can ask?"

The tension in Thane's shoulders didn't relax.

"Someone involved in the reaping?" And maybe after they completed interrogating the Tarka, she could go back and slip a knife between their ribs. Maybe this was the opportunity she needed to exact her revenge.

Her friends' faces flashed in her mind. Memories of their shenanigans were always bittersweet.

"That might tip are hand." Thane glanced down at her clenched hands. "And it's also probably not wise to let you question them. Besides, I don't think it will be helpful."

"Well aren't you a ray of sunshine."

Thane scowled. "There are three things going on here. There are the reapings, where Arkavia opens a portal to another world to reap the resources and power of that land. There's the leaching, where someone has somehow tapped into the reapings for personal gain, and there are the sacrifice circles. We believe the circles are somehow linked to the leaching. The thing is, I don't think the leaching spans more than a few generations, or something would've been mentioned in the history books, or at least the family's personal accounting of past events."

"But you just noticed the circles now."

"I never travelled to a reaped world before," Thane said. "I can only guess, but I think these circles have to be new. Surely someone would've said something before now."

"So the Tarka or Tarkas involved have evolved to use these circles for leaching, or our entire theory is wrong and the circles aren't involved with the leaching at all."

"And if any of the Tarkas involved in the reaping of Earth are involved they're hardly going to admit it. We need to find out what, if anything, has changed in the reaping process."

She sat up in her chair. "In order to do that, we need..."

"A comparison." Thane completed her thought.

"Is there an old, crotchety Tarka stashed away somewhere?" she asked. "One involved in previous reapings? Preferably ones from a long time ago? In a time before the leaching presumably began?"

Thane hunched over the table and examined his calloused hands. "There is a guy."

"But?"

Visibly stealing himself, he straightened and removed all emotion from his face. "But nothing. We'll leave tomorrow."

Though she'd found a possible lead to solving the circle mysteries, Thane didn't seem very grateful. If anything, he'd become more hostile.

Why?

CHAPTER 26
A HORSE, OF COURSE

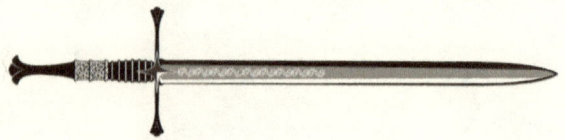

It took over a week of dreary horse riding, uncomfortable nights sleeping on hard ground and tense silence from Thane to make it to the House of Edur.

The usual crew accompanied Thane, but they took their lead from Thane and travelled with the same silent treatment.

Sugar huffed, her warm breath condensing in the dewy morning air. She shifted side to side, restless, but not nearly as tired at Taya. Clearly, her horse was bored and just wanted to get on with it.

Yeah, girl. Same.

Thane had set a slow, agonizingly boring pace, taking multiple breaks for the horses. She'd asked if they had some sort of system involving relay stations set up on Arkavia. Everyone had looked at her like she'd lost her mind, even after she explained how people on Earth used to replace exhausted horsed for fresh mounts to reduce rest stops and subsequent delay during a long journey.

"The horses need to rest," Thane had growled. "We brought our war mounts. Even if we could exchange or trade them, we wouldn't. They're not replaceable."

Sugar huffed again, apparently agreeing with Thane and a pang of guilt stabbed at Taya for asking the question in the first place. Which was totally ridiculous, but true nonetheless.

Lokni pulled up beside Taya, still focused on the small fortress in the valley below. "What do you know about this house?"

Taya played with the leather reins in her hand. "Oh, so now you've decided to speak with me?"

Lokni cut his gaze to her before quickly turning his attention back to the path ahead. "I don't know what you're referring to."

"I was beginning to wonder if he placed some sort of gag order on the team."

"Too tired to talk."

Taya gaped at him.

"What?"

"I find it very unlikely you ever become too tired to talk."

"Taya. Stop harassing Lokni," Thane snapped.

She threw up her hands. "Is anyone going to tell me what's up?"

"No." Thane drew his horse to her other side. "Now pull your face mask up and keep your mouth shut. Under no circumstances are you to speak or ask questions. If you have something to say, do so after we've left this place."

She pursed her lips.

Thane ran a hand down his face. "Taya?"

"Fine." She pulled up the black material that covered the lower portion of her face. Hopefully, the murderous glare she directed at Thane spoke for her.

Shockingly, he didn't fall over on the spot, killed by the potency of her gaze.

"We're not among friends here." He turned away, expression stony and prodded Hades forward.

And she followed like a good little soldier. This servitude itched at her skin. She'd grown to like Thane and his team, but it didn't dull the pain of loss, nor her anger at those responsible for her world's destruction.

She needed to keep her focus on the end game. This was temporary, a means to an end, the best positioning she could manage to get her sweet justice.

Instead of speaking, she trained her scowl on Thane's back. He'd shown her kindness, even vulnerability, but that was gone. Where did that Thane go? Or was the other Thane all an act? Maybe this cold, detached version of Thane was the authentic one.

Sugar plodded along as Taya continued to run through her first memories of Thane. No, he had asshole-like tendencies, but he wasn't actually an asshole. Something about coming here had rattled him. This house had set the entire team on edge, but no one thought to let her in on the big secret.

She studied the simple stone fortress, looking more like some glammed up outpost from medieval times than the house of someone capable of making Thane worry.

Now late spring, the sun should've warmed her back as they made their way into the courtyard. Instead, a frosty chill settled over her.

The House of Edur. Or at least one of them. Cousins from the direct line took up smaller fortresses and buildings away from the main one, choosing to live apart, or being forced to. This must be one such place.

All Taya knew was what Adrianna had told her, which was very little. Now reflecting on their chats, Taya should've picked up on the anomaly. Adrianna normally went into great detail to describe a house and all the gossip surrounding it.

Except this one, and House Jericho. Adrianna had only told her "Edur" meant snow in Old Arkavian.

Huh. Maybe they got the house name for the frosty welcome.

A pale boy, no more than fifteen ran out from some shadowy corner and took Hades' reins from Thane.

"Cool him down, water and feed him," Thane said. "The roan, too. After the horses are brushed, tack them back up with new blankets. We're not staying long."

Taya bit back a groan and dismounted. If they

didn't stay here for the night, that meant another night sleeping on hard-packed, sun-dried dirt again.

Not a fan.

If this was an adventure experience on Earth, she'd rate it one star.

The boy led Hades and Sugar away. The other men would stay and look after their own mounts. Thane must really hate this place. He normally groomed Hades himself. Allowing an unknown stable boy to attend his war mount to decrease time spent here spoke volumes all on its own.

A grizzly old man with white hair and a white beard ambled down the steps from the main entrance. Though stooped with age, his wide shoulders, large hands, and scars lining his exposed forearms hinted at a warrior's past. He squinted at their entourage, the expression looking vaguely familiar.

"Lord Edur." Thane bowed, stiff and shallow.

Taya moved to stand slightly behind him, scanning the courtyard and the parapets for archers.

"You still need to work on your greetings, grand-son," the old man growled.

Shock spread through her body like ice. Lord Edur was Thane's grandfather? No wonder he seemed famil-iar. Thane's mother looked like a female version of him.

"May I have a moment of your time?" Thane asked. "I have some questions I'd like to ask you in private."

The old man heaved a laborious sigh before jerking his chin toward the entrance.

Thane walked up the first few steps and she followed closely behind him.

Lord Edur stiffened. "What is this?"

Thane paused to glance over his shoulder. "One of my team members."

"A girl?"

"A woman."

The man's scowling lowered Taya's opinion of him. So what if she was a woman? Thane had told her how a lot of Arkavian women held positions of power and could be hellish adversaries. Tarka power also didn't discriminate, creating monsters out of anyone, regardless of gender.

"Does she speak?" Lord Edur asked. "Or does she just follow you around like a shadow?"

"My shadow?" Thane's grin was evident in his voice. He stroked his chin. "I think I like that. Yes. She's my shadow. Where I go, she follows."

Lord Edur glowered. "You always were a sentimental boy. Too much like your mother."

Thane shrugged as if the comment meant nothing as if the words glanced off him. Only she caught the tension in his hand as if he fought the urge to grip the hilt of his sword and pull the weapon from its sheath. Instead, he waved at the walkway in front of them.

The older man took the hint and led them through

the entranceway. The inside of this place was just as cold and unwelcoming as the outside.

They followed Lord Edur down an empty sparsely decorated corridor until they reached a heavy wooden door with squeaky hinges. Once they stepped into the dusty sitting room, Lord Edur motioned for Thane to sit in a large chair, one of those with a long, tufted backrest covered with hard creaking leather, narrows arms, and iron-clawed legs that looked like they should be on an old bathtub instead of a chair.

Thane didn't hesitate, sweeping graciously into the chair. A cloud of dust rose around him, but he didn't comment or react to it.

Air whipped around Taya as though someone had opened a window during winter to let a cold draft cut through the heat. Magic. She was somehow sensing Lord Edur's Tarka power. He pushed the cold energy from the room, off to do his bidding. Thane didn't appear overly worried, but he'd probably have the same blank expression on his face if a dragon suddenly sprouted from the shadows and breathed fire at him.

The door creaked behind her. In a flash, she had her dagger out and pressed to the neck of the person standing in the doorway.

"By all means, kill that one," Edur's voice held an indifferent tone. "He's as worthless as the other earthens."

Taya froze.

The man in front of her couldn't be more than

twenty. Long and too lean, his collar bones poked from the drooping neckline of a cotton shirt. He'd synched in the drawstring of his pants to keep them up, but the baggy clothing did nothing to hide his skeletal figure. He held a tray with both hands. An Arkavian tea set sat on the tarnished metal surface of the tray.

Taya dropped her dagger quickly sheathing it.

The entire time, the earthen hadn't flinched or moved, instead, he merely observed her dispassionately from behind his shaggy brown hair.

"This lot of slaves haven't been very good," Edur said.

If only she could place her dagger in his neck.

She stepped to the side and the earthen walked past her without changing his expression. He reminded her of a robot, not that anyone in this room other than her or the slave would get the reference.

"Most of them have died," Edur continued.

Though half her face was covered, Taya forced her expression to remain neutral while she felt each of Edur's words like stabs to the heart. He spoke of her people like someone would discuss a bad crop year, and he crushed one of her dreams. She'd never be able to save them now. She wanted to liberate the earthen slaves from Arkavia, but the truth slapped her in the face. The earthen who just walked past her would never survive on Earth, not without help. His chances of living were better here but only marginally. How could she round up, liberate and care for the handful of earthens left scattered across Arkavia without getting caught and killed?

She couldn't.

Her gut twisted and stomach acid bubbled up her throat.

"If the power levels on Arkavia are dropping faster than the last time, we'll need to do another reaping soon."

"That's actually why I came, grandfather. I'd like to ask you about the reapings from when you were involved."

"Why? You're so big and powerful. What possible information can I provide?"

Thane ignored his grandfather's comment and pressed on. "It's not so much the portal I'm inquiring about, but something I've witnessed on the earthen side. I'm wondering if it's connected somehow."

The old man's eyes narrowed. "Why do you think I would know anything about that? I'm the impoverished, distant fourth cousin to the head of the house. I had to send your mom to that fool just for this house to survive. And look at it." He threw his arm out to wave at the room. "Look at the state it's in. Look what little your mom's life bought. Your father has forgotten me. He left me here to rot the day your mother died."

Thane looked away. The muscle in his cheek flexed and relaxed as he clenched his teeth together. "When you journeyed to the reaping lands, did you notice or hear anything about sacrifice circles?"

"Eh, now?"

"Dead bodies, arranged in a circle in multiple clearings around the portal entry point."

Edur narrowed his eyes.

"Did you see anything matching this description during your trips to the reaped worlds? From the stories I remember you telling, you often had to survey the land around the portals on the other side." Thane's words became more clipped as he spoke, his body tense.

Edur grunted. "I've never heard or seen such a thing. Is that how your generation is running things now?"

"No," Thane snapped back. "The circles as far as I can tell have nothing to do with the actual portal formation, but I wanted to confirm this with someone whose experience can provide a comparison. Can you describe how you formed portals for reapings?"

Lord Edur scowled again before he opened his mouth and a long technical explanation of magic fell out.

Thane grunted, seemingly following all of it. "Nothing has changed. The circles are separate from the portals, or at least the formation of the portals."

"What's the point then?" Lord Edur asked. "Of these sacrifice circles?

Thane clamped his mouth shut. He knew the purpose, or at least highly suspected but was he willing to share his suspicions with his maternal grandfather?

From the closed-off expression, she already knew the answer before he spoke.

"That's what I'm trying to find out," Thane replied. "Thank you for your time, grandfather. We'll take our leave now."

Lord Edur stood with Thane and Taya. "So you got what you came for and now you're off."

Thane clenched his teeth and took a long breath before responding. "This place is full of memories. I'd rather not stay and if you were honest with yourself, you don't wish me to stay, either."

Something flashed in the old man's gaze and his expression softened for the briefest of moments. "You look so much like her." He huffed and looked away, waving his hand in the air. "Off with you, then."

Thane nodded and turned to leave. Taya quietly followed, letting the silence of the building fold around them as they left Lord Edur in his dusty sitting room and made their way to the exit.

Thane stopped abruptly before the grand doors and took another long shaking breath.

"Thane?" She rested her hand on his shoulder.

"This place..." He shook his head.

"Do you need a moment?"

Without turning toward her, he reached up and placed his hand on hers. "This placed used to be warm and filled with love."

When his mom lived.

"Seeing it like this is difficult." He squeezed her

hand before letting his fall to his side. "Now it holds only pain."

"And answers? Did you get anything else from the information your grandfather provided?"

"Like I said before, the process hasn't changed. No one has altered the formation of the portal or the reaping process to allow for leaching."

"So we can rule out that as a potential lead. That's something."

"That's something," he agreed, but his following silence said more than his words.

They might've ruled out a possible lead, but they were no closer to identifying the person or people responsible for the leaching and sacrifice circles.

CHAPTER 27
SWEET WINE

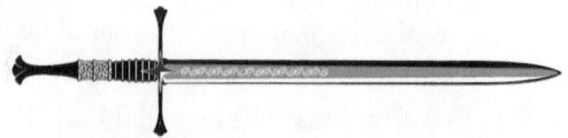

After leaving the minor House of Edur, Thane had dropped all talk of the sacrifice circles, apparently content to let the mystery remain as such, even though it meant the leaching would continue. The status quo remained. With her days filled with weapons and hand-to-hand combat training, history lessons and magic theory, Taya's days blurred together in one exhausted heap. She rarely got away from the main house, but when she did, she tried to savour the moments, so she, too, had stopped investigating the sacrifice circles. What could she do about them, anyway?

The sweet smell of the Arkavian summer drifted over the distant hills and wove through the tall grass surrounding Taya and Adrianna. The long blades slapped against Lokni's armoured shin guards where he stood a few feet away, looking miserable. The sun beat down from above and bathed Taya in its warmth.

The summer after Taya turned sixteen, her family travelled to Hawaii during the summer break. They'd never gone on a tropical vacation before, opting to camp throughout the province and down the island instead. Mom and Dad had saved for years to take them on this trip.

Everything about that vacation had been magical— the plane ride, the lais, the culture and markets, the boys, but what Taya still recalled so vividly, was the smell—hot sand, coconut-infused sunscreen and moisturizer, and the fragrant white flowers from the trees that surrounded the hotel.

Arkavia's sweet summer air smelled like that. Like a tropical paradise from her most cherished family memories, and for some reason, it made her angry.

Okay, she knew the reason.

Arkavia had already stolen so much from her and now, without even trying, it was tainting her memories as well.

When she'd first sat down on the picnic blanket with Adrianna, the floral smells surrounding her triggered memories of Tommy cackling as they attempted surfing for the first time. His white hair had glowed under the hot sun and his nose and cheeks had burned.

"It's been a long time since I've seen your pasty skin without bruises or scratches," Adrianna remarked, bringing her wine glass to her lips.

Taya shook the memory of her brother away. She shrugged and leaned back on the large picnic blanket. "No pain, no gain."

Adrianna liked to haul Taya out of "House Jericho's evil clutches" when she had a rest day. Though Taya enjoyed the time and gossip, she couldn't help suspect Thane had put his cousin up to these outings. Or at least planted the seed for Adrianna to eventually come up with the idea.

The Arkavian noblewoman spent most of the time educating Taya on the houses and their politics, under the ruse of gossip. Without television or any other form of entertainment from Earth, Taya enjoyed the stories. So whether Thane orchestrated the outings or not, Taya didn't mind.

"Are you sure you don't want a glass?" Adrianna turned to Lokni and raised the wine bottle. "Thane's not here."

"No, thank you," he said.

"You could sit on the blanket with us and join the conversation."

"I'd rather die, thank you," he growled.

Adrianna rolled her eyes and turned back to Taya.

"You never finished your story," Taya said. "What happened to this Izar?"

"Well, no one really knows." Adrianna's eyes widened with delight and her smile grew. "What I want to know is what family you come from."

Taya shrugged. "I don't know."

"But who raised you? And don't tell me the wolves. Thane might enjoy spreading that particular story, but I don't buy it."

Taya took a sip of red wine. It was heavier and spicier compared to what she'd had on Earth. Not particularly a fan of wine, she'd rather have a beer, but at this point, she'd willingly accept anything Adrianna shared if it meant getting away from the House of Jericho.

"I was raised by a loving couple. They took care of me and my brother."

Adrianna perked up. "A brother? Why am I only hearing of this now? What's he look like? He must be handsome. Where is he?"

Lokni grumbled and shuffled his feet. God, he was so obvious. Why couldn't Adrianna see it?

The Arkavian noblewoman's excitement sent a bolt of pain through Taya's heart. Where was her brother? She knew the likely answer to that question and it crushed her. "Most likely dead like the rest of my family."

Adrianna sat back, wine momentarily forgotten. Her smile disappeared. "I'm so sorry, Taya. I didn't realize."

"I know. But hopefully, you can understand why I don't like to talk about them."

She nodded, white hair falling over her face.

"I've been on my own ever since," Taya said. Though the words hurt, sticking as close to the truth seemed like the best course of action. She didn't have to fake any of the emotion. She didn't have to act or pretend. The feelings were so real and still so very fresh.

"On your own with the wolves?"

"With the wolves." Taya held up her wine glass and clinked the edge against Adrianna's.

The noblewoman narrowed her eyes at Taya's glass. "That's looking suspiciously full."

"I have another training session tonight. I can't get plastered."

Adrianna pouted, her bottom lip sticking out and her shoulders drooping. "This is supposed to be your day off."

"It is."

She glared.

"Sort of."

"What's so important it can't wait until your regularly scheduled program?"

Taya looked down at her wine glass, wanting to disappear into the dark amber fluid.

Lokni chuckled. "She needs help."

Adrianna's eyebrows crept up. "With what? You're a skilled warrior."

"With my magic," she said. It still felt silly to say the word.

"Not all Arkavians can become Tarkas, even those with the correct hair colouring." Adrianna tugged on

232

her platinum hair. "Or they have so little it's barely notable."

"Thane's convinced I have magic"

"Thane's an idiot."

Taya choked on her wine. "I'd like to see you tell him that."

Adrianna brushed the hair from her face. "I tell him that all the time. He's just too pigheaded to listen." Adrianna placed her empty wine glass on the ground near the edge of the picnic blanket so it wouldn't topple over, and scooted closer to Taya. "What Thane has always failed to understand is not every powerful skill has to be offensive. He relies on brute force, skill and the potency of his magic. Not everything needs to be beaten down or bashed on the head."

Taya frowned. This didn't sound like Thane at all. He had more finesse and cunning than Adrianna's words implied and she said as much.

"No. That's not what I meant." Adrianna glanced at Lokni for help, but their somewhat silent guardian shrugged and went back to scanning their surroundings.

"Thane has never struggled to grasp anything. If a new problem arises, he meets it head-on."

"Are you trying to say he's direct? But in, like, the most indirect way possible?"

"Yes." Adrianna breathed out a sigh. "And he's pigheaded. I stand by that one. If something doesn't work, he thinks trying harder will result in success because that's what's always worked for him. He never thinks to stop and look at things from a different angle. Changing approaches will not occur to him."

"So you're saying I should ask for a second opinion."

She shook her head. "Ask for a different explanation."

Taya grunted. Like that would go well. Thane didn't take criticism well and asking for an alternate method might be taken as exactly that.

"Do you have anything to lose?" Adrianna's eyebrows crept up.

Just her life. "Not really."

CHAPTER 28

JERKS TRAVEL IN PACKS

Taya kicked a pebble and watched it bounce down the overgrown path to the House of Jericho. The tall grass swayed in the gentle breeze. She closed her eyes and stole a moment to enjoy the feel of the sweet air over her skin.

Taya enjoyed the combat defence training, the magic lessons...not so much. Taya reflected on what Adrianna had said about Thane. And in a way, she could relate. Taya never struggled to master a concept or skill before, at least, not like this, not to this extent. Picnics with Adrianna helped take her mind off her failure, but even these outings involved lessons and learning. And she sucked at languages almost as much as she did magic.

It was moments like this. The solo walks from one point to another that she truly savoured, and found herself wishing the trip took longer.

Taya hadn't argued when Lokni offered to stay behind to help Adrianna clean up their picnic while Taya had to leave for training. It meant she had another stolen moment of solitude.

Sleep didn't count. Thane dominated her dreams.

"Look what we have here," Chadwick spoke as he stepped from a bush lining the path not looking surprised at all. His acting skills needed work. He'd obviously hid and waited for her return.

Had Julian sent him? Or Lane? Or did he have his own secret agenda?

A dry twig snapped behind her and she cursed. Where there was one, the other two usually followed close behind.

Chad wasn't alone.

She should've realized. Julian's henchmen only had half a brain put together. They never operated alone.

"To what do I owe the honour?"

Orrin and Steele chuckled and stepped onto the path behind her. They must've used some cloaking skills. They weren't full-blooded Tarkas, but they possessed a little magic, enough to be a nuisance.

"Does Julian know you're here?" she asked.

Chad scowled and sheathed his sword, apparently determining it unnecessary.

First mistake.

"We don't need his permission to move about the grounds, but I doubt he'd disapprove."

"Of what?" Exactly what did they plan to do? Kill her? They must not know about the bond between her and Thane.

"Consider this an extra training session," Orrin spoke behind her, still several feet away.

Taya groaned. Her body existed in a perpetual state of aches and pain. An "extra training session" wasn't needed or welcome, but the glint in Chad's eyes told her they didn't give a shit about her progress or improvement.

"Wow. Three against one. You must be really desperate for validation." She turned slightly to get the other two in her field of view and shifted her weight to her toes.

Steele attacked first—it was always the quiet ones. He leapt at her with a flying right knee, his fist raised to follow up his attack. Stepping to the side, she blocked his knee by driving her own into his thigh. At the same time, she slipped past his punch. His massive fist grazed the side of her head. If he'd connected, she'd be flat out on the ground.

Quick as a snake, she struck out with a bladed hand and aimed at his throat as his momentum carried him past her. He gurgled in surprise.

Not wasting any time, she threw her hands up to block Orrin's attack. He grabbed her wrists, his strong hands clamped down. Crap. She couldn't let him neutralize her.

Twisting her wrists, she brought her arms down

and across her body to break his grip. She countered with a vicious punch to the head, but it barely fazed the large warrior. He stepped to the side, shook his head and swiped the blood away from his mouth.

"You'll have to hit harder than that." He leaned to the side and spat on the ground, his saliva tinted red from blood.

The crunch of dirt gave her the only warning that Chad had decided to participate while Orrin sneered at her from a few feet away and Steele tried to regain the use of his esophagus.

Chad lunged at her exposed back. She kicked her leg out behind her, right into his jaw. His eyes widened before they rolled up into the back of his head and his legs gave out beneath him.

Orrin and Steele gave her no time to catch her breath. They attacked in unison this time. She blocked, stepped and slipped away from their strikes. With each step though, she got slower, and the attacks got closer. Orrin and Steele relentlessly kept coming at her. Orrin's fist grazed her. Steele caught her with a bone-crushing kick to the side and knocked the wind from her lungs.

She stumbled, her foot catching on an upturned rock, mind frantically trying to come up with an exit strategy as she continued to try to avoid getting pummelled to death. Pulling on her magic as Thane taught her, the power whispered along her skin, teasing and tempting.

And then fizzled away.

Again.

Orrin's fist slammed into her jaw and she lurched to the side, staggering to keep upright.

Chad had regained consciousness and scrambled to his feet, murder in his gaze. He unsheathed a dagger and stalked toward her.

"Enough." Thane's low voice stopped the men mid-attack. They straightened and scowled.

The Tarka walked down the overgrown path to stand by her side.

"Leave us," he said to the other men.

Chad, Orrin and Steele walked away without a word.

Thane waited until they disappeared before he turned to her, his gaze scanning her from head to toe. "Are you okay?"

"I totally had that." She panted for air and straightened. Pain shot through her mid-section and she winced.

Thane grunted, eyes narrowing. "Totally."

She'd smack him, but then she'd have to reach out and with a rib most likely broken, the idea didn't appeal to her.

"Rib?" Thane always saw too much.

"Yes." She hissed.

"They will pay for this." His voice held the cold tone of promise. He kept his hands clasped behind him. "I can heal it for you."

Memories from the last healing session flooded her mind. "No, thank you. I think I'll let these heal the old-fashioned way."

Thane remained expressionless, her response hadn't surprised him, or if it had, he hid it well. "You tried to use your magic."

"Tried would be the keyword in that statement," she said.

"I felt it."

"Oh?" She turned to walk down the path. "Is that why it didn't work? Does the bond bind all my power up somehow?"

Thane walked alongside her, following her leisurely pace. "No, that's not how it works. I can control the flow for you if you lose control, and I can siphon the power away if you built up too much. But I would have to actively try to block you from accessing your power, which I've never done."

"Oh."

"I suspect it's a mental block." He tapped his temple. "You haven't quite wrapped your head around the existence of magic, nor accepting that you have a well of it inside you. Understandable, given you spent your formative years living in a magicless world"

Taya sighed, knowing what Thane planned to follow this explanation with, yet powerless to stop it from happening.

Thane leaned in. "Today's incident has highlighted the need for three things."

Taya groaned.

A smile tugged at Thane's lips. "You will wear your swords with you everywhere. No exception."

Now that, she could live with.

"Until I say otherwise, you will always have one of us with you at all times. While my men will never harm you unprovoked, I cannot control my brother's or father's men."

Taya flinched. He didn't need to specify who "one of us" referred to. He meant his trusted inner circle. And while Taya knew and respected all of them, she could kiss her moments of solitude goodbye.

"And last we need to up your magical training sessions."

And there it was. The death knell.

CHAPTER 29
MY MOTHER GAVE ME THE MOON

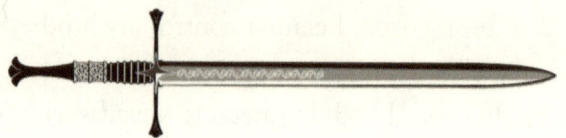

Taya stepped around Thane to view the drop-off to the ocean below. The sweet pine scent of the surrounding forest curled around her. "Why are we here?"

Thane unbelted his sword sheath and rested it against a stone bench facing the water. "This is one of my favourite lookouts."

Okay. Sightseeing wasn't exactly in the training regimen.

"During this time of year, the moonlight hits this spot perfectly.

"For seducing young, unsuspecting women? For shoving someone off a cliff to their gruesome death below, or...?"

Thane smirked. "We've been going about your magical training all wrong."

"Ah...it's to be torture, then." Tension automatically built up in her shoulders.

Thane narrowed his eyes at her. "We've practiced in the fortress and outside. We've never tried accessing your power at night."

"Will that make a difference?"

He shrugged. "Maybe. I can feel your magic. You have a lot of it. Drawing it out, even while bonded, should not be difficult or dependent on the time of day, but if it's linked to the night or the moon, it might be easier to learn about your power here. Now."

"Isn't the House of Jericho all about the moon?" She kept her gaze out, watching the waves crash against the jagged rocks below.

"Of course. Jericho means moon in Old Arkavian, but it is not the only house with its magic tied to the night."

That made sense. Kind of. If she was being honest, nothing about magic truly made sense to her. It went against all the things she learned on earth about math, science and technology. It defied the law of nature. It laughed in the face of logic.

Thane was right. Her inability to wrap her mind around having and using magic undoubtedly caused her failures in learning to master her own power.

"You can feel my magic?" She turned to Thane to find him watching her. "What does it feel like?"

His gaze flashed in the moonlight, unguarded and

wild for a brief moment before he shut it down. "You're not ready."

Fine. Whatever. "What am I ready for then?"

He sat down on the bench and patted the space beside him. She walked over and slipped out of her double sword sheaths, propping them on the other side of the bench.

She took a deep breath in and blinked at Thane expectantly. This was it. He planned to kill her with magic.

Thane's lips twitched. "Relax."

"Easy for you to say," she grumbled. "I bet you probably tell women to calm down when they're upset, too."

His smirk spread into a large smile, his teeth glinting in the moonlight. "I'm smarter than that."

She grunted and closed her eyes, letting the gentle touch of the wind and the repetitive sounds of the waves flow over her. The breeze whipped stray strands of her hair across her face. She breathed in the sweet-smelling air, holding it for a three-second count before releasing it. The tension eased from her shoulders.

"Good. Now reach for your magic. Don't try to control it. Just touch it."

She bit her lip, but instead of making a joke, she did as he suggested. This was the moment she encountered failure. Her power would either flare up before burning out or fizzling to nothing.

She kept her breathing regular, reaching for that

mental space her mind went to during a fight—the quiet place where she existed with all her senses and none of her doubts.

Her magic responded, rising up to coat her mind and her skin.

"There it is," Thane whispered.

She opened her eyes, magic thrumming through her veins. Ribbon-like bands of silver wound around her creating a layer of power over her skin and clothes.

"You're a creature of the night." He nodded at her arm.

With the power wrapped tightly around her, she looked down. Her arm had become translucent in the moonlight. Instead of stiffening or panicking, she took another deep breath and raised her other arm. Also translucent.

"It's called Tarka shielding, though few can achieve this state of invisibility."

"Will it protect me from what Julian and Lane did?"

He smiled, his teeth flashing in the moonlight. "Absolutely. It also explains why you found the other magical activities so frustrating. Your magical strength lies in defence, not offence."

Her magic pulsed as if in agreement. "And how does my magic feel now?" Surely, she was ready to hear the answer.

He leaned in, slipping his hand up to cup the side of her face. "Delicious."

His answer shocked her and she let the magic go. It fell away like shards of glass, bouncing along with the surrounding stones and glinting in the moonlight. Thane pressed his lips to hers, his magic winding around her. She leaned in, wanting more, running her hands up his armoured chest. He deepened the kiss, angling his mouth and flicking his tongue. He kissed like a man on a desert who finally got to drink a glass of water, he kissed her like he'd been starved of this his entire life and finally had what he wanted.

Wrapping her leg over his thigh, she arched her body into his, trying to get closer. She'd let him do anything right now. She was clay in his hands, ready to be worked and moulded. She wanted their clothes off. She wanted his skin on hers. She wanted him inside her. All of it. She would die if he stopped touching her.

Thane broke away first, gaze flashing.

She had no words. Speaking required air and she struggled to breathe.

"We can't do this." Thane abruptly stood from the bench, grabbed his sword and stalked off into the night.

Taya remained on the bench, her fingertips lightly pressed against her still-tingling lips. Whatever was happening between her and Thane, it threatened his resolve to stay away, and the promises she made to seek revenge on all Arkavians.

PART THREE
RECLAIM

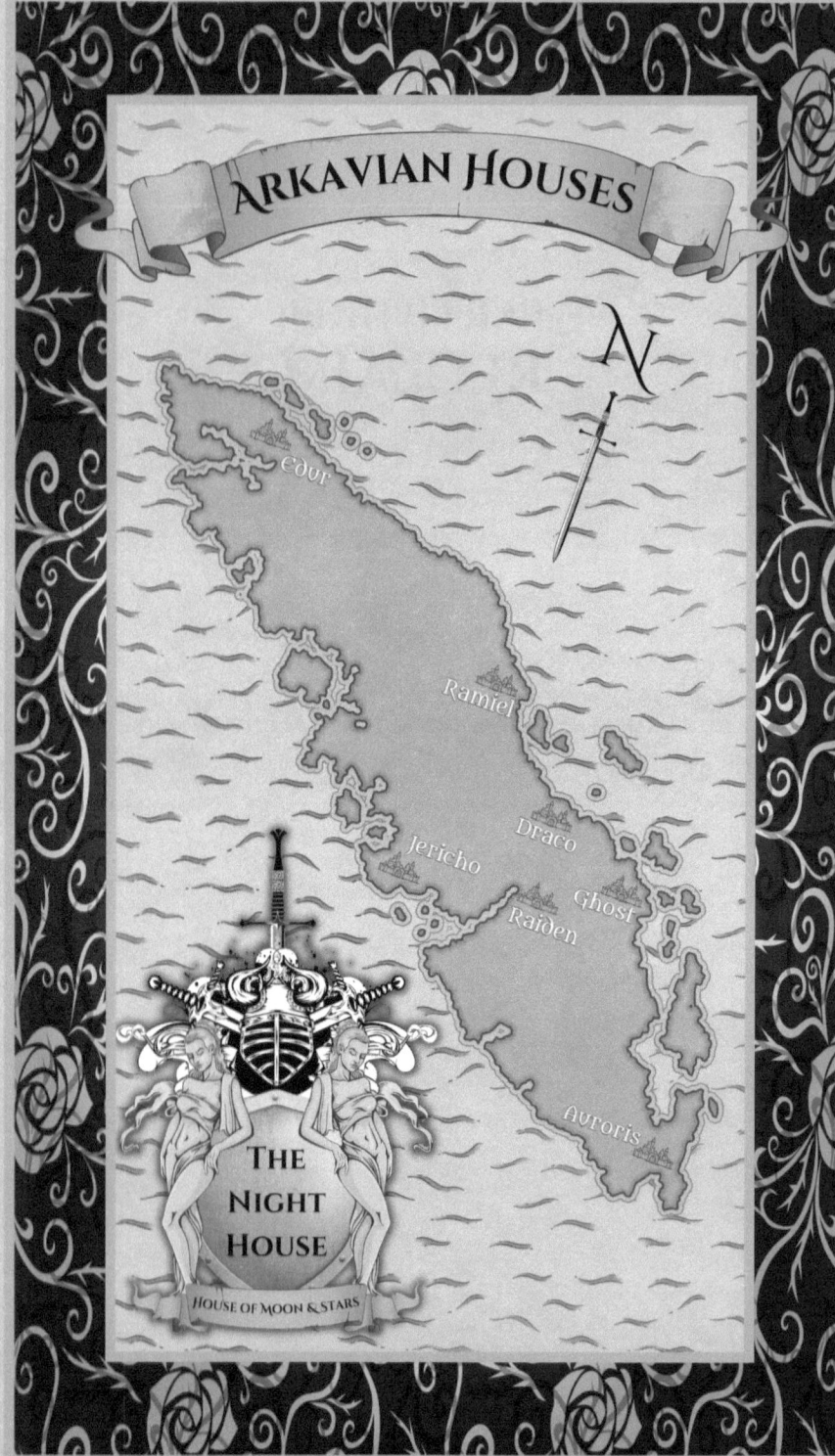

ARKAVIAN HOUSES

N

Edur

Ramiel

Jericho

Draco

Ghost

Raiden

Avroris

THE
NIGHT
HOUSE

HOUSE OF MOON & STARS

CHAPTER 30

FRIENDS OF MY FRIENDS

ONE YEAR AND THREE MONTHS AFTER
ARKAVIA

Taya surveyed the fortress in the valley below. The wind brushed against her leather pants and hooded vest. She'd pulled down the face covering she usually wore in public to enjoy the fresh air on her skin.

The House of Auroris wasn't as grand as Jericho, but in the eleven months she'd served as Thane's bodyguard she hadn't grown accustomed to the opulence of Arkavian architecture. This particular monstrosity belonged to Alexis' family. The building's position ensured it caught the full magnificence of the sunrise, even in winter, and the sight stole Taya's breath away.

Thane stepped up beside her on the bluff. "It's beautiful. Isn't it?"

"It's not the House of Jericho."

"No, it's not." His lips twitched. "But the Sun House holds a radiant beauty we'll never capture."

His visible melancholy hurt. She still kept his painful memories a secret and as a reminder of his family's great capacity for cruelty. Although he never spoke on the topic, he never seemed at home when at home. His brother and father made certain of that. The House of Jericho was a part of his legacy, but in the last year, he used every excuse possible to be away, taking his elite team on the road with him. And Taya. Just as his grandfather predicted, she became his shadow, protecting his back when he couldn't take the team with him, and even when he could.

"You narrowly escaped this disaster." Axel walked over to join them.

"Don't remind me." He stepped away from Taya and swung up into the saddle with a seamless vault. Hades snorted approval.

Taya followed suit, settling into Sugar's saddle. She pulled her face covering over her nose and patted the roan's coat. In the summer, Sugar would shed the darker, shaggier hair to reveal a glistening coat. She looked like liquid silver under the sun and wicked shadows at night.

Axel clucked at his mount and moved alongside. "I never thought Julian would marry. I was sure this debacle would be called off."

"He just needed to find someone as miserable and self-serving as he is," Thane said.

"And now we get to watch them tie their cruel lives together in wedded bliss," Taya said. She'd rather gouge her eyes out with a blunt fork, but she followed where Thane led.

"Come on then, my trusty shadow." Thane leaned toward her. "Let's not delay the inevitable."

The horses thundered down the embankment and galloped across the field of dead grass and frost toward the House of Auroris, the sun rising against their backs. Grass, twigs and small branches snapped underfoot as they sped along, the winter meadow breeze whipping past Taya's face.

Their group travelled unhindered through the already open gate. The jagged end of the portcullis gleamed in the morning sunlight. If someone released the wheel holding thick metal chains that kept the gate up, they'd be crushed by solid metal spikes. What a horrible way to go.

She dismounted with the men and handed her reins to a stable boy with skinny arms and dark bags under his eyes. She patted Sugar's rump as the boy led the mare away. Sugar snorted and flicked her tail.

Music drifted down from the main building along with the din of chatter and clinking glassware. The party had already started and the sun hadn't fully risen above the horizon yet. Fucking animals. How did anyone function this early?

"Lord Thane." A man with a deep voice and thick fur cloak stepped down the stairs leading to the main building's entrance. He had platinum-blond hair that curled around his ears, sharp gray eyes, and the chiseled features she now associated with Arkavian nobility.

"Lord Aries." Thane stepped forward and grasped the man's forearm.

Oh, finally one of the lords Thane said relatively nice things about. The heir to the House of Auroris looked no different than any of the other aristocracy she'd met. Instead of hair with blue undertones like Thane's, Lord Aries' hair had hints of sunshine, resembling dying wheat on a prairie field in autumn. The crinkles around his eyes and mouth suggested a life filled with laughter, but his centered posture and pulled-back shoulders spoke of regimented training and years of swinging a sword.

"I'm glad you made it. I won a wager."

Thane scratched Hades' cheek before another stable boy lead the stallion away. "Your mother bet against me? Again?"

Aries nodded. "She underestimated you. Again."

"She never liked me."

"That might have something to do with our many ill-fated outings as adolescents."

Taya shifted her weight from foot to foot to get the blood flow going. Though she'd spent much of the last year on Sugar's back, memorizing the varying shades of her blue roan coat through the seasons, her legs still ached after a long trip.

"We should grab a drink and reminisce about the good old days," Thane said.

Taya nearly toppled over. She could count the number of times Thane voluntarily invited another Arkavian lord out for drinks. She could keep track because the count was at one. As in right now.

Aries face split into a dazzling smile. "We should. For the moment, though, you should get your party settled. The festivities have started."

Soka groaned. Taya wasn't the only one who hated mornings, but he had no right to complain. He didn't have to attend half the events.

"Is your cousin with you?" Aries smile widened and he scanned the group.

Lokni scowled. "She arrived before us. She must be avoiding you."

Aries smirked at Taya's violet-eyed companion before his attention snagged on her.

Of course it did.

It always did when they ran into Arkavian nobility. Though Thane avoided the "big houses," run-ins still happened.

"So it's true?" Aries' eyes widened and he turned to Thane. "I heard rumours about your shadow. I figured you made her up and that's why you've avoided me."

"As you can see, she's very real," Thane replied.

Aries nodded and dipped into a shallow bow. "Milady."

Lokni coughed.

She stomped on his foot and bowed like a man. Curtseying in leather pants with a dual scabbard strapped to her back looked as ridiculous as it felt. "Lord Aries."

"I hope to speak with you later," Aries said.

"Of course." Geez. Did all the other Arkavian nobles sound as pretentious as this guy? She thought only Julian and Lane talked like this. At least her face covering concealed her scowl.

"Later, Thane." Aries nodded at the other warrior. "We have much to discuss."

Thane dipped his chin and Aries left the same way he came.

"Are we going to have to talk like that?" Taya stepped into the heat of Thane's body. She'd only accompanied Thane to the lower houses and they didn't prance around like the people here. Mainly they cowered and scurried away from their party. Or died.

Thane leaned down, his face impossibly close. "Not in private and not around Aries. Not usually. He put on an act for our witnesses."

"He's a good actor," she whispered.

"That's what makes him dangerous."

"As dangerous as you?"

That earned her a real smile. "Not even close."

CHAPTER 31
SMALL SPACES, DARK PLACES

Taya trailed Thane as he meandered through the crowded ballroom. The grand reception ball was the final event of a long, arduous day and it couldn't end soon enough. Full gem-laden gowns and stylized armour meant more for show than practicality glittered under the magically-lit candle chandeliers. The chatter drowned out much of the music threading through the room from harmonizing string instruments. Taya had walked into Cinderella's ball, except she knew damn well this wasn't a fucking fairy tale.

She eyed the chocolate balls on a nearby platter and her mouth watered. With most of her face covered with black fabric, popping a sweet dessert in her mouth right now was out of the question. Too bad. If she closed her eyes, she could taste the sweet cocoa exploding on her tongue and the velvety smooth flavour coating her mouth. The server and his platter of Arkavian delicacies grew more distant as she followed Thane across the room.

Dangit. Maybe he'd circle back and she'd slip one into her pocket.

She envied Lokni, Soka and Axel who got to stay in their rooms and visit the barracks, drink and tell tall-tales of their exploits to anyone who'd listen. Watching women fawn over Thane and men puff out their chests while speaking to him, all the while she stood nearby to be ignored, set her teeth on edge.

Everything here was so fake. No wonder Thane avoided court.

What she didn't understand was what drove Thane to propose to Alexis in the first place. Didn't he see how conniving she was? Had he fallen for all the bells and whistles of her and this place? Or had he truly fallen in love with her?

As much as it sent a little knife through her heart, if she had to put down money, she'd bet on the latter. Thane struck her as the type of man to give everything to a relationship. When he fell, he'd fall hard. He wasn't the type to half-ass anything or do things in parts. His love would be all consuming.

Too bad it would never be with her.

Jealousy continued to stab at her. She'd never be the source of his desire. He'd established that boundary well over the last year. Despite his passionate words at the beginning of her service and a heated kiss, he'd given no indication he still felt the same way.

While he might've moved on, her feelings for him had only grown. Now she'd become a quivering mess of longing and she could never let him know how much she wanted him. She'd train for him. She'd kill for him. She'd bleed and even die. But she wouldn't fall in lust. Or love. That was the silent promise she'd made to herself almost a year ago. And that was the promise she'd broken.

She watched a young lady with silver-white hair lean into Thane's imposing body.

Why did she have to fall for him? Not only had she not found a way to stop the leaching or save earthens, but her year was almost up, and she'd only killed a handful of Arkavians stupid enough to attack Thane while she was near.

"Taya, isn't it?" Aries cut into her path and blocked her view of Thane.

She scowled and stepped around him into a wake of perfumed air. Music jingled all around them.

The Arkavian lord chuckled and followed, the candlelight dancing along his gold-embroidered court armour. "I see you take your job seriously. He won't come to any harm here. You can speak with me."

She ignored him and followed Thane as he brushed off the young woman's attention and walked away.

Aries sighed and walked beside her. "Is it true? Are

you some scandalous love child from an illicit affair, left for the wolves to raise you in the wild forest?"

She groaned. Without a doubt, the twins helped spread that ridiculous rumour. And Adrianna.

"Stop harassing my bodyguard." Thane stopped to face them.

"It got your attention, didn't it?" Aries jerked his thumb in her direction. "You're one of the most feared Tarkas. You don't need her. Give her the night off like your other men."

Taya narrowed her eyes. This guy tried awfully hard to get her away from Thane.

"Ah, but I want her."

A couple of other courtiers stopped talking and turned to watch.

Her heart fluttered at his words. *For fuck's sake, woman. Pull your tits up and focus.* Aries was up to something. She stepped to the side to get a better view of those gathering behind Thane.

Aries frowned. "Why?"

If only Thane let her show him why. She longed to grip the leather-bound handles of her blades.

"You wouldn't ask if you saw her fight," Thane said.

Aries perked up and leaned forward. "Maybe a demonstration then? A break from the wedding festivities for a duel? Your shadow against one of my finest?"

Thane leaned forward. "No."

"You used to be more fun."

"We're not here as entertainment," Thane growled.

Oh, no. Thane quickly approached his limit for bullshit. She stepped closer.

"Fine, Fine." Aries flung his arm around Thane's shoulder. "Let's get a drink and let Taya guard us both."

He steered Thane away from the dance floor and toward the far end of the room.

Taya glanced over her shoulder and nearly stumbled. The first Arkavian lord she ever saw stood three feet away. She'd never forget his face. It was etched into her nightmares. He wore a scowl and watched them leave. His gaze settled on her shoulders and narrowed.

Why wasn't he dead? Wasn't he in the sacrifice circle? How did he survive and what the hell was he looking at? She froze. Her eyes widened. Her swords tingled and burned against her back where her dual scabbard held them. The twin blades of House Raiden.

These belonged to his brother.

Her lungs snagged in her chest. The lord never spotted her crouched in the bushes. If he had, she would've joined the others in the sacrifice circle. His eyes held no recognition when they glanced at her face. Hell, only her eyes were visible, anyway. He stared at the blades. That was it. Anyone travelling through that town could've and would've picked them up. He couldn't jump to the conclusion she'd connect him with bloody massacres.

"Taya?" Aries held a door open.

She winced and followed Thane through the side entrance. As soon as it clicked shut, Thane brushed Aries' arm from his shoulders. "Why the theatrics?"

The other man shrugged. "Why not?"

They'd entered some dimly lit passageway with stale air. Dust motes drifted in the candlelight and their voices and the scuffle of their feet against stone echoed down into a dark abyss.

"We're too exposed. Should you be discussing this?" She nodded down the dark hallway and shuddered. Anyone could lurk on the other end. How much did Thane trust this guy?

"The area is secure." Aries lifted his chin.

Sure, it is, Big Guy. Ever since Elliot Mansfield told her he wouldn't share *that* picture with anyone, and then preceded to show the entire senior class of their high school just how good her rack looked in a balconette, she never trusted anyone on their word alone—no matter how pretty or self-assured they came across.

"What the hell is going on?" Thane asked.

"You tell me," Aries said.

"What are you talking about?" Thane hissed.

"You brought your pet shadow as your plus one to a wedding reception. Are you trying to piss off everyone in my family?"

Oh. That explained why Aries had tried to get rid of her. Maybe.

"I just watched my former lover wed my narcissistic brother because she'd rather a lifetime with his douchery than risk the gossip about me being true. I think they can forgive me this break in etiquette."

Aries paused and glanced at Taya. "Dismiss her. We need to talk candidly."

"She's under a geas."

Aries nodded. Thane's explanation apparently sufficient enough. "Are you still in love with my sister, then? She dropped you faster than a whore's knickers."

"God, no. One stupid rumour and she was gone."

"I warned you she was vapid. She always tried to make up for a lack in power by assuming others."

Pot, meet Kettle.

"I thought you just hated the idea of me banging your sister."

Aries' face scrunched up. "That, too."

"Have you accompanied any of your family's gathering trips to Earth?" Thane asked.

Aries' face remained scrunched. "Why the hell would I do that?"

"So that's a no?"

"You know I hate reapings."

Well, okay. Maybe this guy wasn't so bad after all.

Thane crossed his arms over his chest. "Who in your family went?"

"No one in my direct family. Father normally sends my cousins. Fuck knows why. Those two are useless."

Thane nodded. "Have you heard anything about the other families?"

"Going to Earth?" Aries blanched. "Not really. Draco and Ramiel lost some family members to earthen savages. Raiden as well. What's this about?"

"I'm not sure, yet."

Thane knew the family involved in the reapings lost at least one soldier because he'd seen her memories. After encountering the Tarka lord in the ballroom, hale and hearty, she knew which family was caught up in this dark magic. She kept her mouth firmly shut, though. Thane might trust Aries, but she didn't. She'd tell Thane her discovery when they were alone.

Aries grumbled and jabbed the air in front of Taya with his forefinger. "Can you at least tell me about her? Everyone's been talking about your shadow at court and your obvious avoidance of the main houses."

"Let them talk. Their stories will be more entertaining than the truth."

"Which is?"

Footsteps padded down the hall toward them.

"I thought this hallway was secure?" Thane asked.

"It is."

"Was." Taya unsheathed her blades. The lightning coursed up the steel and licked her skin. The high pitch whining of the energy danced along the metal and sung to the power flowing in her blood.

Aries sucked in a breath.

The footsteps quickened. Three men turned the

corner, faces and hair covered with black cloth like hers so only their dark gazes peered out.

Aries muttered something.

"Just watch," Thane said.

The men charged.

Taya's magic merged with the blades and she moved, stepping, spinning, slashing, in a deadly dance of sharp edges, cutting one attacker down at a time until three bodies lay in a bloody pool at her feet.

"Fuck," Aries said.

Thane elbowed him. "Now you see why I like her at my back."

Aries closed his mouth and visibly shook himself. "That was worthy of the Night House."

Of course it was. She worked hard to excel and maintain her value to the House of Jericho. She wanted to give Thane zero reasons to regret the offer he made almost a year ago.

She knelt at the nearest body and wiped her blades with his shirt. Thane could've crushed all three men easily with his power. He chose to let her dance with her blades to show off her skill to Aries. Did he do so out of pride or as a warning?

"Did she fuse her power with the blades?" Aries asked. "And I saw a glimmer, too. Tarka shielding?"

Taya straightened. "She's right here and she's getting pretty tired of you talking over her." She sheathed her swords in her back scabbard. "But yes. I fused my magic with the blades." She didn't confirm the Tarka shielding because it was none of his business.

Aries whistled.

Thane knelt down beside her and tugged off the material covering their would-be assassin's face. Shaggy brown hair surrounded a smooth face and blank brown eyes.

"Know him?" Aries asked.

Thane shook his head and moved to the next body. He should've taken care of the attack instead of showing her off. They might've captured one alive and used him for information.

"Who would want to kill both of you?" she asked.

Aries sighed. "The easier question is to ask who doesn't."

CHAPTER 32

DOUBLE TROUBLE

Back in the grand ballroom, Taya waited until Aries walked out of earshot and the din of gossip to surround them before she turned to Thane. "Trust me?"

He raised his dark eyebrows, but nodded.

"I'll be back." Without waiting for a response, she slipped from his side and wound around the milling socialites and nobility. Even with her face guard covering everything but her eyes, their perfume clung to her nose and left her throat dry.

Adrianna stood near two Tarka men. They watched her like vultures waiting for a sign of weakness to swoop in for a piece of the prize while she recanted some story requiring a lot of hand gestures, hair flips and smiles. Her gown cascaded to the floor in beautiful, blue satin folds and the bodice hugged her curves.

Taya smiled behind her face covering. She spent a lot of downtime hanging out with Adrianna, learning Ancient Arkavian, drinking wine and gossiping about soldiers, staff and house politics.

"Come with me." Taya hooked her arm with Adrianna's and pulled her away from the men. They grumbled complaints, but she ignored them and continued tugging.

Adrianna giggled, a bell-like sound, and spun to walk with Taya.

Good. At least she didn't have to drag her.

"What's this about?" Adrianna laughed.

"Later," Taya rasped. Since when did she sound part snake?

Adrianna snapped her mouth shut, but amusement danced in her eyes. They stepped through the large double doorway leading into the ballroom and left the music and chatter behind them. Adrianna's dress rustled against the floor and her satin shoes made a cute pitter-patter against the shiny stonework.

"Who would be a believable 'guest' for you to entertain in your rooms?"

Adrianna's brow arched.

Taya rolled her eyes. They turned the corner toward their rooms. An Auroris servant waited at the hall entranceway. He stiffened at their approach and drew himself taller, tugging down on his blazer with gold trim to signify his house.

"Fetch Lokni from the barracks and send him to Lady Adrianna's room."

Adrianna gasped.

Taya dug her fingers into her friend's forearm.

The servant's eyes widened, but he bobbed his head and took off down the hall.

"What are you doing?" Adrianna hissed.

"Oh, stop." Taya released her friend's arm and held up her hand. "You two aren't fooling anyone, and I need your help."

Adrianna clamped her mouth shut again and unlocked the door to her room. The hinges creaked when she swung it open, waving Taya to enter ahead of her.

Taya stepped into the dark room and quickly checked the corners and closed the windows while Adrianna used magic to light the candles and bask them in the soft glow of fire.

"What's this about?" Adrianna balled her hands and placed them on her hips.

"I'm assuming you arrived with more outfits than you could possibly wear for your visit here?"

Adrianna nodded.

"Perfect. We're the same size. I need a dress."

Adrianna's brows shot up again. "Is this for Thane?"

"This is for the house."

Adrianna's head snapped back.

"I need to go back to the ball where no one but Thane will recognize me as his shadow, and I need you to wear my clothes and follow him as if you're me."

Adrianna shifted from one foot to the other. Her dress swayed back and forth, brushing the throw rug at the base of the large four-poster bed. "I'm not made for fighting."

"I'm sure there's another f-word Lokni thinks you're made for."

"Brat!" Adrianna searched the nearby dresser, found a silver brush and threw it at Taya's head.

Taya laughed and caught the brush in the air. She placed it gently on the bed covers and turned back to her friend. "Relax. Thane's capable of taking care of himself at this event. We'll switch back before he leaves."

"Did someone figure out you're earthen?"

Taya balked.

Adrianna rolled her eyes and dropped her arms. "Oh, please. You're not fooling anyone, either. I've been your friend for almost a year and you say the most bizarre things."

Taya's mouth dropped open. Thane never referred to her as an earthen, but she'd grown accustomed to identifying with the word. At least mentally. She kept her promise and never spoke of her origins outside of Thane's trusted team. Why would she? Most Arkavians still viewed earthens as less than and it would blow her cover as Thane's mysterious Tarka shadow.

But now she regretted her silence with her friend. Adrianna's tone and body language carried no judgement or derision. Only annoyance.

"Come on." Adrianna nudged her in the ribs. "We better swap clothes now. It'll take a miracle to get you into one of these contraptions before Lokni gets here."

Taya snorted. Her comrade was probably sprinting over here as they spoke. "He'll just have to wait at the door."

A small smile spread across her friend's face. "He's good at waiting."

Taya held her hand up again. "Stop right there. I don't need to know details. Let's do this."

Taya took a deep breath of perfumed and powdered air and re-entered the ballroom. Though she technically wore more material than when she worked as Thane's shadow, she felt naked. The absence of her head covering left her face fully exposed to the judging eyes of Arkavian aristocracy and the skin-tight, lung-crushing bodice, displayed her chest like some smorgasbord of bosom. How did Adrianna breathe in this? How did she move so freely?

She read a feminist article a long time ago, in a different life, that claimed men came up with these ridiculous fashion trends to prevent women from running away. At the time, she'd laughed. Right now? It made a bit of sense. This outfit would become completely debilitating if she had to fight or run.

Taya lifted her chin and walked passed the guards. They didn't take names or check a list. She needed no ID or hall pass. Her hair and Arkavian looks were her ticket into this high society event. Luckily, she spotted her mark nearly right away.

The Tarka lord.

Should she slip a dagger between his ribs and walk away?

No.

One, she didn't have permission. Two, although he deserved death for his role in the earthen slaughter alone, she hadn't determined exactly what was at stake here.

Swiping a glass of sparkling booze in a tall flute from a tray perched precariously on the hand of a servant, she trailed the Arkavian lord. He walked with purpose, eyes narrowed, and made his way toward the head table.

She'd missed Julian's and Alexis' grand entrance and making all the appropriate sounds of admiration like some baying cow.

The Tarka stepped close to Julian and held out his hand. While Julian took his hand, Taya slipped past his line of sight. She hadn't factored in the happy couple when she made this plan. Had they seen her? Would they spot an employee amongst their brethren? Would they rat her out?

She had to see this through.

"Congratulations on your nuptials," the Tarka lord said.

Julian muttered a response, sounding somewhere between a grunt, sigh and growl. Oh happy day.

"Your brother's shadow..."

The hairs on her arms stood up. Why was he asking about her?

"What about her?"

"She's been with Thane for about a year now?"

Julian shrugged. "Sounds about right. I don't keep track of his servants."

Huh. His constant attempts to insert spies into their team suggested otherwise.

Two women brushed past Taya in the packed room. Their perfume stung her eyes and sucked the moisture from Taya's throat.

Oh no. Taya rapidly swallowed spit. Her dry throat itched.

"Where'd he find her?" the Tarka asked.

"Why are you so interested?"

The Tarka shrugged. "She reminds me of someone. I heard she has unknown parentage."

That was absolute bullshit. He hadn't seen enough of her to remind him of anyone.

Julian muttered another response, too low for Taya to hear. Both men barked in laughter. She downed the rest of her drink to clear her throat and placed the empty glass on a waiting tray. Hopping on her toes, she looked for another drink tray.

Come on. Come one. Say something important! She could only loiter nearby with no one to talk to for so long before someone noticed she faced everyone's backs like a simpleton.

"He found her near the gate. Why? Is there a problem?"

"Of course not. Just curious."

Taya slipped passed two men with shoulders as wide as old growth tree trunks and weaved around groups of gossiping nobles. Snagging another drink, she pressed the cold glass to her lips and let the soothing liquid slide down her throat like a soothing balm. Hints of fruit and oak teased her senses.

Now. Where did the Tarka lord go?

She turned to find her target and stopped short of ramming her face into a man's chest.

"Oh! Pardon me." She stepped back, dress swirling against her legs and looked up. Her mouth dropped open.

Thane's eyes widened. His grip on his glass tightened.

"Lord Thane?" Some curvy brunette pouted beside him.

"Not now."

The woman glared and stalked off into the throng of guests, but Thane didn't notice. Nope. He hadn't taken his eyes off Taya. His gaze raked her body and grew wild. His lips peeled back into a ferocious, predatory smile.

"Lord Thane. What a pleasure to meet you." She spoke from the throat and dipped into an exaggerated curtsy, making sure to bat her eyelashes excessively. Ow. That kind of hurt.

Someone snorted behind Thane. He whipped around to glare at Adrianna. Her friend, dressed in her fighting garb, waggled her fingers like a socialite on reality television in response. Her gray eyes crinkled.

Great. Way to make it obvious.

Thane shook his head and glanced at the ceiling.

Taya kept her wide smile plastered to her face and bit back the many inappropriate responses and comments she'd like to use right now. She couldn't though. If anyone overheard, she'd break her own cover.

Over Thane's shoulder, the Tarka lord stalked from a group of courtiers. He brushed past two men who turned to scowl after him, but the Tarka didn't acknowledge them. He left the grand ballroom's wide, double-door entrance. Alone.

Dang it.

"Lady?"

"Huh?"

Thane held his hand out, palm up, in front of her. "Would you honour me with this dance?"

Behind him, Adrianna's eyes crinkled more.

Oh no.

Her mouth dropped open again. She snapped it shut and rocked back on her heels. "Uh..."

"Excellent." Thane's grin grew and he reached forward to take her hand. He drew her into the heat of his impressive body. His formal court attire accentuated his broad shoulders, formidable stance and the brutal efficiency from a lifetime of war. He would take her in his arms and carry her off into a world she had no right or desire to be in.

Dance? With Thane? Pressed against his strong chest? Held in his powerful arms? Moving together rhythmically to seductive music? Nope. She couldn't let that happen. She snatched her hand back. "I'm so honoured, Lord Thane, but...I'm not feeling well."

"Please, let my servant attend you." He snapped his fingers at Adrianna.

Adrianna straightened and scowled at her cousin.

Of course, Taya couldn't see the actual scowl with the fabric covering most of her friend's face, but she felt it.

"You're too kind, Lord Thane." She dropped in another deep curtsy.

Thane nodded, sagely. "Please don't linger too long in the halls. I'd like my shadow back promptly so we can discuss the many advantages and disadvantages of hasty retreats."

Ass.

"Of course." She dipped her chin and walked past

Thane. His shoulders shook in silent laughter. Adrianna followed. Though she couldn't hear or see him, Thane's deep chuckle trailed behind her and his heated gaze remained trained on her back until she left the room.

CHAPTER 33
THE TASTE OF SIN

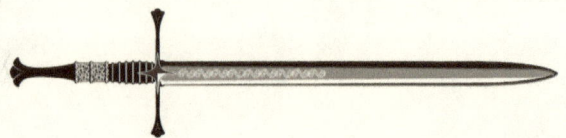

Taya waited for the door to shut behind them before she spun to face Thane. He'd waited three long minutes after she returned as his shadow before leaving the ballroom. She pulled off the mask and cool air brushed along her now-exposed mouth, cheeks, and chin. The guest room was almost as big as Thane's personal one back at home. A giant bed sat in the center. Rich linens and textured throw pillows decorated it. Intricate carvings on the polished wood bed posts came alive under the flickering candlelight.

"These are for you." He held his hand out.

Taya stared at the chocolate balls resting on his palm. Where had he stashed them? How had they not melted? Then reality hit her. Magic.

"Aren't these your favourites?"

"You know they are." She plucked them from his

hand and placed them on a silver dish waiting on a side table. She'd gobble them up later, but first she needed to talk. "Thank you."

Thane remained near the door. He folded his arms over his chest and waited.

"So, to clarify, Aries purposefully tested my professionalism and poked the bear so you had an excuse to speak with him in private," she summarized.

"Poke the bear?"

"Made you angry."

"Ah." Thane tracked her movement as she paced back and forth. "Yes. Pretty much."

"Why go to all that effort? Why not ask to speak with you in private and skip all the mind games and public dramatics?" Taya chewed the inside of her lip. She needed to clear this up before she told Thane what she'd discovered tonight.

"Aries would probably tell you it was more fun the way he did it." Thane's dry tone expressed how little he shared this sentiment.

"And you believe him? He wasn't trying to isolate you for those men to have a better chance?"

Thane laughed. "Those men never had a chance."

Crap, he was right, which meant she was also probably right with her own deductions. "I think I was the target."

"What?" He unfolded his arms and straightened. "Why?"

"I saw him."

Thane frowned. "Who?"

"The leader guy. The one who led the slave procession that ended up getting sacrificed."

Stillness swept through Thane—the same serene calm he embodied before he attacked.

Crap.

"You saw the group before they died?"

How did he not know that? Oh, wait. He'd stopped the memory sift once he got to the sacrifice and hadn't gone farther back in time. "Yes. I hid in the bushes and watched Arkavians lead them away. A lord stopped his horse near my hiding place. I assumed he died in the sacrifice circle, but I never looked at all the bodies."

"And you got a good look at his face?"

Didn't she just explain all that? "Yes."

Thane grabbed her hand and tugged her toward the door.

"What are you doing?"

"Taking you back to the festivities so you can identify the man."

"There's no need."

Thane froze.

"I know who he is."

Thane turned toward her and dropped her hand.

"You named him already. Sort of. You said my swords belonged to his brother. He's from the House of Raiden."

Thane snarled. "Lord Gale."

"I guess so."

"Wait. Gale of Raiden led the slave procession that ended up butchered in a sacrifice ring and you just thought to mention it now?" Thane's silver gaze flashed. He stepped into her personal space. Large and looming, he towered over her, breathing hard.

She yearned to spread her hands across his chest or grip his hair and haul him down for a kiss. Would he taste as sinful as he did in her dreams?

His mouth parted. He leaned down, so close the heat from his skin bathed her face.

She licked her lips.

His gaze flicked to her mouth. His large hands clamped on her shoulders and pulled her close. Finally, she'd feel his lips on hers again.

A delicate knock tapped against the door.

No!

Thane released her and straightened. He opened the door without looking or securing the safety chain. "What?"

Alexis jumped.

What the hell was she doing here? It was her wedding night. She should be basking in the glow of everyone's attention, not skulking off to her former lover's bedroom.

Alexis recovered and smoothed down her voluminous wedding dress. The garment fit her upper body like a glove and cascaded to the floor perfectly. It didn't need any smoothing.

"May I come in?" She stepped across the threshold without waiting for a response.

Taya had to step back or risk getting taken out by tulle.

"Now is not a good time, Alexis." Thane reverted back to his statue impersonation.

Damn skippy this wasn't a good time. This selfish bitch had ruined a perfect moment, one Taya might never get back.

"It's never a good time." Alexis threw her arms around Thane and sagged into his body.

Oh. Oh my. Not at all how Taya expected this conversation to go. Didn't Alexis marry Julian mere hours ago? They'd watched her breathless reciting of the Arkavian wedding vows through her pouting, painted lips.

Thane stiffened. He patted Alexis' back like he wasn't sure if she'd snarl and bite his hand off. "What are you doing here?"

As if noticing Taya's presence for the first time, Alexis flicked her wrist and twirled her finger in Taya's direction. "You can leave."

Taya folded her arms.

Alexis scowled and turned her attention back to Thane. "I miss you."

"You just married my brother," Thane said. "You'll see me quite often now."

"Not the way I want to see you." She dropped her

voice, making it low and raspy, and leaving zero doubt to what she desired. "I miss you. I miss the way you made me scream your name."

Alexis pulled back and batted her long eyelashes at Thane.

Taya shuffled her feet. Developing the skill to disappear would be fabulous right now. Well, actually, she had learned how to make herself almost invisible at night using a Tarka shield, but Thane told her to keep it a secret. Alexis had already proven herself incapable of keeping a promise, let alone a secret.

Thane maintained his stony expression. "You should have thought about that before you broke off the engagement."

"I had to do it. I couldn't risk..."

"My father disowning me?"

She sniffed and nodded.

"If he hasn't disowned me in thirty-one years, I highly doubt he'd consider it now."

And Lane probably never would, either. Over the last year, Taya figured out an important fact—the House of Jericho needed Thane. Neither Lane nor Julian had as much power as Thane, nor were they as feared. The threat and danger the second son of the House of Jericho posed to others was enough to dissuade the majority of attacks and backstabbing. If they lost Thane, or disowned him, they lost their shield and security.

Alexis pulled herself up and pressed her lips against Thane's.

A wild surge of anger rumbled through Taya's veins. She had no claim on him. No right to be jealous. Yet here it was, ugly and real, twisting in her gut. Taya clamped her hands into fists. One step and she'd be close enough to sink her fist into Alexis' pretty face.

Maybe she should put the shield up and disappear.

Thane remained motionless.

Alexis pulled back, probably realizing she kissed a cold rock. Her lips bunched up and her brows puckered. "Don't you miss us? We were good together."

"You did both of us a favour when you broke things off."

Maybe Taya could sink into the floor. During her training sessions with Thane, they determined she had little offensive skills and her strength came in the form of defensive shields and merging with her weapons. Maybe she could merge with the tiles?

She shifted her weight and eyed the door. With three long strides, she'd escape the room.

Alexis' gaze cut to her. "Is it her? Is this shadow the reason?"

Maybe she could make it with two power lunges.

"My reasons are solely based on you, Alexis. On us." He leaned forward. "Did you honestly think you could cast me aside like unwanted trash and I'd come running back to you the moment you crooked a finger?"

She pursed her lips.

He stepped to the side, gripped the handle and opened the door. "Your husband is waiting for you."

Alexis pulled herself up straight and lifted her chin. "You'll regret this."

Oh, wow. She parted with that line? So cliché.

"I doubt it." Thane closed the door on Alexis' heels and turned the deadbolt. When he faced Taya, the bags under his eyes looked darker. He hadn't been sleeping well.

The exchange with his ex may have exhausted him, but Taya found it quite satisfying to watch. She smiled.

"Don't say it," Thane said.

She lifted her arms out to the side. "What?"

"You can wipe that smug smile off your face as well."

She jabbed her forefinger into her breastbone as if to say, "Who, me?"

"Yes, you," Thane bit out.

She tried, but her mouth twisted and sprang back into a smirk. She gave up and let it widen. "If you want private time with your brother's wife, just say so. I can leave."

"Leave? That woman poses a threat." Thane flung out his arm to point at the closed door.

Taya snorted. "Not to your physical safety. I visually checked her for weapons."

"That dress could've hidden anything."

Not the top part. "True, but it would take her

awhile to get anything out of those skirts and I'd hope by then, you'd figure out her intent and defend yourself."

"There are other reasons women lift their skirts." Thane ground his teeth. "That woman is nothing but calculation."

"She's definitely up to something." Most likely wanting the security of marriage to Julian and the passion in Thane's arms.

Thane nodded. "Let's put Alexis and her question-able motives to the side right now. You never answered my question."

She made a habit of not answering his questions.

"Why didn't you tell me you saw Gale on the Earth side?"

Her hands flew to her hips. "This is the first time I've seen him or heard any mention of him being alive after the Arkavians invaded Earth. I thought he died in the sacrifice."

"Did you check for his body?"

"Of course not. I had no reason to." She mostly tried not to lose everything she'd eaten that morning. All the faces had blurred together. "I didn't keep the information secret. You knew I had his brother's swords. Why wouldn't you assume our paths crossed? Why wouldn't you mention that Elias' brother was still alive?"

"I assumed you stole or scavenged the swords. I

didn't realize the House of Raiden and the sacrifice circle were connected. I didn't mention he was alive because I didn't want you to get altruistic and try to return magical swords you're under no obligation to forfeit. If he wants the blades of Raiden back, he has to take them. It's Arkavian Law."

Understanding clicked painfully in place. What a pair they made. "I didn't realize Gale was a part of the sacrifice stuff. We each held a piece to a two piece puzzle." Cool air pebbled her skin. She rubbed her arms. "But Gale survived. He must be part of the leaching. If I had to guess, he saw me tonight with his brother's swords and suspects I know of his involvement. After the failed assassination hit, I followed him and he asked your brother about me. He wanted to know who I was and where you found me."

"Is that what you were doing at the reception? Trailing mysterious men in a dress?"

"He's hardly mysterious. You know who he is." Why did he sound angry? She did a great job improvising. She lifted her chin. "But yes. That's what I did and I looked good doing it."

Heat flashed in Thane's gaze. "Yes, you did."

Oh my. He could melt polar ice caps with that look. "How'd he explain his brother's death and the loss of his men and slaves?"

"He said a nasty group of rabid earthens attacked him and he was the sole survivor. His Tarka skills are so weak, everyone believed him. We believed him. He went on that supply run for the House of Jericho."

"He has an interesting interpretation of the truth."

"Don't we all?" Thane asked.

What the hell did he mean by that?"

He stepped close, his body inches from hers. Without an explanation, he gripped her face and leaned down to kiss her. His lips pressed against hers, hot and demanding. He tasted of sweet chocolate and sin. She inhaled his fresh pine scent and drank in more.

Well, maybe he meant this. She could lie with her words, but her body told the truth. She melted into his arms and lost herself in the heat of the kiss. He pulled her closer. She ran her hands up his chest, enjoying the hard compact muscles under his soft shirt.

A cool draft ran along her back as her nerves sang for more. Thane's mouth moved to her jaw, then her neck, sending chills down her body.

Thane shoved her to the side without warning, breaking contact and sending her flying. He flung out a hand.

Taya hit the cold stone ground, rolled and sprang to her feet, weapons drawn. The blades whined for blood.

Suspended in the air, mid-leap, a man had his arm drawn back with a throwing knife in one hand. Black garb covered his face and he wore plain leather armour with no house insignia. Cold air blew in from a window. The late night visitor hadn't properly closed it.

"Assassin," Thane said. He continued to hold out his hand to keep the man frozen in place. His Tarka power rolled off him, radiating invisible waves toward their attacker. "That's two hits in one night. Even by Arkavian standards, we're very popular."

"I should've seen him," she said.

Thane walked over to the man and stopped a couple of feet away. "You were distracted."

"A mistake I won't make again," she said. Though she meant the words, her body begged for his touch. The taste of him lingered on her tongue and her lips still tingled from the pressure of his mouth on hers.

He looked over his shoulder. "Worth it."

Honestly, what a silly thing to swoon over, yet here she was. Swooning. As if Thane contained a magnetic pull, Taya walked over to him. "Will he talk?"

They turned in unison to the assassin. His dark eyes had glazed over and foam bubbled out of his mouth and through his face covering. Saliva dripped to the floor with a patter.

Thane sighed. "Death tablet. Assassins often have a tooth pulled so they can store poison in their mouth."

"Why don't I have one?" Apparently, her mouth wasn't through talking before thinking.

Thane chuckled. "I've seen how you shovel food in your mouth. You'd most likely dislodge the death tablet by mistake and manage to kill yourself." The laughter drained from his expression. "I'm not letting that happen."

"Why not? It's a part of the deal. I knew when I signed on I might die for you."

"This is non-negotiable." His jaw tightened.

"I made a promise, Thane. To kill for you. We both know what dangers this job entails. Nothing's changed." And back to lying, apparently. If her heart had a choice, it would punch its way out of her body cavity and spill the whole truth at Thane's feet.

His large hands curled into massive fists. "Everything's changed."

She blinked at him. What did he mean by that? Had things changed for him, too, or did the kiss tell him exactly how enamoured she'd become? "You should reconsider. If I'm caught, you'll wish I had one."

He frowned.

"I'll sing like a canary." Her mouth kept moving.

"No, you won't."

"You sound so sure." If she couldn't kiss him, she may as well poke the Thane bear.

"There are many things about you I don't know or understand," he said. "Your integrity is not one of them."

Warmth swept her body. Seriously. It had been over a year since she had any male companionship, but this was ridiculous.

He unclasped his dress scabbard and propped his weapons against the bedside table. "Come on. We both need sleep before we head home tomorrow." He pulled back the covers.

"Um..."

"What?"

She jerked her thumb over her shoulder. "The dead guy?"

Thane grunted. "I'll take care of it." He stalked across the room. The assassin's body floated through the air and trailed behind him. Thane flung open the door and stepped into the hallway.

The assassin had come through one of the windows, which someone must've left unlocked for him. No wonder she felt a draft. While Thane dealt with the body, Taya secured all the points of entry and checked the rest of the room to ensure no other surprises leapt from the shadows tonight.

During her circuit through the room, she passed the metal tray with the chocolates and popped them in her mouth. The intense flavour exploded in her mouth and brought back the memory of Thane's kiss and the taste of him on her tongue. Her skin warmed. Nope. This wasn't a good time to revisit that kiss.

Instead of turning into a love-sick tween, she shed her various weapons and scanned the room for the cot. *Where the hell was it?* The other houses always brought a cot in for Thane's shadow. Was this an oversight or an intentional slight? Where would she sleep?

Thane returned, shut the door, turned the lock,

and brushed off his hands as if he actually got them dirty.

That was fast. Did he just dump him in the hall-way? "Do I even want to know?"

"Probably not."

She shook her head. No doubt she'd find out tomorrow. "They forgot to leave a cot."

Thane shrugged. "Climb in. You can sleep with me."

Well, he seemed unconcerned. If the House of Auroris tried to insult him, they failed. And now he wanted to sleep with her.

Sleep. Just sleep. Right? The pressure of his phantom lips still pressed against her own. She raised her eyebrows.

He held his hands up in mock surrender. "Best behaviour. Promise."

He might manage to keep his hands to himself, but she didn't trust her own intentions.

Thane waited, his expression an open challenge as if he knew her exact concerns. He waved his arm out in a sweeping motion toward the bed.

Ass.

She walked to the opposite side, pulled back the thick covers perfect for staving off the cold in a damp castle, and slid into the bed. Her body thrummed with anticipation.

For what? Get it together, woman.

Thane snuffed out the candles with a flick of his

wrist, and climbed into his side. The mattress dipped with his weight. He rolled toward her. His arm slipped around her waist and his hand splayed against her flat stomach.

What was he doing?

He pulled her into the heat of his body, surrounding her with his dizzying scent. He nuzzled his face into her neck and hair, and took a deep breath.

"You said best behaviour."

"This is my best."

"And it's terrible."

"And if I hadn't caught the draft in the air, you might've died tonight. Someone tried to assassinate you. Twice," he growled.

"I'm your shadow. It's what I do."

His grip tightened. "Let me hold you."

Her nerves sang with his proximity. Her memory replayed their kiss and demanded more. She still tasted his sinful tongue in her mouth, and if she were honest with herself, she needed him to hold her, too, but it was wrong. She swore to her dead friends to avenge them. Sleeping with the *enemy* conflicted with her promise. Yet...yet she wanted Thane. She craved him. Shouldn't she be happy, too? Wouldn't her friends want that?

"It's a good thing the assassin interrupted us." Thane's breath brushed against her neck while his words pierced her heart.

"Wow. Regrets already."

"Absolutely not," he growled. "But you have a

couple of weeks left before you're free from your service."

Apparently, they were having this conversation now, to hell with the dead guy Thane disposed of and the spooning.

"Did you question my consent a moment ago?" Her consent had grinded all over his rock hard body and begged for more.

His fingertips stroked her stomach. "No, but nothing can happen between us while you work for me as an indentured servant."

"Why is it so important to you that I'm free?"

"Besides it being the right thing to do?"

"Yes."

Silence descended on the dark room. It stretched until Taya was certain he wouldn't answer her and closed her eyes to sleep. The heavy sheets rustled as he pulled her closer. His legs pressed against the back of hers.

"My mother," he whispered.

She tensed. The memory rushed forward. Thane rarely spoke of his mother.

"What happened?" she asked.

Thane shrugged, his hand sliding along her stomach, as if to say it was not a big deal, but the tightening of his hold and shallow breathing said otherwise.

"She never wanted to marry my father," Thane said. "He scooped her up from an impoverished line under the House of Edur. He saved her family from financial ruin and held their livelihoods in his grasp."

"Isn't Edur a big house?" Her brain ran through the genealogy of the houses Adrianna gossiped about incessantly.

"Yes, but my mother's family was a small branch under a large tree. They weren't important enough to the head of the house—a distant fourth cousin—to risk defying the House of Jericho. My father could crush my mother's immediate family at any point."

"So she did everything he wanted."

"Yes. That's why the infidelity rumour was so preposterous. She'd never jeopardize her family, especially her little brother. She loved my uncle very much and would do anything to protect him."

"What was in it for your father? Surely he could've found a more willing bride."

"Willing, yes. Controllable and predictable, no. He wanted guaranteed compliance. He wanted someone from a big house with a high probability of producing magically gifted children who he could control at all times."

"And so he found your mother."

Thane nodded, his chin brushing her back. "Julian never forgave me for her death."

"His hatred is misplaced."

"Maybe." He placed a light kiss on her shoulder. "I spent a lot of my life blaming myself, too."

Oh, Thane.

She should say something, anything, but what? What could possibly remove a lifetime of hurt and anger?

She placed her arm over his and squeezed. He held her closer and nuzzled his nose into the crook of her neck. Maybe words weren't needed right now. Maybe silent support was enough.

CHAPTER 34

A QUICK SKINNY DIP

Taya kept her attention on the path in front of Sugar, but the weight of Lokni's gaze irritated her skin. She gave up. "What?"

Lokni had kept his mouth shut about her and Adrianna swapping outfits last night, and he never elaborated or explained what happened between him and Thane's cousin after Taya left them to return to the ball. From Adrianna's wide grin this morning, Taya assumed all was well for both of them, but something obviously ate at Lokni. They were now half a day away from the House of Auroris. How had he managed to keep his mouth shut this long?

"Have an eventful evening?" he asked.

Ah. She knew he wouldn't last.

No one had said anything about the assassin's body the next morning. She still had no clue where or how Thane disposed of it, but apparently Lokni found out about their late night visitor. "I've never seen a man foam at the mouth like that before."

Lokni's mouth turned down and his brow bunched as if someone took a corkscrew to his face and twisted.

"What?"

He opened and closed his mouth, and then opened it again to speak. "That was more information than I needed."

"What are you talking about?" She hadn't explained what happened when she swapped places with Adrianna or the unexpected visit by the assassin and Thane's mysterious cadaver removal skills. How could he accuse her of saying too much?

"What are *you* talking about?" Lokni asked.

Taya blinked.

They stared at each other.

"No cot..." Lokni leaned in. "You and Thane..."

Heat flushed her cheeks. R-rated images flooded her mind. She might dream about Thane, but why would Lokni think anything happened between them? Had Thane said something? How'd they know about the cot?

Understanding rang the little bell inside her head. She winced. Lokni, and probably Soka. Those rat bastard twins must've removed the cot. She should've figured it out sooner.

"Thane and I killed an assassin," she said. Better to fess up now than let Lokni run around with rumours about Thane foaming at the mouth.

Lokni straightened in his saddle. "Oh. That explains the body outside Julian and Alexis' bedroom."

"He didn't."

Lokni grinned. "He did. Special wedding gift."

Idiot. The last thing Thane should have done was antagonize his brother. She'd have to talk to him about that later. Right now, she needed to confirm the cot situation before she started plotting revenge. "Why do you think something happened between us?"

"What are you two gossiping about?" Thane grumbled as he brought Hades to the other side of Taya's horse.

"Your unusual wedding gift," she said.

The horse hooves clip-clopped along the narrow bridge as they crossed a raging river below.

Thane's gaze darted to the river. Something about running water disrupted Tarka power—not fully, but significantly enough that most Tarkas avoided rivers, lakes and oceans. They didn't like to make themselves vulnerable. And unsurprisingly, most attacks on Tarkas occurred near water. Some Tarkas took armed guards into the bath with them. Not Thane. He took a sword and said he never wanted to rely solely on his powers for survival.

"A dead assassin is a lovely way to say, 'I love you,'" Thane said.

Sugar snorted and tossed her black mane. Some of the hairs whipped across Taya's face.

"Unless your brother takes it as a threat," she said.

"It's only a threat if he's the one who sent the assassin. He'll take it as a gesture demonstrating the might of the House of Jericho." He pulled his shoulders back. "You should practice your Tarka shielding to—"

Something large flew through the air, passing inches from Taya's face and lodged into Thane's chest with a sickening thud.

Thane grunted and the impact knocked him over. He hit the railing on the side of the bridge and tumbled into the river.

Lokni spun in his saddle, pulled his bow, notched an arrow and released it in one fluid motion. The arrow sailed through the cool air. A man cried out. A body dressed in black and green fell from a thick tree branch jutting out from the forest over the river. The body hit the rocky bank with a terrible slap.

Heart in her throat, Taya dismounted and ran to the bridge railing. A long, javelin-sized, spear-like arrow stuck out from Thane's chest on the right side as he flailed in the water.

The men ran up to her.

"He can't swim," Axel said.

She looked at them.

"None of us can," Soka said, gaze darting left and right.

She shed her dual scabbard and dropped them on the bridge. Metal clanked on wood. She pulled her boots off and swung onto the railing.

"Make sure you shield," Lokni said. "If you touch him without it, he'll sap you for healing."

And then we'll both drown. What a comforting thought. She took a deep breath of cold air and jumped into the icy river. The frigid water enveloped her, shearing her skin with its near-freezing temperature. She surfaced a few feet away from Thane, his gaze wild.

Unflappable, rock-solid, immoveable Thane was terrified.

She threw up a shield. The power wove around her. The water rammed against her magic as if trying to knock the barrier down. She clenched her teeth and pushed forward.

"Stay away," Thane barked before his head dipped under. He bobbed back up. "I can't shield."

"I can." She swam over.

"Don't..." *Glug, glug.* "Don't touch me." Thane flapped at the water. His head plunged below the surface again. His face grew pale.

"Shut up and stop flailing." He would knock her out if he clipped her with one of those clobber fists. She couldn't get close enough to grab him. How would she pull him to safety? Her chest tightened. Her mind spun. *How? How? How?*

"I...don't—" His lips turned blue. His gaze wavered. Blood flowed away from him in the water. "—flail."

His body went limp. She dove under the surface

and gathered him in her arms. She pushed off a large rock and with a powerful kick, pulled them to the surface. She hooked an arm under Thane's so she could clamp him against her body. The javelin sized arrow stuck out of the water. Even if she could pull it from his chest, he'd bleed out.

She leaned back and let the buoyancy of the water support their combined weight. She used her free arm to paddle backward and frog kicked to propel them faster. The rushing water battered at them, splashing icy water in her face. She couldn't feel it anymore. Everything was going numb.

Probably a good thing Thane was unconscious. If he panicked again while she rescued him, he'd push them both under.

The river carried them down the bank and smoothed out. Ripples of water danced along large rocks jutting out from below. She didn't fight the current. Instead, she angled them and used the power of the river to push them to safety. Her feet found the rocky ground and her legs shook. Her teeth chattered. Hypothermia was kicking in. She needed a fire and body warmth. Thane needed to heal. Time was running out.

The thunder of hooves grew louder.

She hauled Thane out of the river and dragged him away from the water's edge. God he was heavy. With more distance from the water, her shield grew stronger. She needed to drop it soon. Thane couldn't heal from the men and he'd already lost a lot of blood. His breathing didn't look good either. Shallow and raspy. His skin pale.

No. He wasn't allowed to die like this. He wasn't allowed to die at all.

She hooked her arms under his armpits and hauled him to a nook in the treeline.

Horses burst from the forest. Axel leapt from the saddle. "What can I do?"

"Build a fire." She turned to Lokni. "Make a bed for us." Then to Soka, she said, "Help me with him. He needs to be stripped down."

Her teeth wouldn't stop chattering. The air sliced at her numb skin.

Lokni and Axel jumped into action and Soka took Thane from her and carried him with ease. No one mentioned the large arrow jutting from his chest.

"He'll be fine once he heals from you." Soka walked Thane over to the bedroll Lokni had already laid out. "He won't need body heat."

"But I will." She dropped the shield. A disturbing warmth spread through her limbs. Her heartbeat slowed. Oh no. She'd run out of time. "Hurry."

Soka flipped Thane onto the bedding and pulled off his clothes. While he worked on Thane, Taya stripped down. Her legs wobbled. Her stupid hands and arms fumbled with the buckles and clasps.

"Let me help." Lokni grabbed her shirt hem and pulled up.

"Don't...get...any...ideas," she chattered. If anyone could help any woman undress, it was Lokni.

Lokni said something about Thane, but the world wavered around her.

Fire crackled in the distance.

"Get...that out first," someone said.

Her vision blurred. Light headed, she careened forward. Strong arms caught her and she floated.

CHAPTER 35

A DONE DEAL

Crackling heat from a fire bathed her face. She opened her eyes and her lashes fluttered against a broad chest.

She froze.

Events stampeded back into her memory.

With her ear pressed against his naked chest, Thane's heart pumped away in a healthy greeting. His strong arms held her close and their legs intertwined. Her limbs had that "too-warm" swollen feeling she used to get after coming inside from playing in the snow.

She pushed away from Thane. His arms tightened and held her close. If she pushed again, he'd release her, but she didn't want to leave the heat of his body. Not really.

"Shhhh," he said. "Don't ruin the moment." His

voice sounded rough and raspy, as if he ran it over gravel and let Hades stomp on it. He did have a javelin sized arrow embedded in his chest not too long ago.

"You should've let me go," he said.

She relaxed into his warmth and ran her hand over his chest. A new circular scar marred his right pec. Angry and raw, the puckered red skin stared back at her only inches from where the skin dimpled from his last arrow wound.

He rumbled approval.

"You're okay?" she asked. *And are you part cat? How many lives did Thane have? How many has he already used up?*

"All healed. Thanks to you."

"And the men. If they hadn't set up camp, I'm not sure either of us would've survived." *Where was the rest of the team? No other bed rolls lined the clearing and only Hades and Sugar waited for their lazy humans to get up and feed them. The wind didn't carry any sounds of the twins bickering or the steady cadence of Axel's rumbling voice retelling a story of his youth.*

"You would've managed." He brushed his thumb along her arm. "You're a survivor."

Survive first, feel later...

"Where are the others?"

Thane didn't answer right away. Instead, he lay beneath her and continued to stroke her skin. "I sent them away."

"What?" She pulled away. "Why?"

He clamped her back to his chest.

"We're sitting ducks, right now. Let me go. I need to secure the perimeter."

His chest rumbled. "I've recuperated enough to defend us."

"Why'd you send them away?" she asked.

"I've dreamt of holding you naked for the last year. Now that I finally have you here, I didn't want anything to spoil the moment."

Warmth of a different kind now swept through her body. The twins would definitely disrupt the moment unless Thane remembered his immovable morals first. "Why let others ruin it when you can do it yourself?"

"What's that supposed to mean?" His chest muscles tensed under her face.

"What's changed since last night?" If he wouldn't touch her then, why would he now? She pushed up enough to prop up on an elbow and look into his eyes. Despite Thane's infamous card playing skills, he never successfully lied to her. In fact, he never really tried.

Thane's jaw clenched. His body tensed under hers.

"You could release me early, you know. You're the one who imposed the *year-long* sentence."

Thane grumbled and looked away, breaking the eye contact. "I've thought of that."

Taya waited. He obviously dismissed the idea for some reason. She wanted to know why. "What is it you want, Thane?"

He sighed. "I want you to assassinate Gale."

Okay, not what she'd expected him to say at all.

Then it clicked. Like a cold, wet towel to the face, understanding slapped her brain. He feared she'd leave if he released her, and then he wouldn't have someone trained with her skillset to take out Gale.

She opened her mouth to reassure him, but he kept going.

"I want to set you free."

She shut her mouth.

"I want you to stay with me because you want to, not because you have to."

Her chest expanded with a fuzzy warmth.

"I want to keep the bond in place and claim you as mine. Properly."

Properly? Her imagination filled in the blanks of what a proper bonding entailed. Cool wind slipped over her face from the river, but did little to cool the fire burning inside her.

Thane's hand gripped her arm as if he feared she'd run. Maybe he did. Despite his grip, if she bolted, he'd let her go.

The river rippled and bubbled nearby. And the tree branches swished in the gentle breeze.

"I want you..." He plucked a strand of her hair from his chest and wound it around his finger. "I want you to love me, like I love you."

She sucked in a breath. Her heart hammered

against her breastbone, as if it would bash its way out of her body and latch itself to Thane if she refused to give it to him. Thane had laid out all his feelings, fearless as ever. Yet she *knew* he feared her response.

"Is that all?" she asked. It was a long list of wants, yet she'd grant them all, the yearning in her veins already ramping up in response. In anticipation.

His lips tugged up. "There's one more thing."

"Only one?"

"I want to do very bad things to you."

"Bad things?"

"Dirty things."

She had a fair idea of what he meant. A huge idea. It currently pressed into her hip. She wanted to roll on top of him, impale herself and ride him into the sweet bliss of ecstasy she'd fantasized about since she first glimpsed him sitting like a statue on a rickety supply wagon.

"We have a saying on Earth," she said instead.

He stroked her arm, his gray gaze flashing. "What's that?"

"If you love something, set it free."

His arms tightened around her. He took a deep breath, closed his eyes and nodded. She hadn't told him the second part of the proverb, but from his firm mouth and tense muscles, she didn't need to.

"Taya of Earth," he said. "I release you from your service."

A slip of his magic unwound from her mind and trailed away. The bond remained in place, wrapped around her with its comforting and consistent pressure.

Thane opened his eyes and waited. Waited for her to bolt. To run away. To reject him like his family. Like his ex-fiancé. Taya had no plans to leave. She'd still avenge her loved ones. She'd still search for a way to save earthens, but she had her own happiness and future to consider, and right now, that future stared back at her, open and vulnerable, waiting for her decision.

"There's a second part to the proverb," she said.

His eyebrows rose.

"If you love something, set it free. If it comes back, it's yours." *If it doesn't, it never was.*

His lips compressed into a thin line. His voice growled. "You're leaving then? Is that it? Or are you saying you'll come back and you want me to wait for you?"

She shook her head. "It's a stupid saying. I'm not going anywhere. I don't need to leave to know I'd return." She held her breath.

The confusion fled from his face and his lips twitched. "You're not going?"

She nodded.

His grin turned wicked. He clutched her, his fingertips digging into her side. "But you will be coming..."

Bolts of heat flew straight to her groin. She leaned down. "Promises, promises."

He turned his head to the side. Her lips pressed against his stubby cheek instead of his mouth. She groaned. What now?

"You don't have to sleep with me as payment for your freedom," he said.

Oh, Thane. "You need to shut up, now." She chuckled in his face and pressed her forehead against his. "I've been yours since the moment we met, and it has nothing to do with servitude."

He growled, gripped her in his arms and rolled to pin her beneath his weight. He settled between her legs. "You need to give my mouth something else to do, then."

"Done." She pulled his head down. His mouth crushed against hers. Sin and chocolate played with her senses.

What started as sinful, delicious kisses, turned into ravenous ones. Thane made good on his promise and used his mouth to make her body sing with need. She was about to beg for a release from the torture when he finally flexed his hips and pushed into her slowly.

He paused to study her face. "Are you sure? There's no going back after this. You will be mine and I will never let you go."

"I've never been more certain of anything." She wrapped her legs around his waist and held him close.

He growled and pushed all the way in. With his power released and his body moving with hers, he was *everywhere*. His magic surrounded her and slid inside, pulsing and moving in time with his hips. The pleasure he wrought consumed her, and her world became his.

CHAPTER 36
PRACTICE MAKES PERFECT

Taya stood over Lane's moon-bathed face. Even in sleep, resting his head on a plump pillow with his white hair splayed out, his mouth tugged down in an unimpressed scowl. Did he dream of more takeovers? More wars? He had already amassed so much power in Arkavian society, what more could he want?

More power. There was always more power.

With the window open, the sound of the gentle lapping of the ocean against the cliffs below trickled into the bedroom.

One fluid motion and she'd end Thane's suffering. At least the suffering from his father's abuse.

She stilled, letting the cool breeze slide over her shoulders, and stroked the smooth leather of her dagger's hilt.

One plunge. One slash. That's all it would take to free Thane from this asshole.

She shook her head. Platinum hair brushed against her cheek. She couldn't be the one to take Lane's life. Thane would never forgive her. She knew that.

It'd almost be worth it.

Instead of slitting his father's throat, she pulled her shielding magic around her and backed out of the room. The newly greased hinges turned soundlessly as she shut the door behind her. A few feet away, the guards stood in relaxed postures with their backs facing the door. One of them yawned.

"Stop that," the other hissed, and then yawned.

"I can't help it."

"That saucy wench keeping you up?"

They exchanged a grin.

Taya slipped past Lane's guards and made her way down the hall. She needed to report her shielding success to Thane. Not that her achievement changed anything. Thane refused to send her after Gale until they devised a way to assassinate him so no one would, or could, reasonably point fingers at the House of Jericho. Currently, their houses weren't in a feud and had multiple trade agreements. Thane couldn't risk those. If he had proof of Gale's involvement in the assassination attempts, things would be different.

She passed a large mirror in the hallway, the air wavered as if unsettled by a force. No reflection stared back at her.

Lokni told her once she looked like she lost substance. If he watched the entire process and she stood still, he could make out an outline of her body, but if she snuck up on him or moved too quickly, he had no clue where she was and she became a real life shadow.

The power drained from her bones and her body throbbed. She turned the corner to enter Thane's wing and dropped the shield. Sweat poured down her face and an ache bloomed in her chest. Though she'd improved her shielding, it still took a lot out of her. Her magic had limits.

She knocked on Thane's door. Her arms shook.

The door swung open and Thane's eyes widened. He gripped her face and captured her mouth with a hungry kiss.

Pshhht. Who needed air? She melted into his arms and let the heat of his body consume her. Her skin begged for more. She burned for more. The memories of their time together by the river flooded back and a needy ache expanded through her body.

He pulled back entirely too soon. "I thought you'd sneak in."

"Tapped."

He nodded. "I don't hear my brother bellowing for your head. Success?"

A grin spread across her face. She couldn't stop it if she tried. "Yes, but I didn't stop there."

"Taya," Thane growled.

She loved when he rumbled her name. His deep voice vibrating along her naked skin sent all kinds of shivers to all the right places.

"What did you do?"

"I decided to make it a family affair." She pulled out Julian's comb, Adrianna's earring, and Lane's watch.

Thane hissed and snatched the items from her outstretched hand. "He would've killed you."

"He'd have to catch me."

"Taya—"

The clip of shoes against stone rebounded down the hall. Thane snapped his mouth shut and straightened. Taya took a step back, out of the heat of his body and shivered.

Adrianna sashayed down the hall, her skirts swinging back and forth with each step. She often wore men's clothing when safe behind Jericho walls, but tonight she had on the full get-up.

"Isn't it past your bed time?" Taya called out to her.

Adrianna smirked and slowed as she approached them. "Some of us need more beauty sleep than others."

"Must be why I never sleep." Thane's words were ruined when he stifled a yawn.

"Why are you up, cuzzie? Preparing for the delegation?"

Thane frowned. "What delegation?"

Her pretty lips twisted into a sneer and she crossed

her arms over her chest. "Figures Julian didn't brief you. Edur, Draco and Ramiel are visiting tomorrow to discuss gate access and trade routes."

Thane groaned and ran a large hand through his platinum hair.

Wait. Three big houses, but not the House of Raiden. That meant Gale would be at home toiling over his plans to become Arkavia's biggest douche. Taya turned to her friend. "And Thane is expected to attend this delegation?"

"Of course."

An idea percolated. "Which means my presence is also expected?"

Adrianna cocked her head, her pouty lips twitching down a little at the corners. "Yes?"

This was the opportunity they needed—a chance to eliminate Gale without any suspicion cast their way. If Thane had an alibi from three powerful houses, and witnesses placed her in attendance, too, no one would connect them with Gale's death.

Taya's smile grew. "How would you like to play dress up again?"

CHAPTER 37
SOMEONE HAS TO DO IT

T he cold air stung Taya's nose as she crouched in the bushes in the forest surrounding the House of Raiden. A clear field separated the protection of the forest's shadows and the gray stone walls of the massive building. That didn't concern her. With her Tarka shielding, she became nearly invisible at night. The reflections of moonlight off metal could give her away, but she sheathed her swords and wore leather instead of traditional Arkavian armour. As long as she didn't draw a weapon, she'd remain unseen.

The rotating guards ambled slowly along the ramparts and turrets above. A lone archer sat on a high ledge of a lookout tower.

The house might be smaller than the House of Jericho, but it was well guarded for a family not in an active feud. Anticipation gnawed on her spine. She stretched and forced her breathing to remain steady.

She needed to stay calm and centered in order to pull her magic tight to her skin like Thane showed her.

Thane.

He'd held her and delivered a bone-melting kiss before she left. "Come back to me," he said.

She shook her head and pushed the memory away. She needed to focus on her target. There was no room for lovey-dovey crap tonight. Thane safely sat in a large room with his family and members from the Houses of Edur, Draco and Ramiel. Sure, Adrianna, not Taya, stood behind him dressed in face coverings, fighting garb and imitation swords, but no one else knew that.

Taya pulled on her power and let it soak into her with its soothing energy, coating her like a second skin. The power vibrated against her bones, ramping up with anticipation. The power of her blades ebbed from the scabbard and demanded release. She stepped into the moonlight and in a low crouch, sprinted across the open space. No one called out. No one raised an alarm.

They might keep the main gates closed at night, but they left a side entrance accessible for changing guards, and the shift had just ended. Unfortunately for the new soldier guarding the door, he had to die. He was Arkavian, he worked for the house that lead a procession of earthen slaves to their doom, and he guarded the only feasible entrance. No mercy. No trying to justify his presence. No preservation of life. She steeled her heart and pressed forward.

The door would make a sound and she couldn't

risk detection. As she closed the distance, she flipped her long dagger into her hand with the blade lying flat along the back of her forearm so she shielded the metal from moonlight.

The guard turned toward her and his hand moved to the pommel of his sword. He'd spotted something, or heard the dampened sound of her feet on the hard, frozen ground, or maybe the rasp of her breathing or her racing heart.

The guard frowned and leaned forward, gaze not quite focusing on her. She ducked behind him, clamped a hand over his mouth and slit his throat in one fluid move. He gargled against her hold. His teeth grazed her skin and blood bubbled and splashed on her palm. He sagged and fell back. She braced his weight with her body and propped him against the wall with bent knees. She posed him so he looked like he rested his head on crossed arms to sleep, and wiped her blade on his dark shirt.

The ruse wouldn't last forever. She needed to get in and out before the next change in guard or before someone looked a little too closely.

She took a deep breath and turned the knob. Locked.

Crap.

Taya couldn't wait for the next guard to open the door and walk through and she certainly wanted to avoid scaling walls. She crouched by the dead guard and patted down his pockets.

Bingo.

She pulled the keys from his pants pocket and got the right one on the third try. Her heart raced too fast. She took another deep breath of midnight, winter air, full of damp stone and moss. She needed to calm down. She breathed deeply again.

She turned the handle and pushed open the door.

"Hey!" A man said. "You're not done with your shift—"

Taya lunged forward and shoved her knife into the waiting guard's chest. His eyes bulged and he toppled forward. She caught his weight. *Ugh.* Why did Arkavians have to breed such massive soldiers? Her legs threatened to buckle. Blood soaked the front of her shirt from his wound.

She scanned the inner sanctum of House Raiden. No visible guards. No one had spotted her. No cries of alarm echoing through the halls. She released her breath, ignored her pounding heart and dragged the guard outside to pose him beside his comrade. His boots crunched gravel and drew two rough lines in the dirt. Sweat pebbled along her brow and dripped down her face. She used her boot to scatter the tracks.

Let's try that again. Taya slipped back inside the keep and pulled the door closed behind her. The hinges creaked and the wood groaned.

She had less time now. A missing guard on the inside of the fortress would be noticed sooner than one on the outside.

She cursed and sprinted toward Gale's suite. Luckily, the House of Jericho had detailed schematics and other useful information on the other families. She'd memorized the floor plans and the location of Gale's room. Cold air cut at her face as she ran, landing on her toes and using her shielding to dampen the smack of her boots against the hard tile.

Killing Gale was her first mission as a free earthen and the first notch in her belt to truly avenge her world. Gale had killed so many from that town. He was responsible for the leeching. He needed to pay with his blood, and tonight she'd be karma. Tonight she was vengeance.

She slowed before rounding the final corner. The notes said Gale often had guards outside his door. Constantly paranoid, he rarely appeared without a guard and used his power to scan for archers when he travelled. Other than a public assassination, which might result in witnesses and exposure, or a direct assault on a barren road, which might result in Thane's team taking damage or losses, Taya was the best bet for success.

She peered around the wall's edge. Motherfucker. Two guards, one on each side of the double doors leading to Gale's room. Full metal armour. She either had to kill them both or go around.

Two dead guards would cause a commotion and lead to early detection. Even if she managed to take them down simultaneously, their large, hulking bodies, dressed in armour would make an unmistakable racket when they fell to the stone floor. She might manage to catch one and take the impact of his gargantuan body weight, but two? Simultaneously? Not a chance.

Fuck.

She ground her teeth and backed away. The notes on Gale also said he usually slept with a window open. They'd bribed a bitter, discarded mistress for that particular tidbit.

Hopefully, this personality quirk remained true during the cold winter months.

Out of the line of sight from the guards, Taya propped open the door to the balcony and slipped outside. No rusty hinges screeched and no gusts of air. Only the soft click of the door closing behind her disturbed the silence of the night.

She held her breath and waited. No cries of alarm. She scanned the towers for lookouts. The archer faced the other direction. His job wasn't to monitor the inside of the building. He wouldn't see her with her shield, anyway.

She turned and assessed the siding of the tower Gale slept in. A small ledge circled the tower. Small edges of the stone blocks used to construct the building only allowed a tenuous finger hold. She glanced down. The world tilted.

She wouldn't survive the fall.

Gale knew of her existence. He knew her eyes and she couldn't take the chance he'd recognize her face. He'd never invite her into his room or let her draw him into a private space. Killing him at night was her only option other than returning to Thane as a failure.

Nope, the latter wasn't an option.

She glared at the wall. This left her only one choice.

Taya stretched her fingers to improve the range of motion of her hands and stepped onto the balcony's banister. On her toes, she reached for the ledge. Air pushed past her skin and protective clothing. Her leather pants brushed against the stone and her hood flapped in the wind. The fabric across her face blocked most of the chill. She sucked in a breath of cold air and hoisted her body onto the ledge. Her fingertips gripped the small crevice, but the ledge held her weight and gave her a sturdy base.

"You can do this," she whispered.

Her dad's voice spoke in her head. *Stay light on your toes, let instinct take over. Don't over think.*

She stepped out and readjusted her hold. The safety of the balcony no longer loomed beneath her.

I've got this.

Step by step, she inched around the tower. The wind pressed against her back. She continued her slow, deliberate pace with only the power of her Tarka shield protecting her exposed and vulnerable position.

The cold air continued to slice past her, picking up speed as a small system moved over the keep and she moved out of its direct path. Thunder boomed in the distance.

Her muscles tensed. She pressed her fingers into the rough stone.

No.

A sprinkle of rain pattered against her head and shoulders.

No. No. No.

She picked up her pace. Her heart lodged in her throat and threatened to choke her. The wind wailed in her ears. The rain picked up, splattering the stone siding and trailing down the bricks. The ledge grew slick.

Taya squeezed her eyes closed and hugged herself against the cold surface. Only a few steps to go. The shutters of Gale's window remained open and almost within an arm's reach.

She stepped out again. Her foot slipped. She scrambled and lost her finger hold on the ledge. As her whole body careened, she clawed at the ledge. No! She flung her body out, stretching, lengthening and pushed off the ledge with her other foot. Sailing through the air, she reached out as she plummeted.

She wasn't going to make it.

Her hand slapped the window ledge. She death-gripped the rough stone. Her camouflaging shield dropped. Her body swung up with the momentum.

She grabbed at the sill with her other hand. Her fingers couldn't grip the slick surface. She flailed her legs to find some sort of purchase on the wall beneath. She groped the ledge with her free hand. There! With a tenuous hold, she pulled her panting body over the ledge and into the room as one soaking wet ball. She hit a plush rug, and rolled into a crouch.

Gale stood in the middle of the room, dressed in full armour, weapons drawn and studied her. Candle-light reflected off the metal and the bright sapphire gem of his house ring. "I've been waiting for you."

CHAPTER 38
I'LL CUT A BITCH

Taya stood and brushed the rain from her clothes. Water and sweat dripped from her face and leathers to pool by her boots on the floor. A large canopy bed, topped with throw pillows and furs, occupied one side of the sprawling master bedroom. Beautiful, intricate rugs lined the smooth stone floor and a low burning fire radiated warmth from a fireplace opposite of the bed.

Did he stand by this window and let the night air slide over his shoulders while he enjoyed the silkiness of his favourite liqueur? How could such a vile creature have great taste in furnishings? The hair on the back of her neck lifted. There was something so inherently wrong with this dichotomy.

"If you expected me, why not dismiss the guards instead of making me climb walls? You could've saved some of your men's lives."

He cocked his head. "Obviously, I hoped you wouldn't make it. I should've known. Thane wouldn't employ a subpar shadow."

She forced her lungs to take even breaths of the fragrant wood and oil scented air, though her heart raced and adrenaline pumped through her veins. She wanted to double over and pant. Her shoulders screamed and her hands ached from gripping the edges of stone slabs for her life. To hell with avoiding noise. She'd leave through the doors after she killed Gale.

"You've been waiting for me?" she repeated his words. She needed to keep him talking while she collected herself. He seemed like the type who liked to listen to himself speak.

"The assassins failed to kill you. I knew it was only a matter of time before Thane sent you." He nodded at her weapons. "You've bonded to the swords, haven't you? Something no one in my family has managed to do in generations."

That's right. He couldn't even touch them.

"How did you get them?" he asked. "I know you weren't in that town when we raided it."

"I visited the town after."

"Soon after?" A streak of moonlight broke through the cloud cover and beamed through the open window to illuminate his armour. The reflection bathed him in a white glow while she stood to the side in the dark.

She nodded. What harm would come in telling

him the truth? If he was willing to talk, she might glean more information from him for Thane.

"You recognized me at the wedding reception," Gale said.

"How do you know?"

"Your eyes gave you away. They widened like two saucers. Never play cards." He paused. "You recognized me, but I've never seen you. And you came across my brother's body in the town. That leaves only one possibility. You must've been nearby when we attacked."

"The bushes."

He swore.

"You stopped your pretty horse a few feet away from me to admire your pathetic work," she explained.

Gale's mouth turned down. He shifted back and forth and stared at the ground by her feet. He stilled, gaze cutting to her face. "You're one of them, aren't you? Some dirty earthen whore? And by some sick twist of fate, you look like us." His face screwed up as if saying the words left a vile taste in his mouth. "And you watched the destruction of your comrades and did nothing. You're a coward."

"I'm not a coward, I'm smart. Attacking you then would've been suicide." Wait, why was she defending herself to this asshole?

"And now isn't? One shout and the guards will come."

She shrugged. "Why not? They already think you're weak. Call them. Show them you need defending against a dirty earthen whore."

He hissed, but didn't attack.

What was he waiting for? Was there some sort of trap? She scanned the room. No elaborate pulley system connected to a net. Only tasteful décor and historical artifacts in custom nooks lined the walls. Was he planning something else? Something less obvious? She pooled her power and held her shield closer.

Gale laughed. His magic pulsed in the air. "Your camouflage won't work here. Not against a son of lightning."

Dang it! Why not? She held onto the shield anyway. Maybe he had a way to nullify the camouflaging affect, but hopefully, she still had a defense against a magical assault.

"I'm going to kill you," he said. "I was going to make it swift, but after that weak comment, I'll make you suffer first."

She tried not to roll her eyes and failed. She'd accuse him of stealing the lines from an average C-list movie, but the reference would be lost on him. "What are you waiting for?"

"I want to know something else."

"Ask away," she said.

"Are you here in retaliation for the hit or something else?"

"You know why I'm here. Why else would you send assassins?" She swiped her wet hair out of her face.

"I sent those thugs to retrieve my brother's swords."

Oh. Well, then. Thane had mentioned the weapons belonged to her by Arkavian law and Gale would have to take them back if he wanted them. But why would he put so much effort into retrieving something so useless to him? He left them on Earth. Was his hit on her just to save face? Had they underestimated his pride? Apparently, it outweighed his common sense. "And when those assassins failed, you sent another. Why bother? What could you possibly want with these swords when you can't use them?"

He cocked his head. "I never sent more."

Cold prickled her skin. Who had sent the other assassin then? The one who arrived after Alexis' attempt to throw herself at Thane on her wedding night?

"But now it appears I should've sent more," Gale interrupted her thoughts. "You know more than I thought."

"I'm here to ensure you pay for the earthen lives you took."

Gale snorted. "The House of Jericho gives zero fucks, as you earthens say, about your people."

She bristled. The only way he'd know that saying is if he spent significant time around earthens. How many slaves did he lead to the slaughter? How many did he bring home to do his bidding? "One does."

Gale sneered. "Thane should be more careful not to pull down the very house he lives in."

"What the hell does that mean?"

"Do you honestly think someone from the House of Raiden could do anything, let alone set up multiple anchoring sites for power leaching in a zone claimed by the House of Jericho on the other side of a portal the same family opened and operates, without them knowing about it? Without them approving it?"

Taya snapped her head back as if he slapped her with his words. Unease shimmied up her spine. The House of Jericho knew?

Gale leaned forward, a smug grin spreading across his face. "I'm just a minion and if you kill me, you'll bring the house down on your darling master."

That's why he'd stalled. He wanted to know what she knew because he counted on her standing down. Oh, he wouldn't let her go. He'd either imprison her or kill her, but afterward, he'd go to Lane with the information he pulled from her brain. Damn it! She shouldn't have revealed Thane's knowledge. She had no choice but to succeed tonight. If she failed, it wasn't just her life that was forfeit, but Thane's as well. "Why wouldn't they tell Thane?"

"The same reason they keep it secret from everyone else," Gale said. "Thane doesn't need the leaching. He's strong enough on his own and they hate him for it. They're weak in comparison, even with their stolen magic. They've been weak for generations. Admitting to the leaching admits their weakness."

"You kept their secret."

"I need the leaching, too." His hands balled into fists and shook. "My silence and our families' agreement is mutually beneficial."

All the pieces fell to the floor and snapped together in a perfectly completed puzzle. Lane and Julian's mistreatment was designed to groom Thane and keep him ignorant and in his place. Too busy trying to earn their approval, he never realized the truth.

Oh, Thane.

Gale snarled and lunged. Apparently, their chat had ended and imprisonment wasn't an option. She ducked out of the way and drew her swords.

The lightning sparked and whined, running down the cold metal. The energy fused with her power and intensified. She whirled away from Gale's strike and counterattacked, deflecting his blades and pressing forward.

He glared at her on the other side of the attack, expression livid. His sword punched through her defences. She side-stepped and kicked up, bone snapped. She danced out of the way of his next swing.

Gale staggered back, blood spurting down his face from his nose. His lip curled up, letting blood drop into his mouth and coat his teeth. He turned to the side and spat.

She attacked, spinning in a whirlwind of blades, drawing on her family's move. He scrambled to swat the swords out of his way and stepped back, eyes wide.

"The Makani?" he breathed, chest heaving. "The Ghost House is dead."

Instead of replying, she jumped, still whirling and kicked out again. Her foot slammed into the side of his face and sent him reeling. He landed, bent over one knee. She dodged his weak defensive swings, stepped in and drove her blade into his back.

He cried out and arched, head flung back. She gripped his platinum-blond hair and pulled so his face was inches from her own.

"Ilta..." he whispered. "Night..."

Yes, she worked for the Night House, for the House of Jericho, and technically she was here on Thane's orders, but this wasn't for them. This was for her.

"For the earthens," she said, and yanked her blade free from his back. Blood sprayed against her leather pants and splattered to the floor. She shoved Gale's now-limp body to the ground. His strangled cries hadn't raised any alarms, but she didn't have much time left.

She cleaned her swords and sheathed them in the dual scabbard on her back, cutting off their whines.

The selfish beasts wanted more blood. She pulled Gale's house ring from his forefinger, slipped it into her pocket and drew her daggers. With her shield back in place, she headed to the exit. She might've killed the intended target, but this assignment was far from over.

CHAPTER 39
HORSING AROUND

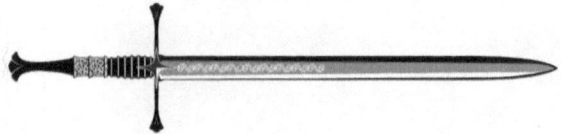

The bite of conifers and damp soil wound around Taya as she picked her way through the floral winter forest. Her feet hit the frosted ground and exhaustion pulled at her limbs. She'd killed the two door guards and made it through the fortress to the safety of the woods. Surprisingly, the clatter of their armour didn't raise an alarm. Without needing the element of surprise, she'd let their bodies fall and clatter on the stones before booking it.

As soon as she stepped into the deep shadows, she dropped her shield and lay down in the dirt. The last drops of rain splattered against her face before the bulk of the storm moved on.

She couldn't rest. Not yet. Shouting echoed through the trees. Someone had found the bodies. Damn it.

If she had any energy left, she'd climb one of these

behemoth trees and shield until the search parties gave up and returned home, but her arms shook. After scaling the tower wall, fighting Gale, and dragging multiple bodies for concealment, her physical strength had depleted significantly. And she'd shielded for hours. Her Tarka power was also drained. Tree climbing was out.

She needed to get to where she left Sugar tied up.

Originally, she'd balked at the idea of leaving the horse vulnerable to predation, but Thane assured her the anti-predator charm would keep Sugar safe.

Dogs barked in the distance. *Crap*. She had to go. They'd catch her scent. She'd dripped sweat all over Gale's chamber.

She rolled to her feet, muscles screaming, and broke into a run. The air burned her throat and lungs. The straps of her sword scabbard chaffed her skin and dug into her back. She dropped her chin and pushed forward. Sweat ran down her forehead.

A branch slashed her cheek. She stumbled on a root and flew forward. She hit the ground, rolled and sprang to her feet.

Faster.

The barking drew closer.

Sugar nickered in greeting when Taya broke through the forest. Why the hell had she tied the horse to the tree branch? Sugar wouldn't have gone anywhere.

Taya leapt on Sugar's back, grabbed the reins and

slashed the ends free with her dagger. She dug her heels into Sugar's belly and the horse charged into action.

She made—

Pain exploded in her chest. She looked down. A bloody arrowhead protruded from her chest.

"Go!" She slapped Sugar's flank.

The horse bolted into the trees. Men yelled, the dogs howled. Their noise grew more distant with each thundering hoof beat.

God she loved this horse. She whipped the reins and urged Sugar faster.

Pain erupted through her torso.

Two arrows.

Taya wheezed. Each breath hurt. She couldn't get enough air. One arrow must've nicked a lung. The other missed her heart. She needed to get to Thane so he could heal her.

Something wet trickled down her back. She slid her hand under her shirt as Sugar raced forward. Her hand came back bloody. Really bloody.

Sugar continued to sprint, each stride sending a bolt of pain through Taya's body. Tree branches whipped by, blurring her narrowing vision.

House Raiden didn't know her destination. They'd have to take time to track her and once she hit the main road, even their tracking dogs would prove useless. Sugar had rested for hours in the forest and was almost unparalleled for speed and stamina.

They'd never catch her now. As long as she stayed conscious and stayed on the horse, she'd make it.

Her vision wavered. She couldn't pull the arrows out. One, her arms didn't bend like that, but even if they did, the arrows were the only things stemming the flow of blood. She panted and braced as Sugar thundered down a hill. A river loomed ahead. She tugged the reins and directed the horse to follow it downstream.

Taya had planned an escape route, just in case. She didn't figure in how jarring the trip would be with two arrows protruding from her body.

Sugar charged forward, sure-footed and fierce, passing multiple crossing points without hesitating. Either the mare anticipated her needs or the horse didn't have any sense of self-preservation. She'd take her hardworking mare over those testy stallions any day.

There! Finally. The crossing point she wanted. It would take her pursuers forever to pick up the trail again after she crossed.

Sugar surged forward. Water sprayed and splashed against her legs. She turned Sugar to backtrack while still in the river along a smooth ledge. The horse slowed and picked her way up river. The only thing to foil the plan would be the House of Raiden showing up before she had a chance to disappear in the forest. Then the backtracking would be for nothing and she would've wasted her lead and precious time.

Her shallow breathing hitched. Pain coursed through her body in crashing waves. She clutched the reins and clenched her jaw.

Dogs barked. Men yelled.

Small breaths. Almost there.

Finally, she tugged on the reins and directed Sugar to exit the river slowly.

Hoof beats thundered in the distance.

The horse picked her way through the rocks, the careful footing making little change to the riverbed. The large warhorse stepped from the rocks onto a well-trodden campsite used by travellers as a waypoint.

Good luck following her tracks now.

Dogs brayed beyond the trees, closer now.

She nudged Sugar and the horse sprang back into action, fresh as a daisy and giving no indication the frigid water bothered or hindered her at all.

The dogs barked, minutes from arriving on the other side of the river. They were too late. Taya and Sugar made it to the protective confines of the old forest.

The pounding of Sugar's hooves against the hard ground continued to slam Taya with waves of pain. Sitting hurt. Holding onto the reins hurt. Breathing hurt.

Her vision blurred. She slumped forward in the saddle.

"Keep going, girl," she whispered into the horse's black mane. "Take me home."

She wrapped the severed reins around her wrists and knotted them together. She draped her arms on each side of Sugar's thick neck and let darkness descend.

CHAPTER 40
THE TRUTH HURTS

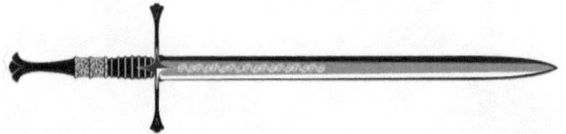

Taya woke to find her sore body cocooned under heavy blankets and a large fire roaring nearby. Her lungs and back ached, but not with pain. Not exactly. They felt more like muscles the day after a massage therapy session where some buff guy named Bryan with mammoth hands worked out a horrendous knot.

A branch snapped. She turned her head while keeping her body prone. Though pain no longer throbbed through her body, exhaustion weighed down her limbs.

Thane walked out of the surrounding forest and into the small campsite. He dumped an armful of wood into a pile near the fire. They clattered against the ground in a heap and stirred scents of wet soil and dead leaves.

"I didn't make it back to the house?" she asked.

Instead of answering her, he clenched his jaw, picked up a piece of wood from the pile, and threw it into the fire. Flames leapt up and sparked. A plume of smoke from the fire travelled over her body.

Thane brushed off his hands and crouched down beside her. Lightning flashed and firelight danced in his gaze. He pulled his power around him like an impending tsunami about to crash down on her.

"No," he said.

Huh? No, what? No, he wasn't a giant tidal wave? Did he read minds, now?

He smoothed the blanket over her and tucked the ends in. His wild gaze settled a little. "No, you didn't make it back."

"How'd you find me?"

"I used the bond. I found you miles away from the house, tied to your horse, bleeding out. If I'd stayed to listen to the rest of Julian's whining, you may have died."

"If you left the delegation, they might suspect your involvement."

"Doubtful. I left my shadow, remember? And even if they do suspect, I don't give a damn."

Despite the warmth of the bedding, ice stabbed at her skin. It had been close then. Too close from the look Thane gave her. "I'm glad you found me."

He gripped her head in both hands and kissed her. Hard. It wasn't a tender kiss. It was a harsh, claiming kiss that spoke of fear and the promise of passion. He stole her breath away, and she loved every second of it.

He released her and pressed his forehead against hers. "You scared me."

"Sorry."

"You will not do that again," he rumbled.

"That's a big ask."

He sighed. "I know."

"You scare so easily. The smallest thing could set you off."

He pressed his lips together, unamused. Why not? She was hilarious.

"You've been out for two days since the healing," he said. "I wouldn't call that a small thing."

She bolted upright. Her vision swam. "Two days?"

He nodded, face grim and pressed his palm on her chest to push her down to the soft bedroll laid over rocky, cold dirt. He knelt down beside her.

If he hadn't left the house when he did... Wait a minute. "How'd you know when to leave?"

"What do you mean?"

"You said you left in the middle of a conversation with Julian, but I didn't send a message. How'd you know I was in danger?"

Thane looked away.

Busted. "Thane?"

"The bond."

"I think it's time you gave me more specifics about this *reversible* bond." First, he learned of her impending doom through their link, then he used it to find her. What other information could he glean from the magical twist-tie?

Thane sighed again, a long exasperated whoosh of air like her request was somehow tedious or meant as a slow form of torture.

She glowered. Really, she should've asked more before she let him place his magic inside of her, but she hadn't been thinking with her brain at the time.

"It was only reversible so long as we didn't consummate the link. It's too late to remove it now."

She squeezed her eyes shut. When she'd asked him what he wanted, he'd told her he wanted to keep the bond in place and claim her properly. That had been her opportunity to ask some clarifying questions, but she'd wanted everything he had to offer. She still did.

Was she mad the link wasn't reversible?

Nope. Not at all.

She opened her eyes to find dark shadows across Thane's face. She squeezed his hand. "But *what* is it?"

"The bond is a magical link formed between two Tarkas," he said. "It allows us to sense each other and to feed off each other's power."

"You've been feeding off me?" Surely there was a dirty joke in there somewhere, but this wasn't something to laugh about.

He grinned. "Well, I—"

"Thane!"

Thane's head whipped back as if she flung a rotten

cabbage at his face. "No, Taya. I didn't feed off you. That's not something I can take. Not with a bond. You have to open your end of the link and allow access. When I originally formed the bond, your end remained closed. It can only be opened from within."

She folded her arms over the rough, woolen blanket.

"Technically, I can barge through, but that might destroy your mind and I happen to love what's in there."

Swoon.

Keep it together, Taya. Don't let his pretty words distract you. Focus. "If my end remains closed, how did you use it to find me?"

"I don't need you to open the bond for that. The presence of the link allows me to sense certain things like intense emotions, physical trauma, and proximity. The bond has grown stronger since we consummated the relationship."

"Sounds like marriage." Not that she disliked the idea...

Thane nodded. "It often is. Centuries ago, bonding was a part of the marriage ceremony between two Tarkas."

She ran her hand along his face and teased the silky strands of his white-blond hair. "Why'd they stop?"

He leaned into her hand. "Would you want to be

in the head of the spouse forced to marry you through an arranged marriage?"

"Too many intense emotions?"

He smiled, flashing white teeth. The shadows around his eyes eased away.

"Why'd you do it?" She let her hand slip from his hair. "You didn't know me at the time. Why would you bond with an earthen slave?"

A gust of wind moved through the forest. The branches laden with deep green, fragrant needles brushed against each other and played in the breeze.

"I never thought of you as a slave and I knew you were powerful," Thane said. "We needed a way to contain your power until you could control it on your own. That was the only way I knew to accomplish it while you kept some semblance of freedom and an intact mind. I never planned to consummate the bond." He paused, his gaze heated. "At least not at the time. That was one of the reasons why I tried to stay away from you."

Taya nodded. His words made sense, but she hoped he had more reasons than he listed to keep the bond in place. She'd taken control of her powers months ago, and he'd granted her freedom. He had no need for the bond to remain, yet he wanted to keep it.

He said he loved her, and he'd given her no reason to doubt the truth in those words.

Thane's stern expression softened and he leaned

forward. Though hard and battle worn, he was such a contrast from his cold and cruel family.

His family.

"Thane."

He stilled.

"Gale said something."

"I'm sure he did. Rats will do anything if they know they're going to drown."

"He said he acted under your father's order."

Thane straightened. His mouth twisted into a snarl. "You're mistaken."

"He was very clear."

"He's mistaken." Thane took a step back.

She pulled the blanket away and stood on shaky legs. "Was he though?"

Thane stepped forward and steadied her with a hand under her arm. "What's that supposed to mean?"

"Your father's an asshole."

He released her. "That doesn't make him a leech."

"He beat your mom to death in front of you when you were a child." Surely Thane saw how such an action meant his father had little sense when it came to discerning right from wrong, and good from evil.

Thane balled his hands and rocked back onto his heels. "He's my father."

She reached forward and smoothed her hand down his forearm. His muscles tensed underneath, but he didn't pull away. "You've been too busy trying to earn their approval to see their animosity was aimed to hide their own weakness and keep you in line."

Thane opened his mouth and shut it again. The muscles along his jawline bulged as he clenched his teeth. His eyebrows dug in and gave him a murderous expression. He couldn't scare her with his death stare. Taya stepped in and ran her hands up his arms to grip his broad shoulders.

He pressed his lips tight and watched her.

"You're stronger than them," she continued. "You're better than them in every way and they know it. The men know it. I know it. The only one who doesn't is you."

He stepped back and shook her hands off. "My brother and father are cruel, cold and calculating. They're not good men, but they've never shown any signs of being leeches."

"Haven't they though? Isn't the act itself dark magic? Doesn't the taint leave a mark on the soul? Doesn't it twist the wielders power and mind? Your father married your mother with the hopes the power from her bloodline would provide an heir with stronger magic. When she birthed a powerful Tarka, he flipped because the child wasn't the firstborn and accused her of infidelity. Does that sound like a sane conclusion to draw? For someone cold and calculating, that reeks of mental instability. Has he done anything else to defy logic? Dark magic has corrupted your family. I felt it the first time I met your father but thought that was how magic was supposed to feel."

Thane jerked back. "Does my magic feel like that?"

"Not at all." She swallowed and looked away. "I've always craved the touch of your magic. I thought my reaction to your family's magic was due to my addiction to yours. Like nothing else was good enough. Like everyone else's magic was gross and disgusting compared to yours. But now I realize that although I'm still very much addicted to your touch, your family's magic is tainted because of more nefarious reasons."

Thane shook so hard he vibrated. His wild gaze shifted back and forth as if flipping through a family album at super speed. His breathing hitched. His mouth turned down and his shoulders sagged. "Motherfucker."

She waited.

He pulled Tarka power around him, into him and through their bond, so much power, the air pulsed around him. It dripped from him, radiated from his skin. "I'm going to kill them."

"Later."

He turned to her.

"Right now, I need you to show me this is real. That I survived and you're mine."

His gaze flashed. Without a word, he reached out, gripped the back of her head and pulled her in. His mouth pressed on hers. His power surrounded them, caressing her skin and flowing into her like an incoming tide crashing against rocks. The ebb and flow of his magic coupled with the intensity of his kiss ignited a fire in her core. She burned for him, her bones turned to molten lava. She melted in his arms. Again. His passion might consume them both, leaving nothing but burnt husks, but she didn't care. She wanted to dance in the flames with him and revel in the pleasure.

CHAPTER 41

TWO TRUTHS AND A LIE

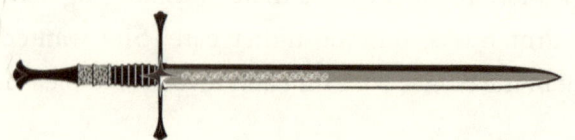

Taya sat forward in the saddle when they crested the hill. The horses drew to a stop. The sight of the House of Jericho still awed her. They approached from the opposite direction the first time she'd arrived at Thane's home, but the fortress was stunning from all angles. Despite all the grand fortresses she'd seen since arriving on this side of the gate, nothing surpassed the raw magnificence of the House of Jericho.

The dark forest spanned the cleared field in front of the castle and a blue haze glowed in the distance, marking the location of the portal.

She turned to Thane. "Gale said something else..."

Thane's brows rose. "I'm afraid to ask."

"He said the portal belonged to your house. What did he mean by that?" Is that why three houses had formed a delegation to discuss access and trade routes with Jericho?

Thane shifted in his saddle. "We own it."

"But it's the only portal." At least, it was the only portal she knew about. How could one family own the only portal without the other houses fighting for it?

Thane nodded. "It is."

The only way the other houses would concede this imbalance of power was if Jericho... Tension knotted at the base of her skull. "Did your family open the portal?"

Thane nodded again, expression grim.

"Did your family send the death wave?" She held her breath.

He gripped the reins hard. His mouth turned down. He obviously didn't like where this line of questioning headed.

"Yes." He hissed the words as if it sent a knife straight into her chest. In a way, it did. Fear pulsed through the magical link between them.

"Did you send the death wave?" Pain bloomed in her core. *Please say no. Please say no.*

His shoulders stiffened. He hesitated.

"I need you to say it," she said, heart sinking. "I need to hear the words."

"I helped." He bowed his head.

Her vision wavered. No. Not her Thane. Not him. She sucked in a deep breath and forced the next question out. "What does that mean?"

"It was a powerful spell that required all of us to work together. They needed me." He met her gaze, his expression sorrowful and pleading.

Her stomach twisted in a giant knot.

He'd seen her memories.

He'd seen through her eyes while she watched the blue death wave turn her friends into dust.

He'd heard her promise to avenge her friends and family and kill the man or woman responsible.

And here he sat.

And he knew he was her target all along, and said nothing.

Nothing.

The nausea dissipated, her vision crystallized and molten hot anger spread through her core.

"I didn't want to do it," he said.

"You could've refused." She gripped the saddle horn. How could he keep this from her? He'd let her love him. He'd bonded to her. Yet this whole time, he held this devastating secret to himself. What the hell would she do now? Where would she go? What would she do?

"I tried."

"Not hard enough." Her pledge to her friends replayed in her mind. Would she attack Thane? Could she? The idea of harming him sent a sharp stabbing pain through her chest. Drawing air into her lungs hurt.

She'd promised her friends.

Michelle's final sad smile flashed through Taya's memory.

Thane shook his head. "They had my uncle."

"The much-loved brother of your mom?" she whispered, mind still reeling.

He nodded. "He's still alive. He's Adrianna's father, and they threatened to kill him if I refused to help. They would've done it, too. They don't bluff. My uncle is one of the few people in this dysfunctional family who's ever shown me kindness."

His words made sense and quelled the anger a little, but nothing stemmed the sinking of her stomach. If she closed her eyes, she could imagine Thane defying his father, face inches away, snarling, only to have Lane smirk and calmly inform him of the consequences of his refusal.

Her heart tore, ripping painfully in multiple pieces. Her friends' faces streaked across her mind. Thane's wild and intense gaze when he drove into her. Her family. Her home.

Her lips quivered. Invisible weights pulled down her limbs. She loved Thane, and loved how he loved her, but... "I can't do this."

"Taya." He reached out.

She yanked the reins and Sugar danced sideways out of reach.

Thane dropped his hand. His lips turned down.

The wind wrapped around them, whipping her platinum hair into her face. The trees swayed and clouds gathered.

"I'm not letting you go," he said. His magic encircled her.

"You have no choice." Her chest tightened. Taya closed her eyes, savoured the warmth of the caress, and shrugged his power away. She was free. She didn't have to take orders from him anymore.

His mouth turned down.

"Would you force me to stay?" He wouldn't. It went against everything that made him...him.

"You know I won't. Where will you go?"

"Home," she said. Earth had limited time left before Arkavia drained it to a barren husk. She needed to find out if any loved ones remained to save.

"I will find you," he said.

"Don't." She blinked back tears. The words slipped past her lips, but he'd ignore them. She wanted him to ignore them. But she also needed time to sort through the whirlwind of emotions boiling within her.

She dug her heels into Sugar. The horse surged forward, barrelling into the forest. Cold air sliced past Taya's cheeks. Tears streaked down her face. The bond pulled her back toward Thane, but she pressed on, urging Sugar to run faster before she changed her mind. She couldn't look back. She couldn't see his face, his pain, hurt, and loss. She'd never leave if she did and she'd hate herself and him more if that happened.

She had to decide whether to fulfill her promise to her dead friends and kill the man she loved, or go back on her word and die from self-loathing and guilt.

CHAPTER 42
TO A PLACE I BELONG

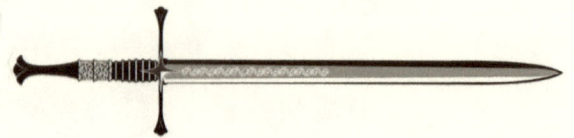

Taya stepped onto the sandstone rocks and pulled the kayak out of the water. The salt air brushed her face and the familiar smell of the winter forest greeted her. Although she grew up on a small island, she'd never manned a sailboat on her own and certainly not one without a motor. Instead of risking the wrath of the ocean and getting swept away to sea, she opted for a kayak instead. She had plenty of practice with kayaks, but it still took all morning to make the trip across the water that normally required a half hour ferry crossing. Her arm muscles screamed and her back complained.

She hauled the kayak to the entrance of the beach access path. Decayed leaves and needles mixed with packed dirt marked the area her family often walked to take a dip in the ocean. Most people dreamed of tropical white sand beaches. Not Taya.

Nothing beat sprawling out on smooth sandstone while the waves lapped nearby, the sun beat down, and the sweet smell of an arbutus summer forest washed over her.

She closed her eyes and took a deep breath. The familiar scents calmed her nerves. In five minutes, she'd complete the short trek through the woods and arrive at her parents' place. She opened her eyes, turned to the path and braced herself for what she might find. Or not find. She pulled the swords from the kayak and strapped them on her back.

Taya forced one foot in front of the other. Her feet pressed into the soil. No matter what she found, she needed to return to the main island tonight. She'd left Sugar tied up in a shed. Though the structure and the anti-predator charm would protect the horse from wolves and mountain lions, neither warded off thieves.

Taya knelt and placed her hand against the short cement block with crusted yellow paint marking the roadside entrance of the path.

Be strong, her dad said.

She gulped and turned down the main road toward her childhood home. The wind barrelled down the open road, brushed past her leather pants and pushed her hood back.

Smoke.

Taya froze.

Chimney smoke. Could it be them?

She jogged.

Metal clashing broke the silence up ahead. Sword-fighting.

Taya ran.

She pumped her arms and pressed forward, muscles screaming. She turned the corner and the front yard came into view. Two men practiced sword maneuvers in an overgrown lawn.

Taya cried out and sank to her knees. Plush grass surrounded her.

She'd hoped. Then she'd chastised herself for daring to hope. She'd prepared herself for the pain and hurt. For more loss.

She hadn't prepared herself for this.

Her dad and brother called out.

Tears streamed down her face. Strong arms wrapped around her and hauled her to her feet. Dad and Tommy held her as she sobbed.

Forget feeling later. A year and a half of grief welled up and spilled over the walls she'd built around it.

She cried.

Her brother cried.

Her dad cried.

"We're a mess," she said when the grief ebbed enough for her to speak.

Her dad pulled back and held her face, wiping her tears away with his thumbs and squishing her cheeks a little. His platinum-blond hair was more white than blond and had grown out to brush his shoulders. More lines crinkled his face. Sad lines marred his forehead.

"We thought we lost you," he said.

Her brother still hugged her, holding her as tightly as he had when he was younger and scared of the dark. He used to clutch her like this when he believed a monster hid under his bed. Tears threatened to fall again. She blinked them back. Her baby brother, now in his twenties, who towered over her at six foot two, clung to her.

"I thought I lost you, too," she whispered. "Mom?"

Dad shook his head.

The grief welled again. She blinked rapidly, but now released, they refused to stop.

Tommy's arms tightened, almost suffocating her.

Dad gathered them both in his arms again.

"We were swimming and she went back to the house to get lunch started," Dad said. He man-swiped the tears off his face.

"I offered to help," Tommy said. "But she told me to stay. I was visiting and she wanted me to relax."

Oh, Tommy.

Dad pulled back and studied her leather fighting gear still caked with blood. "Let's go inside. I think we have a lot to discuss."

Tommy and Dad blinked at her once she finished her story. Silence settled over the room. Normally, a clock her brother won at an amusement park filled the silence with its incessant tick-tocking, but now the crackle and snapping of a low burning fire took its place.

"So you're in love with an Arkavian?" Tommy said.

She turned to her brother. "I never said that."

"You didn't need to," Dad said.

"Out of everything I told you, that's what you picked to focus on?"

They shrugged in unison, carbon copies of one another.

"The Arkavians never came to the island. Without technology or any word from anyone, we didn't know what was going on until we went to Nanaimo."

Her dad named the closest town on the larger island, the one where she'd found a shed to stash Sugar.

"What happened?" she asked.

"Survivors attacked us," Tommy said.

"We've all done things since that blue crap came out of nowhere," Dad said. "We got answers from the attackers, but they refused to go away or leave us alone."

So her dad and brother killed them. She didn't need him to explain. She'd done worse.

"Thane believes I'm a descendent of an Arkavian Tarka from a Ghost House who ventured to Earth a few generations ago."

Dad nodded, reached behind him and pulled an old leather-bound book from the nearby bookcase. He placed it on the dinner table in front of her.

"What's this?" She'd never seen it before and she'd scoured her parent's bookcase through the years. Her mom had an unhealthy obsession with romantic suspense, which Taya shared, and her dad relished historical fiction.

"The journal of Izar from the House of Ilta, son of Aello from the House of Ilta, and Corentine from the House of Raiden."

"Why didn't you tell us?" she asked. The House of Ilta. That was the name Gale had spoken with his dying breath after she used the family move.

"Ilta..." Gale whispered, blood seeping from his wounds. "Night..."

Ilta. Ilta. Ilta.

Why did that sound familiar?

Lazy afternoons drinking wine with Adrianna stumbled through her memories. Adrianna gossiping. Adrianna laughing and sharing stories. Adrianna's lessons on Old Arkavian.

Like a giant elastic band snapping her brain, realization hit her.

Ilta meant night.

The Night House.

This whole time, she'd assumed the House of Jericho was the Night House. Every time she heard whisperings or mentions, she attributed the wary comments and trepidation to Thane's house.

Thane's theory from a lifetime ago flared up in a vivid memory, so real, she swore his voice rumbled against her skin.

"Everyone figured the scout was lost. He was the last son of his house and it died with his disappearance. They call it the Ghost House, now," Thane continued. *"But what if he didn't disappear altogether? What if he found a lovely woman and made a family and life in your world? What if his house lives on?"*

The House of Ilta *was* the Ghost House. And the Night House. They were all one and the same.

Her thoughts crystallized and her mind cleared.

Her family was the Night House.

Dad shrugged. "I never put much weight into my ancestry. It's not something I cared about. I believed this old book was a useless journal from a European ancestor and kept it locked in the safe. I didn't read it until after the survivors attacked us and called us monsters. They thought we were Arkavian, too." He lifted his hand and rotated his wrist so the back of his hand faced her. The afternoon sun streaked through the windows and danced on the surface of a large black gemstone. "This ring used to be his, too."

"The house ring," she breathed. The black gemstone must be the house colour. Ilta meant "night" in ancient Arkavian.

"Apparently." He pulled it off and turned to

Tommy. "It gets passed down to the firstborn son. This is yours, Tom."

In Arkavia, they gave every son in the direct line a family ring in case any of them got taken out, but it made sense that this ring got passed down to the oldest son. There was only one.

Her brother stared at it.

Dad opened his hand, rolling the ring to sit on his palm.

Tommy sighed and plucked it from his hand. He glanced at Taya. "Sorry, sis."

She shrugged. "I got swords that shoot lightning. We're good."

Her brother laughed and slipped the ring on his finger. It fit perfectly.

Her dad nodded at Tommy and nudged the journal toward her.

"Can you summarize it?"

Tommy chuckled.

Her dad shook his head, not in refusal but in exasperation. "Izar was the fourth son of Aello. He was never supposed to lead the family and instead was sent to the Tarkavian Order to study magic so he could be useful to the family cause. He lost all three of his brothers and his father in a war for a realm the Arkavians invaded, eventually dominated and subsequently sucked dry. He became disenchanted with the Arkavian way of life and suspected someone from a powerful house used the portal his father opened for personal gain. He couldn't prove it. He didn't have any spies and his knowledge of house politics was weak as he only had rudimentary training on the inner workings. When the houses approached him and asked him to pick up his father's mantle and open a new portal, he agreed. He was supposed to use his advanced Tarka training to scout the compatibility of Earth and return with the information. With no family or attachments to Arkavia left, he took his father's portal-opening notes and left. He liked Earth. He fell in love. He started a family. He also feared the return of Arkavia and ensured his knowledge was passed down through the generations. He'd lost access to his powers when he shut the portal, but he trained his children how to fight and made them promise to do the same when they had children. He wanted us prepared."

"He didn't prepare us for a blue death wave," Taya said. Okay, maybe that was a little harsh.

"No." Dad sighed. "From what I gather, that's a relatively new development. I don't think they did that for previous takeovers."

"And that's probably why he lost all his brothers and father," she said. And probably why the House of Jericho decided to make a pre-emptive strike. She flinched.

"This Thane. Is he a cruel man?" Dad asked.

"No," she answered without hesitation.

He nodded as if she answered more than one question.

God she used to hate when he did that. Instead, she just wanted to hug him again. She pushed away from the table. "I need to get my horse."

Both men raised their eyebrows.

"You'll understand when you meet her. I can't leave her."

"She's not going to fit on a kayak," Tommy said.

She frowned. Her brother had a point.

"She's not going on a kayak, Tom," Dad said.

She wasn't?

"She's going on the boat," he continued. "With us."

Her brother and father stood.

"We just found you," Dad said.

"Technically, I found you..."

Tommy grunted.

"We're not losing you again," Dad said.

Although she'd taken care of herself since the Arkavian apocalypse destroyed their world and survived, his words sent warmth rushing through her body. She wasn't alone. Her family was here. She was loved.

Yet...

Yet a pit in her stomach told her what her heart already knew. She was still missing something. Someone.

CHAPTER 43
ISLAND HOPPING

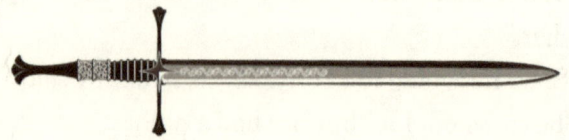

The cool winter breeze cut past Taya's face as she walked down the road ahead of her brother and father.

"I don't see why we couldn't use one of the boats moored in Pilot Bay," she said. Not only did Pilot Bay have a number of boats moored in it, the bay was only a five minute walk away from the house.

Tommy caught up to walk beside her. "None of them could fit a horse."

"Ah, the horse, of course."

Dad groaned. "No more rhymes, please."

They'd been mercilessly playing old games from their childhood for the entire walk and Dad looked about ready to tap out. But just when she thought he would, he'd get a small, somewhat sad smile on his face, and let them continue. He might make a fuss, but he couldn't hide how happy he was to have both his children with him. And how bittersweet the moment was without Mom.

Tommy nudged her. "I think he means it."

She snorted. This was entirely too easy. "Does anyone want a peanut?"

Dad rolled his eyes in a manner that would've made her fifteen-year-old self proud. "Come on, you two jokers. I know the Philips had a boat moored in Degnen Bay large enough to transport your magical horse. I even know how to sail it, so that's a plus. We'll cut down Gray Road."

Right. No motoring over to Nanaimo.

Taya readjusted the backpack she wore over the dual sheaths and trudged on. They were almost there. "I could use a nap."

"Don't worry. The refreshing swim to the boat will wake you up," Tommy said.

Taya snorted. "I'll take one of the rowboats that are always stashed on the shore, thank you very much. I'm not getting the supplies wet."

"Sure, it has nothing to do with the weather..." Tommy shrugged. "If you're chicken, just say so."

She scowled at her brother. "If you're stupid, just—"

A branch snapped in the forest.

Taya had her swords out, lightning blazing down the sharp blades before her brain registered what stepped out on the road ahead of them.

A large llama blocked their path to the beach

access, chewing something in its mouth and looking at them as if they were the most boring things in its day.

"Get out of the fucking way, Darla!" Dad yelled.

Taya sheathed her swords and bit her lip. Darla?

Tommy chuckled before glancing at the hilts of the swords that peaked out past her shoulders. His gaze widened. "Those are dope."

She flashed him a smile. Her hands drifted to the hilt. No harm in showing them off again. Darla didn't look ready to move any time soon.

An older man with sagging skin stepped onto the road behind the llama. He was completely naked. In winter.

"Why are you upsetting my girl?" the man yelled out.

"Why are you naked, Bill?" Dad called back.

Bill leaned forward and squinted. "Is that you Knight? Thought the blue blaze got everyone."

"Not everyone," Dad replied, though his shoulders dropped. He was thinking about Mom, again. He had to be, because she was, too. They all were.

Sadness clung to the air.

Dad cleared his throat and waved his hand at the llama. "What is this? Your security llama?"

"Eh? Don't be ridiculous." Bill placed his hands on his hips and straightened with zero concern that he thrust his exposed junk in their direction. "She's my therapy llama."

Of course. Only on Gabriola Island would they run into a nudist with a therapy llama.

"Well, get her out of the way," Dad said. "Please."

Bill scowled and walked to the side of the road. "You know, Knight. You've become a real dick. Come on, Darla. Let's find some better company."

The llama gave their group a final dismissive look before haughtily turning away. She sashayed over to Bill and the two disappeared into the treeline.

Better company?

"I know, sweetheart," Bill spoke loud enough for them to hear. "You'd think they'd be nicer to the only other survivor on the island."

Dad shook his head before walking toward the beach access. "This way."

CHAPTER 44
HAVE FUN DOCKING

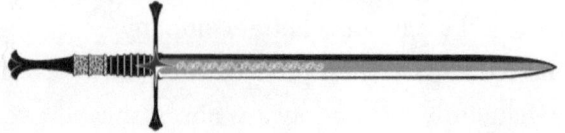

Taya braced against the mast as Dad rammed the boat into the dock. The impact jarred her. Tommy recovered first, jumping from the boat onto the dock to quickly tie the boat down.

"Smooth, Dad," Tommy said. "Like butter."

"That was shit and we all know it." Dad scowled and waved his hand at her.

Without a word, she lowered the last mast. Despite her need to laugh, Dad did a better job docking a boat under half-sail and without a motor than either of them could manage. It's not like they grew up practicing these types of maneuvers.

"Any damage? Dad asked.

Tommy shook his head. "Barely tapped it."

She snorted and grabbed her stuff. "The challenge will be getting back out again."

"You have more to worry about than sailing," a new unfamiliar voice called out from the shore.

Huh? Taya turned to the source to find the man wasn't alone. Eight young men stood at the entrance to the dock with baseball bats and machetes. One held an axe. They wore clothing in various styles, fit and condition. They didn't need to announce they were earthens. Their ragtag appearances and the inflection of their words gave them away.

"What..." Tommy straightened from tying off the boat and scratched his head. His confusion faded to a look of pure sadness. "Oh..."

"Tommy." Dad picked up her brother's sword and tossed it. "Here."

"We're not them," Dad called out. "I know we look like them, but we're not."

"And regular humans just run around with swords, huh?" the leader called out "You made a mistake coming here without your army."

"The only mistake here will be if you attack us."

Tommy's expression turned grim. This must've been what happened last time.

The boat bobbed in the water, doing little to relax any of them. They stood, frozen, waiting for the chips to fall.

Taya stepped from the boat onto the dock, relishing the more stable footing. She strapped on her sheaths and continued to wait. She'd killed earthens before but had no wish to do so again. There weren't that many survivors left on either side of the portal.

"My name is Tommy Knight," her brother said. "I went to high school here. Played for the Islanders."

The men hesitated, turning to look at one another. Their brows furrowed, they glanced at each other, sharing looks of confusion, then determination.

Ah. It didn't matter whether they were Arkavian or not. Taya, Tommy and their father were a threat, and that's all that mattered to them.

Please, just go away.

The men rushed the dock.

An amateur move. They gave away their advantage in numbers by filing themselves into two rows on a narrow dock.

Taya unsheathed the swords. The blades flared to life, thirsty for blood. The man at the front of the line faltered, nearly tripping over his own feet. His friend shoved him from behind.

"I knew you were lying," another man in the line yelled out, followed by a string of curses.

The other men join in, bolstering their confidence as they closed the distance to her and her family at the end of the long dock.

They met Taya and Tommy in a clash of metal.

She danced around the men, who swung their weapons wildly. Her brother moved seamlessly around the inexperienced fighters as well, cutting them down. The afternoon sun glinted off their blades.

Dad had joined them on the dock and protected their backs from the few who slipped past them. Three experienced swordsmen against eight novices didn't equal a fair fight.

The battle ended almost as quickly as it began.

Taya flicked blood from her sword and knelt by the nearest body to wipe both of her weapons clean. Though she didn't hesitate, and she understood the alternative was dying, the knowledge didn't lessen the weight pressing down on her shoulders and twisting her guts.

"Such a waste," Dad said, mirroring her actions.

"Is this what happened the last time you came to town?" she asked.

Tommy nodded. Having already cleaned his blade, he sheathed the weapon. "Pretty much. There were more last time and they caught us off guard and in the open. We had to cut our way through to run."

Taya sheathed her swords across her back and looked toward the shed where she'd housed Sugar with plenty of feed and water.

"That horse better be a fucking unicorn that shits gemstones," Dad grumbled.

CHAPTER 45
TUMBLEWEEDS NEEDED

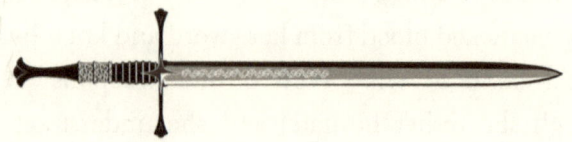

Sugar nickered when Taya approached the shed. The sun dipped behind the trees and cast her into a world of shadows. The cold condensed her breath in little puffs of air, and the sharp pine and ocean scent burned her nose. Her dad and brother waited on the sailboat, not wanting some "dog fucker" to steal the fully loaded vessel.

Her dad had the oddest sayings sometimes and now it all made sense. He was a descendent of Arkavia, like her. An alien.

She clucked her tongue. Sugar stomped her hooves a couple of times and settled.

Taya smiled and unlatched the shed door.

"I knew you'd return for that stupid horse," Julian said.

Taya whipped around.

Thane's brother stepped from the dark shadows between two identical storage sheds, swords drawn.

She pulled her magic close and her shield snapped in place.

"Thane finally detached himself from his shadow and we didn't have to do a thing," he said.

"Why are you here?" Taya unsheathed her swords. Lightning danced along the blades and their power screeched for blood. They demanded she quench their thirst. She merged her magic with theirs and promised them victory.

"That should be obvious," Julian said.

Three more Arkavian soldiers stepped from the shadows. Julian must've shielded them. She would've sensed them otherwise now that she had better control of her power. She recognized the men—Orrin, Chadwick and Steele—Julian's henchmen. They followed him around like evil, lost puppies and did his bidding whenever the jobs were too dirty for even Julian to carry out.

Thane never spoke about how he'd punished these three after they'd attacked her, but no one saw them around the House of Jericho for months. When they finally returned still bruised and limping, they kept far away from her. Their position in Julian's inner circle may have saved them from death, but that only made Thane more creative.

No one would tell her what had happened.

Apparently, with Thane absent, they'd grown bold again.

"I know what you plan to do," she said. She was earthen, not stupid. "I want to know why."

"You killed Lord Gale. He was important to house business," Julian said.

If they knew her actions, they must know who ordered her to carry them out. Her lungs constricted. Pain streaked across her chest. The thought of losing Thane cut deep. "Did you kill Thane?"

"No."

She nearly staggered in relief, but this was not the time or place to show weakness. Thane was alive. Everything would be okay.

Julian continued as if he had no idea how much that single word affected her. "Thane will live and remain ignorant, but you must pay."

Ah, they didn't know she already knew about the connection between Raiden and Jericho. Nor did they realize she'd told Thane all about it. They were in for a big surprise, unless...

Unless Thane didn't confront them.

Her stomach sunk. Thane wasn't a coward...was he?

"Are you sure you're not trying to kill me because you don't want Thane to get too powerful and realize how much weaker you and your father are?"

Julian snarled and leapt forward. She met Julian's attack. Metal clanged, sparks flew. She danced between the men and she parried, blocked, and dodged their attacks. A sharp edge caught her midsection. She spun away and slashed out. Orrin groaned and fell back.

A shadow loomed over her. She turned too late to block Steele's attack.

The shed door slammed open, smacking Steele in the face. Bone crunched. Steele crumpled to the ground. Sugar charged out of the shed and reared up, kicking her front legs out.

"Good girl." She turned toward Julian. His sword swung down. Light reflected off the blade.

Someone barrelled into Julian before his sword connected. The two men rolled away from her.

Tommy!

Chadwick surged forward and attacked her. They exchanged a whirlwind of blows and strikes. She turned and sank her blade deep into his gut and pulled the sword free. He collapsed forward with a groan. Blood spurted from the lethal wound and Chadwick fell to the ground.

The fight doesn't often last long enough to go to the ground when sharp edges are involved, Thane said.

She turned to her brother. Julian staggered to his feet, blood dripping down his face. Her brother lay prone at his feet.

No!

Julian studied her brother and his gaze snagged on something—the ring.

"The House of Ilta," Julian growled. "I should've known."

She jogged toward them.

Julian held his hand out, palm toward her. His magic clamped on her body like a vise. Dark and twisted, it pressed against her shield, and tried to crush her.

Taya snarled and pumped more energy into the barrier protecting her mind. Sweat dripped down her face.

Julian flashed his teeth and the magic clamp intensified, lashing against the shield in wave after corrupted wave.

A dark shadow moved in the periphery of her vision. Orrin? Steele? They'd stab her in the back.

Sugar? The horse wouldn't realize Julian attacked her.

Dad? Please, no. She couldn't lose them both. She couldn't lose either of them.

Taya couldn't move. She couldn't feel. She needed to be strong and break the hold of the magically enhanced dark practitioner of Tarka power. She grit her teeth. Pain erupted behind her eyes. The clamp tightened, crushing her shield.

Suddenly the pressure released. Startled, she shook her head and stumbled forward.

A glowing white sword tip protruded from Julian's chest. His eyes widened. His body slumped forward and fell off the blade with a sickening wet sound.

Thane stood behind him, expression murderous.

"You stabbed your brother in the back?" she gaped.

"Nothing he and my father haven't done to me countless times." Thane flicked blood from his blade. "He didn't deserve an honourable death."

She nodded. He might've said more, but she ran to her brother's side. She slid the final distance to him, spraying dirt against his prone legs. Blood pooled under his body. His breathing was shallow, but present. She brushed his platinum-blond hair slick with sweat off his face, and his eyelids fluttered open.

"You can't leave me now," she said. "We just found each other again."

His lips twitched in an attempt at a smile.

She patted his body to find the wound. Everything was wet and her hands came away soaked with blood.

Dirt crunched behind her. Thane approached.

She looked up at his grim expression. "Can you heal him?"

His expression remained serious. "A life for a life?"

"What?"

"Spare my life, and I'll save his."

What the hell? She hadn't planned to kill him and even if she had, this wasn't a decision that required any deliberation. "A life for a life," she agreed.

Thane nodded and crouched to gather Tommy in his arms. "Your brother?"

She swallowed. "Yes."

Thane closed his eyes and pulled his magic around

him. Taya studied the battle scene while he worked. Thane had dispatched Orrin and Steele while she mentally grappled with Julian. He'd saved her life.

Sugar stood nearby, munching grass, ears pinged forward.

Footsteps slapped the ground. Her dad sprinted around the corner and skidded to a stop. His gaze scanned the dead bodies littering the area and settled on Thane holding Tommy. "Who's that?"

"Thane."

"What's he doing to your brother?"

"Saving him."

Dad sheathed his sword and turned to her, checking her body for injuries. "I guess you can't kill him anymore."

A life for a life. "I guess not."

His expression softened and the tension from his shoulders eased away. "You'll have to forgive him instead."

Never question your father, her dad's voice played in her memory. *I'm always right.*

Taya smiled and let the power of her shield flow away. "You might be right."

CHAPTER 46

CONFRONTATION OF
THE HEART

Taya stared at the crackling fire, trying to force her muscles to relax while Thane took care of the horses. They'd decided to camp here, near the river for the night after a long, hard ride toward the portal. If they kept this pace up, they'd reach it in another two days.

She'd left Dad and Tommy in Nanaimo while she accompanied Thane back to the gate. Her family hadn't been impressed and argued for half a day, but she insisted.

She needed to do this alone.

Despite the privacy and time with Thane through the rest of the day, though, they hadn't spoken. At least not on important stuff. It was as if they both silently agreed to postpone any serious conversations for when they could talk in a more relaxed setting.

Well, here she was, supposedly in a more relaxed

setting, tension knotting her muscles, and worry twisting her stomach. The long day gave her time to think about what she wanted, but would she have the guts to say any of it?

Thane finally sat on the log beside her, the warm light of the fire flickering in his gaze and illuminating the sharpness of his features. He'd appeared lost in thought for most of the day as well, and his brow bunched forward.

"I was never going to kill you." She spoke softly, but her words broke the silence threatening to suffocate them and sounded like a death knell.

Thane hesitated. "I wasn't sure."

She waited for him to elaborate. Just when she thought he wouldn't, he cleared his throat. "I saw your memories," he said. "I've felt your loyalty, and your love for your friends as if they were my own. I felt it all. Your need for revenge, even in a memory, was palpable." His mouth flattened. "Not only was I responsible in part for their deaths, but I kept this information from you. I let you remain ignorant of my involvement and the extent of what bonding entailed while we consummated the bond. I am not innocent. I have wronged you, and I'm sorry. I will spend the rest of my life trying to make amends if you let me."

"You expected me to kill you."

He clenched his jaw and nodded.

"And you came anyway." He'd shown up in Nanaimo in time to save her and her brother. He could've hesitated. He could've avoided her altogether. Instead, he tracked her down, fully expecting to answer for his past crimes with his life.

He nodded again.

"To save me?"

He paused and licked his lips. "You're everything to me."

She swallowed and ran her sweaty palms down her dirty leather pants. When he asked for his life as payment for saving her brother's, he'd given her an out from her promise to her friends. He'd given her a way to make peace with sparing his life even though she'd already decided she couldn't live in a world without him. "What is it you want, Thane?"

He stared up at the night sky and studied the stars. His Adam's apple bobbed as he swallowed and visibly sorted through the words to use next. "I want to close the gate and stay here with you."

She waited, not daring to attempt words. Pain clenched her heart. Could it be that simple? Could they find happiness? As soon as he spoke those words, they *felt* right. She wanted that, too.

"If you want me," he added.

She took a deep breath. If she wanted to hurt him, she could draw this out. She could lie or evade. But they'd already suffered enough. Both of them. "Along with all that other stuff, you've seen yourself in my memories. How can you doubt how I feel?"

Something intense flashed through his gaze and he

gathered her in his arms. He kissed her and stole her breath away. Her mind spiralled and her thoughts became a muddled mess, but a persistent worry pinged in her mind.

She tore her mouth from Thane's, panting to catch her breath. "What about your friends? Your family?" She didn't particularly care about Thane's evil father, but he had people he cared about on the other side of the portal.

"I killed my father," Thane explained like it was no big deal. "And assumed control of the House of Jericho."

She blinked at him. "You killed him?"

Thane nodded.

"And you're just telling me now?"

"I was processing. I still am," he said. "I confronted him and he confessed everything. He expected me to accept it and fall in line. Like every time before. I can't believe I didn't see it sooner. Before he died he told me he killed Adrianna's father and sent Julian after you as punishment." Grief clouded his expression. "They'd sent the assassin who interrupted us after the wedding reception."

She nodded. "I figured that out. I think Alexis was meant to distract you."

Thane scowled, but continued. "When I dropped the body at Julian's door, they assumed you'd sent them a warning message. The javelin arrow that almost killed me was meant for you, too. After the failed attempts, they decided to wait until they could get you alone. My arrogance and willful ignorance almost killed you."

She cupped his square jaw, his stubble rough against her fingers. "You're not responsible for their actions."

He reached up and gently wrapped his hand around hers, pulling it from his face. "I have no wish to remain in a broken world. I want to build a new one with you."

"Here?" How could he want to give up everything he had in Arkavia to struggle for existence here? No wealth. No status. No fucking castle. Would he be happy in this mundane world?

"You have asked me more than once what I want," he said. "But what do you want? Will you have me?"

She licked her dry lips. "Yes."

He leaned forward.

Before she got lost in his dizzying kiss, she needed to tell him something else. "If you close that gate, you will likely lose access to your power. I will lose my power. It happened to my ancestor."

He shrugged. "Then I won't be a Tarka, and neither will you."

"What about our bond?"

His gaze flashed. "Our bond will remain. Nothing can break it. Not even a closed gate. It is more than magic now. It is who we are."

His words comforted her. Now that the bond had

settled in place, the idea of losing it was almost worth closing the gate from the other side and staying on Arkavia. Almost. One thought of her brother or dad quelled that notion.

"And your friends?"

"*Our* friends are already on their way here."

If she had been drinking anything, she would've sprayed it out over the fire or choked on it. "W...what?"

"I left my cousin and the inner circle with instructions to pack up and follow."

"As an order?" She cringed, feeling icky just for asking the question. Thane didn't operate like that.

He narrowed his eyes. "As a choice. They all accepted. None of us are disillusioned with the current state of affairs. Arkavia is dying. The leaching has slowly poisoned our world. The House system is a broken, antiquated establishment that is falling apart. Closing the gate won't condemn everyone on that side to death, but it will ensure our safety here. We have the opportunity to start something new and I'm not the only one thrilled with the idea. I wish we could scour the land and save everyone, but I'm not some kind of hero. I'm not willing to sacrifice you to save the world. I will shut the portal to save you. And us. Your family. Those I care about most."

She squeezed his hand, not quite sure words would work for her right now.

"I love you, Taya. You're my redemption. You're the light that staves off the darkness. Though I had wealth, fame and power, I used to feel so alone in my world. It took a trip to yours to find what I've been missing all this time." He slipped his hand to the back of her neck, tangling his fingers in her hair.

She could answer with some corny line about how he completed her. She could make a joke to try to lighten the mood. Instead, she slid onto his lap to straddle him, the campfire heating her back. "I love you, too."

They still had a lot to say to each other, but the rest of the night they didn't speak with words. Instead, Thane proved how much he loved her with his teeth, and tongue and lips, with his body pressed to hers. And she lapped it up, enjoying and responding to every second of it. For Thane was the light to her darkness, too. He kept her grounded and her nightmares at bay. He might think he wasn't a hero, but he had the heart of one. And it belonged to her.

EPILOGUE

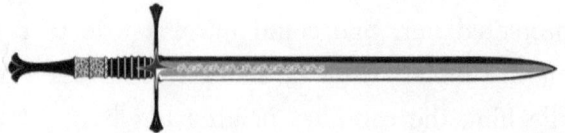

Taya sat on Sugar and glared at the portal. Thane drew up beside her on Hades and stopped. They sat in silence, letting the sounds of the forest wash over them. Time stretched, Thane apparently as lost to his thoughts as she was.

Finally, Taya slipped from the saddle and walked toward the gate. Gravel crunched under her boots. Thane mirrored her actions and approached. His armour clanking with each step and glinting under the sun.

"They're not here yet," she said, though Thane could very well see this for himself.

"We should make camp."

"You don't think anything bad happened to them, do you?" She bit her lip, unease clawing at her stomach.

Thane turned to face her, his large hands slipping

to each side of her face. "It would take a lot to bring my team down. Besides, packing up a house isn't a fast process."

She shuffled her feet, turning up dust from the dry ground. She didn't like the idea of the others still on the Arkavian side, but she also didn't relish the thought of going back through the portal to get them. She would, of course. She wouldn't hesitate. But that didn't make travelling to Arkavia one more time any more palpable.

"Let me take your mind off it." Thane's mouth quirked before he brought his mouth down to hers. God, he could kiss. He could take all her worries away with the flick of his tongue, and create an inferno burning low inside her. She grabbed his armour and pulled on the straps.

"Um, can you guys maybe hold off on all that lovey-dovey crap until later?" Lokni's voice sent Taya jumping from Thane's arms and reaching for her blade.

"Wha—?" She spun to face Lokni, Soka, Axel, Bertrand and Adrianna.

They grinned at her.

She dropped her hand from the pommel of her sword. "What took you so long?"

"It takes time to defect from our homeland to follow our exalted master," Soka said.

"Deflecting isn't quite the right word," Adrianna chimed in. "There's no house left to defect from. I want to be with my friends...and..."

Come on, say it.

She drew herself up in the saddle. "And I want to be with Lokni."

Wide smiles erupted across everyone's faces. Lokni swung his arm over Adrianna's shoulder and leaned over for a kiss.

"Ugh." Axel looked away.

Bertrand scowled.

Soka shook his head and tugged on the supply mule's reins. The beast ambled forward, bumping into Lokni's horse. Lokni drew back, and straightened in his saddle.

"About time," Taya said. Though she knew Adrianna had her reasons for keeping silent about her affair with someone not from Arkavian aristocracy, she didn't need to maintain the lie with them. And not here. Lane couldn't punish her.

"They're all accounted for," Taya peered at the group before turning to Thane. "Should we do this now or wait to see if any one follows?"

Axel slapped Thane on the back. "We'll go ahead and make camp."

"Let's get it over with," Thane said. "I don't particularly like the idea of any one following."

"There might be Arkavians on this side of the portal still. We'd be trapping them here," she said.

Thane nodded. "We'll have to deal with them as they come, I guess. I don't think there will ever be a perfect time to close the portal, but I feel the longer we delay, the more likely something or someone will try to prevent it." His gaze blazed. "I won't let anything stand between us."

"Are you sure? If you close the gate and there's no more magic, you'll leave yourself vulnerable?" The guy struggled to cross bridges for fuck's sake.

He ran his hands up and down her arms, rubbing her woolen shirt against her skin. "I'm more than my magic, Taya. I never let it define me like my brother and father. You of all people should know that."

She snapped her mouth shut and folded her arms over her chest.

He leaned forward, armour creaking. "Or do you only want me for my magic?"

A smile tugged at her lips, but she refused to let him derail her from her questions. "What about my swords?"

"They probably won't shoot lighting anymore, but a sharp blade is a sharp blade and you'll still be deadly with them if need be."

She nodded, but a small pain punched her in the gut. Losing the ability to merge with her swords was a huge personal loss, but a small price to pay for closing the portal and saving Earth from the Arkavian locusts. "What about next time?"

"What next time?"

"The next time evil Arkavians figure out how to open a portal to Earth?"

"It took us a hundred years to reopen this one."

"What if?" She dropped her arms.

"We won't let history repeat itself." He took her hand and squeezed. "Everyone involved with opening this gate, aside from myself, is dead. I destroyed the notes on Earth's location. Arkavia is a dying realm. Closing the gate will cut off the leaching, but also the energy and supply chain. If they don't figure out a way to open another gate to another realm, there might not be anything left to fear."

They turned to the portal together. Thane held out his free hand and pulled his magic. His power tugged on the bond. Without hesitation, she opened herself, allowing her magic to flow to Thane. The blue light of the portal flickered and faded, dimming gradually until it snuffed out.

And just like that, it was gone. A mere shimmer in the air marking the location where a portal to a parallel universe had once stood.

"But what if?" she repeated, reaching out internally for the reassuring presence of the link that bound them together. Awareness of Thane pulsed in her mind and relief swept through her.

Thane took her other hand and brought them both to his face to kiss her knuckles. "If they ever figure out how to reform a portal to Earth, we'll be ready for them."

His words held ice and deadly promise for their

enemies, but they sent warmth through her body. She believed every word.

If the Arkavians ever came back, they'd regret it.

She drew the twin blades of Raiden. At first they did nothing. They flickered, the light sputtering. Then, like the hope in her heart, the blue light flared to life.

CHARACTERS AND GLOSSARY

Adrianna: from the House of Jericho, niece of Lane, cousin to Julian and Thane

Aello: father of Izar, "whirlwind" in Ancient Arkavian

Alexis: from the House of Auroris, sister to Aries and Ayden

Aries: head of the House of Auroris, brother to Alexis and Ayden

Auroris: the House of Auroris, "sun" in Ancient Arkavian

Ayden: deceased, son of the House of Auroris, brother to Alexis and Aries

Axel: one of Thane's men

Bertrand: Thane's Steward

Bruno: one of Thane's men (sort of)

Chadwick: one of Julian's men

Chantelle: earthen survivor

Corentine: from the House of Raiden, Mother of Izar, "storm" in Ancient Arkavian

Draco: the House of Draco, a constellation

Edur: the House of Edur, "snow" in Ancient Arkavian

Elias: second son and heir to the House of Raiden, brother to Gale

Gale: head of the House of Raiden, brother to Elias

George: earthen survivor

Ilta: the House of Ilta, the Ghost House, "night" in Ancient Arkavian

Izar: Son of Aello, head of the Ghost House, the name of a star

Jericho: the House of Jericho, "moon" in Ancient Arkavian

John: earthen survivor

Julian: first son and heir to the House of Jericho, son of Lane, brother to Thane

Lane: head of the House of Jericho, father of Thane and Julian

Lokni: one of Thane's men, twin brother of Sokanon, "rain" in Ancient Arkavian

Makani: whirlwind combat move from the House of Ilta, "wind" in Ancient Arkavian

Maris: from the House of Edur, mother of Thane, the name of a star

Orrin: one of Julian's men, a constellation

Raiden: the House of Raiden, "lightning" in Ancient Arkavian

Ramiel: the House of Ramiel, "thunder" in Ancient Arkavian

Sokanon (Soka): one of Thane's men, twin brother of Lokni, also "rain" in Ancient Arkavian

Steele: one of Julian's men

Thane: second son of Lane from the House of Jericho

Tommy (Tom): Taya's brother

AUTHOR'S ENDNOTE

I first wrote this story when I recently returned to Canada from living abroad and found myself in that awkward "I'm broke and have no job" stage of life. Like any other time I faced anxiety-inducing events, I turned to reading for an affordable escape from reality and stress relief. After binging on several fantasy series, I started having strange dreams and the urge to write them down. I hadn't had this feeling since high school, which I ignored at the time, because I was too busy withering in self-doubt like pretty much every other teenager on the face of this Earth (but that's another story).

This time, the push was more forceful. I wanted to write a story of a fictitious woman who wasn't me, nor meant to be a fantastical version of me in any way. I viewed the characters like a spectator and the dreams of the woman's life and journey were so vivid and real,

I *HAD* to write them down. And since I had no job, I had the time! This woman's story ended up being the first manuscript I ever completed. I called it "Earthen." The manuscript was 80 000 words, 300 pages, and a hot, hot mess. It collected proverbial dust on my hard drive while I went on to write other stories. Ten published books later, I decided to try again.

And I started from scratch.

Nothing from the original manuscript was salvageable. At least not the words. The ideas behind the words—like the inciting event, overall plot arch and character development—remained true, and I wove them into this book.

I hope you enjoy reading my first story—the story that started my journey as an author—as much as I enjoyed writing it (twice).

Acknowledgments

I'd like to thank the following people:

Karilyn Bentley, Charlotte Copper and Nicole Flockton for beta reading and providing feedback. Their critiques are always on point and this story is better because of them.

Lara Parker for the fabulous editing, especially for switching to "Canadian Mode," which I appreciate.

Book Nook Nuts for the proofreading.

Jacqueline Sweet for the stunning cover and JV Arts for the alternate illustrated cover.

Linda Marrs for her wealth of horse knowledge and for answering my many, many questions about horse coats and colour genetics. I might've still messed things up, but that's on me.

My friends on social media for answering random questions about clucking and klicks.

My family and friends for their support.

My readers for reading.

As always, any mistakes found in this book are mine alone and made in spite of everyone's best efforts to support, guide and inform me.

ABOUT THE AUTHOR

J. C. McKenzie is a book loving, gumboot-wearing, unapologetic science geek. She predominantly writes urban fantasy and post-apocalyptic dystopian fantasy with strong romantic elements. When she's not spinning tales, she's in the classroom sharing her passion for science and mathematics while secretly warping the young, impressionable minds of our future to carry out her evil plans for world domination. She lives in the Pacific Northwest with her family.

Visit her at jcmckenzie.ca

facebook.com/j.c.mckenzie.author

twitter.com/JC_McKenzie

instagram.com/j.c.mckenzie

www.ingramcontent.com/pod-product-compliance
Lightning Source LLC
Chambersburg PA
CBHW030549020726
47494CB00005B/1535